ARCHANGEL RISING

ALSO BY EVAN CURRIE

Archangel One Series

Archangel One

Odyssey One Series

Into the Black

The Heart of Matter

Homeworld

Out of the Black

Warrior King

Odysseus Awakening

Odysseus Ascendant

Odyssey One: Star Rogue Series

King of Thieves

Warrior's Wings Series

On Silver Wings

Valkyrie Rising

Valkyrie Burning

The Valhalla Call

By Other Means

De Oppresso Liber

Open Arms

The Scourwind Legacy

Heirs of Empire

An Empire Asunder

The Atlantis Rising Series

The Knighthood

The Demon City

The Superhuman Series

Superhuman

Superhuman: Countdown to Apocalypse

Superhuman: Semper Fi

Other Works

SEAL Team 13

Steam Legion

Thermals

ARCHANGEL RISING

EVAN CURRIE

47N RTH

Published by 47North, Seattle

www.apub.com

Amazon, the Amazon logo, and 47North are trademarks of Amazon.com, Inc., or its affiliates.

ISBN-13: 9781542004879
ISBN-10: 154200487X

Cover design by Mike Heath | Magnus Creative

Printed in the United States of America

ARCHANGEL RISING

Prologue

Fleet Commander Birch wondered if she was perhaps being overly cautious. The enemy was a cunning sort, of course, but there was a point at which no level of cunning could survive against superior power.

She was quite certain she had that level of power, if not considerably more. Yet the powers the enemy held in reserve stayed her from actions that might more befit her comrades among the other fleets of the Empire.

The superweapon.

Indeed, that alone was enough to make her reconsider whether her overly cautious approach was, in fact, cautious enough. The enemy's fleet disposal was . . . interesting, not impressive. She'd studied their combat capabilities, and while they showed an aptitude for battle admittedly beyond that of any she'd encountered in the Empire, including within herself if she were being harshly honest, they simply did not have the firepower to turn that difference into something that truly mattered.

Facing them with a parity of forces would be the ultimate stupidity, but she had no intention of doing that, and so ending them as a threat in fleet-to-fleet actions would not pose a serious issue, if not for the superweapon they had deployed.

A weapon she was beginning to think was only the more obvious of the daggers this enemy had at their disposal.

"Show me again," she ordered.

"Yes, My Lady."

The screen cleared, showing a stylized starfield that encompassed the region in which the fleet had deployed. It was a time-lapse map, including reports from her scouts and date stamps to isolate precise periods when the reported incidents were created and covered.

Enemy fleet movements were shown with an unusual pattern that she could not quite figure out.

"The enemy appears to have built up their fleets from previous estimates," her second in command said softly from her side.

Helena nodded slowly. "Yes . . . not a surprise, Robe, but they appear to have done so faster than expected given what the analysts had to say."

Sub-Commander Robe Havreu nodded in agreement.

"However, the data speaks for itself," he said, pointing to the varying reports and time stamps. "That's at least eight new squadrons showing the flag across the perimeter systems of the Oather territory."

Helena nodded reluctantly, but grimaced as well.

"There's something about them that bothers me," she admitted, "something I cannot put my brain on."

Robe frowned, considering her words. "I'm not sure what it would be, though I do admit that they are well coordinated."

"What?" she asked, looking over at him sharply.

"The time stamps," he said. "No two squadrons are in system at the same time. One appears, does its patrol, and then departs. Almost immediately afterward, another appears a few hundred light-years away, does its patrol, and then departs, then the third . . . and the fourth, and so on."

Helena looked at the time stamps more closely, realizing that her sub-commander was correct.

"What an unusual level of precision and coordination," she said after a moment. "Why would they deploy in such a manner?"

"I have no conception of how this enemy's mind works, My Lady," Robe said with some chagrin. "They are tactically unpredictable, strategically unique, and the method in which they dealt with the Third Fleet leaves me questioning their sanity."

"Oh?" Helena asked, amused. "How so?"

"They left the fleet largely *intact*," he said flatly. "No sane commander would have done that. Why not wipe out the Third and give their ultimatum directly to the Empire, along with some pointed demonstrations of their power?"

Helena gestured idly. "The destruction of the Third would not have significantly impacted Imperial power, and leaving them intact rings as a disregard for the power of an Imperial Fleet. It was likely a show of confidence more than a lack of sanity, though whether that confidence is valid, overestimated, or entirely false is one of the things we're here to determine."

She sighed, looking over the data again. "Thank you for pointing out the time stamps, Robe. I have a feeling they're important, but I am not yet certain how."

He bowed slightly. "I will examine them more closely, My Lady. Perhaps something more will come to me."

"Do so," she ordered. "In the meantime, see to our disposition as well. Continue the operation as planned."

"As you will it, Commander!"

———

Destroyer Dutchman, *Free Stars*

Steph stood at the command station of the captured destroyer, looking over the layered displays that lit up to show the system beyond the hull of his vessel. He would have preferred to be on his own fighter-gunboat, the now aptly named *Gaia's Revenge*, but the current mission had other requirements.

"Passive scans have picked up a signal from the expected region, Captain Teach."

Steph suppressed the urge to grin at the moniker, merely nodding.

"Thank you, Lieutenant Kora. Respond with the countersign."

"Yes Captain."

The lieutenant, one of the original crew that Steph and his Marines had captured along with the ship, had decided to stay on with his forces for reasons that Steph both understood and yet had trouble wrapping his head around. Steph noted that the man was amusingly stiff, but that was to be expected. He was trying to get the new recruits *mostly* used to using proper discipline, if not fully Confederate or Earth style in nature. The original crews had been somewhat lax in that area, and for someone like Steph to think so . . . well, it meant something.

He'd confirmed a lot since taking on the locals to crew the captured ship. His hunch that most of them were press-ganged into service was, if anything, understating the situation.

Free Stars my ass, he thought sourly.

If anything, the so-called Free Stars were more tyrannical than the Empire. At least, as best they could tell, there was some semblance of freedom for citizens of the Empire within Imperial-controlled areas. He could see arguments over just how much that really was, and how much of it was illusion, but that was a matter for philosophers.

Freedom was really more of a subjective quality when applied to civilization, in his experience. There was a balance between restrictions and freedoms that ultimately defined if a people were free; merely having fewer restrictions wasn't enough, nor was having more "freedoms" sufficient.

It was all very fine to claim that people were free to work hard and find their own success, but it was another thing for avenues to actually exist that allowed them to do so . . . And it was yet a third thing for those avenues to be reasonably accessible to most people.

In the case of the Free Stars, it was actually a lack of restrictions that led to the worst of their tyrannical nature. Laws were more than limitations, they were boundaries within which you could grow more freely than you could without them. Take down the law, and people inevitably began to carve out mini-empires where they could . . . And those sorts didn't rule through order, they ruled through power. Growth within that sort of arbitrary chaos was all but impossible.

He got headaches just thinking about it, honestly, because he knew how very counterintuitive it was, but that was the nature of people. The more people you put together, the more of a mess you got, and the less that logical solutions seemed to fit.

"Captain."

Steph was gladly broken from his thoughts as he heard the familiar voice approaching from behind. He rose from the command chair and turned, smiling.

"Milla, welcome to the bridge."

Milla Chans nodded, glancing over the sprawling deck with a keen eye. She had a large part in rebuilding much of the captured vessel after the last battle and was a careful guardian of her work.

"I see you have not broken anything yet," she said dryly, her eyes dancing with some amusement.

Steph clutched at his chest. "Ouch, Ms. Chans. That's uncalled for. When have I ever been that hard on equipment? Don't answer that."

Milla closed her mouth and lowered the hand that had come up to start ticking off examples. She sighed. "Very well. I will merely inform you that the engines are now repaired, and the *Dutchman* is similarly fully operational."

Steph nodded. "Thanks for that. I know it's been . . . troublesome."

Milla scoffed.

"Troublesome is a problem that is difficult to work out," she said. "The state of repairs that this vessel had been in was not troublesome, Stephan. It was abhorrent."

That didn't surprise him.

"This ship was likely overdue for standard maintenance by, at least, several tens of thousands of hours," she fumed, "and that's only if the builders were *far* better engineers than I give them credit for. More likely, the ship was more than two decades overdue for a basic maintenance pass. Frankly, Stephan, I'm not sure how it was still flying before we shot it up, let alone how the ship survived what you did to it *afterward*."

That, he didn't want to hear.

Steph winced, thinking about the strains they'd put the destroyer through in escaping the Empire in their last run, and really didn't want to know just how close they'd come to pushing the ship past its limit.

"The systems are now at a state that I am no longer afraid to be present on board," Milla went on. "And most of the internal structure has tested out as acceptable . . ."

She scowled slightly, sighing. "Which I should say does actually speak well for the engineers who designed and built her, so perhaps my earlier estimate is slightly excessive."

"Do we need to arrange more . . . *proper* maintenance?" he asked carefully as he glanced around.

Most of the crew were rescues from the battle, either already members of the *Dutchman* or one of the other vessels they'd removed people from ahead of the arrival of the Empire during the last mission. None were remotely cleared to know that the little merc unit they'd "joined" was actually linked to another stellar power, let alone one that had just forced the Empire to back off. Steph didn't see anything good coming from them finding out either. Earth's link to his mission had to remain hidden.

Milla shook her head. "No. The hull and internal structures are solid, no signs of microfractures. The design and materials were of quality make, even if the vessel has been horribly mistreated since it was launched."

"That's good," he said.

Steph didn't know what, if anything, the Forge or its Terran counterpart would be able to do anyway, and they were months away from even Priminae space if they limited themselves to the *Dutchman*'s drives.

Transition drives could get them home in a slice of an instant, but only the Archangels were so equipped and they were considerably smaller than the *Dutchman*, so no chance of getting a tow there.

Steph chuckled at the idea of an interstellar towing company transitioning busted ships around the galaxy. He didn't have a clue if that was remotely possible, but it was a funny thought.

"What?" Milla looked at him, confused by the chuckle.

"Just some amusing imagery," he said. "Nothing to worry about. So we're good to take the *Dutchman* operational?"

Milla nodded. "Aye Captain. She is ready to fly."

Steph nodded. "Alright, because we have a mission."

A mission and, more importantly, letters of marque.

Imperial Central Command

The command center of hundreds of worlds was an impressive place, no matter your background. For Fleet Over-Commander Sinthra, however, it was home. She walked into the main area, a massive circular construction of metal and transparent composites with terminals dotted all the way around on multiple levels. Each was assigned a specific sector or system, depending on the relative importance of the assignment, and each was tasked with constant monitoring.

She oversaw *everything*, in the empress' name, and took her duties seriously.

The empress, like the emperor before her, did not suffer fools easily in certain positions. In others, the fleets were full of them as best Sinthra could tell, but somehow, someway, certain positions were always kept *pure*.

She'd asked the emperor once, before his death, why he only enforced his will in targeted ways. Why allow fools in so many places, if he had the power to keep them clear of certain spots?

His answer had both opened her eyes and made her deeply cynical of the Empire and people in general.

Fools are a part of life, Sinthra, he had replied. *If you stamp them out wholesale, all you will get is more fools somewhere you've not accounted for. I prefer to keep the fools where I can see them.*

Over her career, she'd seen enough to sadly confirm the emperor's opinion and internalize it as fact. She did her best to ensure that key positions around her were fool free, as it were, but beyond that contented herself with identifying the fools and making note of their presence.

"Status," she ordered as she approached the supervisory console.

"All systems within expected levels, Over-Commander. No new encroachments, reports from the Eighth Fleet and Seventh Fleet indicate mission profiles continue as expected."

Sinthra nodded slowly, thinking about those two *very* different fleets and their equally diverse mission profiles.

The Seventh Fleet had been, until very recently, one of the biggest hammers of the Empire. Called up for the biggest military actions, trusted to solve problems without any further support no matter how troublesome those problems were.

How the mighty can fall, Sinthra thought idly, reaching down to manipulate the controls that allowed her to scroll through the recent fleet action reports.

Sometimes it only took one wrong decision, she knew.

Still, what dropped the Seventh Fleet was troubling the entire Empire. Her eyes lifted to the projected map of the Empire above, noting the harsh yellow icon that *still* remained where the shipyard facilities had once been.

The Empire had been struck at home before, of course. Historically, it was all but impossible for such an event not to have happened, really. They'd never been struck without being able to actively strike *back* before, however, and hadn't *that* set everyone in a buzz when it became clear they were dealing with something very different.

Something very new.

Now, months later, everyone was still waiting for the enemy to press the assault.

Yet, they hadn't.

No one knew what to make of that. Any Imperial force would have attacked again, no matter what, just to ensure that the enemy knew they weren't weak.

Even if they were.

The total silence, that was frightening.

Good.

The Empire needed a scare once in a while. They had been coasting for too long. Sinthra knew this better than anyone, possibly better than even the empress herself.

Fear honed the edge that the Empire relied on, an edge that had obviously been dulled by too many easy victories.

She looked to the icons that showed the Eighth Fleet and the systems beyond, and knew that it was time to hone that edge again.

Chapter 1

Steph sat watch on the bridge of the *Dutchman*, glaring jealously at the sleek profile of the fighter-gunboat flying in close formation with them.

That was supposed to be his ship, his Archangel.

Instead, he was sitting in command of a scow.

Oh, the destroyer was actually a pretty hot piece of kit, by Earth standards at least. It was faster than the cruisers Earth, the Empire, and the Priminae generally deployed, even if it didn't pack much of a punch by the same comparison.

It just wasn't an Archangel.

Steph sighed, wishing he'd turned down the promotion when it was offered.

He had the thought fairly often, well aware that Eric had the same thought as well. The higher up the ranks you climbed, the less fun stuff you got to do. You also endured a lot less shit, mind you, but most times he wasn't convinced the trade-off was worth it.

And the rest of the time, I damn well know it isn't.

Still, he'd taken the bump, and accepted the responsibility. So now he had his duty.

Damn Eric for beating that little trait into his personality.

He checked the telemetry, though he didn't really need to. They were on course and on schedule, a little less than a day out of the target system with all systems running green.

In less than twenty hours, we'll be in the soup again. Oh the things I do for my planet.

Archangel One, Gaia's Revenge

Milla Chans walked the tight halls of the Archangel, making her way to her work space.

The crews of the fighter-gunboats were, by necessity, limited in size, which meant that every person had multiple roles and their work spaces were as flexible as possible. For most, this meant a computer terminal and a desk, a small one of each. For Milla, well, she got a little bit more.

Her primary role consisted of serving as weapons control officer of *Archangel One*, at least in a tactical situation.

She considered her more important role, however, as existing outside of battle.

She was the designer and engineer who had made most of the new class of vessel possible, and this was in many ways their shakedown cruise . . . as the Terrans liked to term it. Milla was fully determined to see her first major work in design through to a successful conclusion.

Designing a new ship was not something that a Priminae Fleet would ever have given her the opportunity to accomplish, and now that she had done it . . . Milla simply could not imagine going back to the *limited* nature of her previous duties.

Maintaining weapon systems, and the mining systems they'd been derived from . . .

Or is that the other way around? Milla wasn't certain anymore. She had always believed that the tools came first, but something told her she'd been wrong.

Her tasks then had been monotonous, but vital. First, to develop technologies such that raw materials could more easily be acquired for the growth of the Colonies and, later, so that the weapons needed to protect lives were available when called upon. Her service hadn't been glorious, but she had taken the work seriously.

Now however, as important as that task had been—still was, even to this moment—Milla knew she could never settle for that again. She had seen more, *done* more. She wanted to do more still, and with the Terrans she was certain she could. Maybe she could show the Priminae that the old ways weren't the *only* ways.

Maybe she couldn't.

Either way, she was on a new path now.

She made her way into her office-slash-lab, really just a small additional section attached to the main engineering section, which was actually more a hallway with access panels that let her get at the power core and other systems for maintenance. Luckily she was hardly a large person, otherwise the basic work needed to maintain the small ship would be a pain.

It was already far from fun, even though she had done her best to make sure that everything was accessible enough to easily repair and maintain. However, even on a full cruiser, that wasn't always the easiest thing to accomplish, considering design constraints.

Luckily, in this case, she'd had very few constraints put on her by her superior officers, and she'd mostly found workarounds for the few that she had to deal with.

Unluckily, there had also been a few imposed by the physical rules of the universe, and those were a lot harder to find loopholes for.

She set her tablet computer down on the desk, letting the magnetic system lock it into place just in case something rocked the ship. Not a concern on a cruiser, but she hadn't had the space needed to put a complete cruiser spec inertial field into the Archangels.

Loose items, particularly hard-edged ones, were to be secured at all times when not in use. The method of securing them didn't have to be anything crazy—if the ship experienced much more than a few g's, everyone on board was probably dead *anyway*—but because the system was limited, it was designed to let some of the force through to the crew as needed in order to avoid overheating and frying vital components. It made for a rougher ride, but added a little more leeway in the performance specifications of the ships as a whole.

None of that was needed for intentional travel, thankfully. Otherwise, a ship the size of the Archangels wouldn't have been possible. The drive system itself took care of that, incidental to its primary function.

"Computer," she said softly. "Status on all primary systems."

"Primary systems are green."

The computer wasn't the most intelligent of conversationalists. She was going to miss working with Odysseus for that, if she was honest, but the system here was responsive.

"Status alerts for secondary systems," she ordered.

"One alert for secondary systems."

Milla frowned. "List alert."

"Secondary weapon systems show yellow. Error Code Four Niner Alpha Two Bravo."

Milla frowned, scraping her memory for what the code meant. Finally she sighed and picked up her tablet, punching it in.

Hmmm . . . an overheat on the relay array. Odd. There shouldn't be anything running through those systems to cause overheating.

"Tyke, Milla."

"Go for Tyke," the pilot's response came back almost instantly.

"I'm seeing an alert on our weapon relay system," she said. "I'm pulling it off the power grid while I find out what's wrong."

14

There was a pause before the pilot came back over the line.

"Roger. Try to get it back online before we make system, okay?"

Milla snorted. "We have almost a day, no? If I cannot have it corrected by then, believe me, Tyke, we have bigger problems than the operation."

"Roger that. Have at it."

Milla closed the connection and grabbed her tool case from where it was stashed.

This will likely be a long night.

———

Dutchman

Traveling this way is creepy, Steph decided as he looked out at the long night that filled the displays around him. *And boring. Can't forget boring.*

They were hours out from their target system, but it felt like days. The squadron was warping space at well over a hundred lights, and for the first time he was really understanding just how damned *slow* that was.

A thousand times light-speed would get you across the galaxy in a mere seventy-odd years. A few hundred was more than enough to handle local travel between stellar neighbors, especially in a cluster like the Free Stars.

But compared to transition drives?

Well, there was no comparison.

It was a quirk of the universe, he supposed, that Earth would simply skip all the apparently most common means of transport and simply jump right to *instantaneous teleportation* . . . or whatever it was they were calling transition now. Honestly, he'd stopped keeping up some time ago. The tech seemed to be constantly redefined by one group or another who were in the know enough to make such declarations.

Probably helps that warping space requires exotic matter, something that you only get when playing with a singularity, and no one on Earth was crazy—or stupid—enough to play with that until we had a stronger presence in space and some tutors to help out.

Not that tachyon transition was really all that saner, to his mind. Probably the least pleasant way to travel ever invented, in fact. The sensory mishmash that followed a multi-light-year jump was enough that ships tended to smell faintly of vomit for days afterward if you were able to get past the charcoal odor of the filters.

That part of a transition, he wasn't missing.

But damn it, he was getting tired of just how much time a normal transit was taking.

I need a hobby.

Hele Protectorate, Free Stars Cluster

Sub-Commander Pirot examined the system in front of him, frowning slightly. His shift in body language was enough for his superior Commander Geth to notice a moment later.

"Do you see something, Sub-Commander?"

Pirot grunted slightly, more focused on the displays than the question for a moment.

"No," he said finally. "I believe it's interference. The stellar cycle has been somewhat more active recently. It's playing games with our scanners."

Geth nodded. "Understood. Stay with it until the interference clears, just to be safe."

"Yes Commander."

It was a pain, but long-range scanners were a required station. One of the most important stations, in fact, which was part of what made them so very frustrating. The sheer size of space made it effectively impossible to scan, no matter what level of scanner you had available or how much power you used.

The leading edge of gravity shifts could be detected relatively easily, but there were literally millions of bodies out there with the mass of a military ship, and that was just within a few light-days of the fleet's scanner perimeter.

Anything else was even worse, just due to the length of time it took for any usable energy to reach the target and return on a bounce. Passives were moderately better, but they suffered from the problem of signal drop-off. That is, a signal dropped in intensity in an inverse to the square of the distance it traveled. In space, that distance was absurd, even at relatively close ranges.

For anything actually *outside* the stellar gravity well?

Absurd wasn't even close to the right word.

Impossible, that was getting there.

Despite that, they *tried*. Everyone tried.

Scanner deployments were placed at likely approaches, along with stealth pickets that would detect any ships within their ranges, and various other sorts of sentry systems. Most of the effort was largely worthless if an opponent wanted to remain hidden, which was why real defenses were pulled back to cover the actual targets of value.

Inhabited worlds, valuable mine sites, those sorts of locations got fixed defenses and fleet protection.

Which left sitting the scanner watch for screwups like him.

Pirot had no real question that he was a screwup. He hadn't held any illusions in that regard for a long time. He had once thought he would be the next big commander, or fleet commander even. One too many disciplinary events put an end to that, his vices not so easily ignored by the Protectorate Command, he supposed. Still, he continued to do the basics of his job if only to keep from getting sent to some even worse location. But he didn't have the heart for his work any longer.

Wasn't like it mattered. No one gave a damn about any of what he did in reality, but it still had to be done. There were worse assignments, though, and at least on scanner duty, he returned home every few weeks and the pay wasn't bad.

Plus, no one wasted energy shooting at the scanners or the stations they beamed to.

The scanner glitch he was dealing with now, however, was just making his job a frustrating pain to deal with.

Damn stellar activity.

It was amazing, as far out as they were, that the energy release of the local star was causing so much trouble. The whole inverse of the square thing and all, but stellar masses were *powerful* sources of energy. When one of them got riled up, literally in this case, it could project itself across quite a shocking range. Planets with magnetic fields were generally well protected, but even out this far, anything with lesser shielding got the worst end of the deal when reckoning with that kind of power.

At least the interference is starting to drop.

He sighed, checking over the anomaly briefly. It was still there, of course, but he'd give it a little bit longer before he made any reports. Not that anyone would bother reading the reports, not unless the commander slapped the emergency override down on the whole system. Short of the Empire showing up in force, that wasn't likely to happen.

"Ah, finally," he murmured as the interference cleared and the anomaly faded.

"Everything okay?" the commander asked.

"Yes Commander," Pirot confirmed. "Systems are clearing up as predicted."

"Good. Continue as you were."

Joy. As he was. So satisfying.

Dutchman

"We just passed through a scanner picket, Captain. Scan intensity never approached detection threshold."

Steph nodded. "Thank you, Ensign."

He'd adjusted the ranks of the new recruits to coincide roughly with what he was familiar with, mostly just so he didn't have to get used to all the damned variations of the word "commander" they used.

Really, sub-commanders, commanders, fleet commanders, over-commanders? What the hell? Use some imagination, you mooks, make some shit up.

Steph sighed, putting the thought firmly out of mind. Time to focus on the job.

They had letters of marque, and a mission to accomplish.

The letter—his term for it, of course, not the locals'—was really just a promise of a port of call where they wouldn't be arrested on sight for whatever their actions were in the Free Stars, as long as they abided by certain rules.

The letter was from the Kingdom, one of the more minor polities in the region, and also one of the only suppliers of natural processing crystals. That gave the Kingdom some power but also made them a few enemies, with not enough friends to tilt the balance. The letters of marque would transfer both the power and the enemies to the Archangels, offering advantages and costs that Steph had to weigh carefully. He had already shipped a sizeable allotment of crystals back to Earth; hopefully they'd be of some use to the system's defense, making the decision shift more in his favor over time.

Resources, in general, were incredibly cheap and easy to come by once you had space lift capability. Need deuterium for a reactor? It exists, literally by the exo-ton, just floating around your average star system. Want gold, for some unfathomable reason? Again, just floating around waiting to be picked up. Useless stuff, really, but it was there.

The same held true for *almost* all materials. Precious metals and stones, base materials galore, it was all there for the taking once you could get a decent lift capacity beyond the gravity of your homeworld.

That made the few things that weren't in abundance *far* more valuable than they might normally be. The processing crystals that were the backbone of the Kingdom's economic, political, and military power? Those were one of a very select list of things that couldn't be more easily and effectively found elsewhere.

Another such substance, one the Kingdom had tasked the squadron with acquiring, was *strange matter*. That was a material the Protectorate had something of a local monopoly on, a monopoly the Kingdom was eager to see broken.

Steph wasn't sure they could do that, but that wasn't the mission. They were assigned something much simpler, and successfully completing the mission for the Kingdom would put his unit in a far better light locally, something that was of real value to him.

In the present time, what the Kingdom represented best for him and his was legitimacy.

By backing him in an at least semiofficial capacity, the Kingdom had provided him with an identity within the Free Stars and, more importantly, to the Empire beyond. Captain Teach, a name he'd tossed out on a lark, was a real person now. He had a background that could be checked, if one had access to the Kingdom . . .

Which most of the region seems to, as far as I can tell, Steph thought with sour amusement.

Unfortunately, that identity and official—or semiofficial—recognition meant taking on the occasional mission to make everything look all nice and on the up-and-up.

Well, up-and-up for mercenaries, anyway.

Steph examined the telemetry as the squadron pierced the heliopause of the target system. The Protectorate was a small multi-star polity, really more of a loose alliance of minor tyrants as far as he could tell. In the files they looked like a real stellar force, but in reality they were like most of the Free Stars, what used to be called paper tigers. All show, no real go.

That was mostly due to the actions of the Empire, as best he could determine. They did semiregular roving patrols and *pruned* the locals down to size on the barest of excuses. According to local sources, the attacks were nearly random, but Steph was convinced that the Empire was also selectively setting up different groups of the Free Stars against one another by greatly reducing the supply of specific resources with strategic precision.

That calculated resource shortage was what brought him to Hele, and what had bought his squadron their letters of marque.

He didn't like it, exactly, as being a mercenary was never something he wanted out of his life, but there was a certain romance to being a swashbuckling privateer. All the more so since he was *actually* infiltrating an enemy group by pretending to be a privateer while really being an upstanding officer of the good guys' Navy.

Completely not complicated at all, and also totally unlike something out of the books he used to spend tons of time reading.

"Avast ye mateys," Steph said softly. "The *Revenge* is in the system. Lock up your valuables if you like, it won't do you any good."

He opened a signal to the squadron.

"Execute the operation as planned."

Chapter 2

Hele Protectorate

"Status of the mining operations?"

"All blue, Commander."

Commander Geth nodded, not having expected anything else. Checking status was one of the things he had to do at the start of every shift, regardless of the fact that nothing changed. The mining facility was entirely automated and had sufficient redundancies that even catastrophic failures were of little import to the overall operation.

Every shift, however, he had to ask the same question, get the same answer, log it in the record, and pretend like the data mattered.

The neutron star that had been here some billions of cycles ago had made quite a mess when it exploded but had also scattered incredibly valuable material all through the system and beyond.

Better than that, the star was stable. Without any of the pulsing bursts of radiation that most neutron stars were prone to, the system was both relatively safe to work in and, more importantly for certain people, almost entirely dark. The Protectorate had located the system entirely by accident, losing half a handful of ships in the process when they entered the gravity well too deeply while at light-drive speeds. The surviving crews realized just what they'd discovered.

Keeping the system hidden had been hopeless in the long run, of course, so instead they had defended it as best they could while trying to keep the secret for as long as possible. Somehow, that had held longer than anyone expected, or the only groups that discovered the system were happier to trade for neutronium than they were to fight over the resource.

Geth was simply happy with each shift that ended without discovery or combat.

The Protectorate had the benefit of being in the system first and establishing strong defenses, but star systems were big things and quite impossible to hide in any reasonable way or properly defend.

So every now and then, some group or polity would take their shot at a raid. Generally, only the larger governments would try to establish any sort of beachhead in the system, of course, but smaller ones and the various mercenary and pirate organizations that existed would often make hit-and-run raids to get away with whatever they could snap up.

Those were the main sources of frustration he had to deal with, and for the most part it was a relatively easy job. No one expected him to actually *catch* those annoyances; space was too big for that. His task was to drive them off as quickly as possible, ideally making them pay for the attempt with more lost lives and ships than the exotic matter they were stealing was worth.

Geth had received worse assignments.

"Keep me apprised," he said as he took a seat and reached for his drink before calling up reports he needed to sign off on.

Another day in the neutronium mine.

———

Dutchman

"Telemetry feeds are live and at full resolution, Captain."

Steph nodded absently, already looking through the feeds as he relayed them from the main system to his personal repeaters. The system was fascinating in a slightly ghoulish sort of way.

The neutron star had gone supernova, a long damn time ago thank God, and left quite a mess within its influence. He was quite certain that there were probably entire *planetary systems'* worth of mass traveling away from the star at high speed, lost to the black. What was left, however, was still a bounty for any up-and-coming civilization.

Neutronium and other exotic materials were the key to faster-than-light tech, at least looking at the way the Empire and its little branch groups did things. Earth tech was a little different. He'd read the brief on the differences a while back and then promptly forgotten most of the details for the sake of his own sanity, but Steph remembered enough.

Instead of using exotic materials directly, since the system around Earth had insufficient deposits, technologies like the transition drive and the counter-mass system used quantum effects to replicate some of the qualities of exotic and strange matter.

The process was crude by comparison, a kludge that really didn't do a tenth of what the real thing managed, but Earth had leveraged what it could do in ways the Empire had never dreamed of.

The Archangels' telemetry put them on course and schedule, but that was as he expected. Steph suppressed another sigh, wishing he was commanding *Archangel One* for this mission, but until he knew the crew of the *Dutchman* better, he didn't feel he could entrust them with much, and the destroyer was important to the operation.

"Any sign that we've been spotted?" he asked, looking up.

"No Captain," Ensign Dumora responded. "All scanner intensities remain stable and well below the detection threshold for the . . . *Dutchman*, to say nothing of your Archangels."

Steph nodded.

"Good, good."

He was looking over the positioning of the Protectorate's holdings within the system, puzzling at some of their choices.

"Is there something wrong, Captain?"

"No," Steph said, glancing up to where the *Dutchman*'s executive officer, Commander Gurenn, was standing.

The commander—well, sub-commander technically, but Steph was having none of that bullshit naming convention—was a squat man with a talent for appearing at the right place and right time. Steph had pulled his name from the list of possible second-in-command options after they'd spent a few weeks repairing the *Dutchman* and he'd seen Gurenn solve multiple small issues without needing to escalate them up the chain of command.

A useful skill, that.

It also didn't hurt that Gurenn was talented, smart, and had been completely wasted in his previous "employment."

"I'm just trying to work out a few of these extraneous facilities," Steph said, gesturing to the screens. "The processing, mining, security, even administration are all pretty obvious, but what are these massive facilities here? They don't seem to have the traffic for anything productive."

Gurenn leaned in to look closer before nodding. "Holding pens, I imagine."

"Holding pens? For what?" Steph blinked.

"Slaves, sir."

Steph frowned. Now he was just confused.

"I thought the workers were held in these areas," he said, gesturing.

"Yes sir. Those are the workers' sections, as we discussed."

Gurenn was now looking puzzled as well, leaving Steph to wonder what the obvious miscommunication between them was.

"The workers aren't the slaves?" he asked.

Gurenn's expression cleared. "Ah. Yes sir, they are. The workers are taken along with their families from various planets and ships, wherever really, and assigned to various duties. Those with appropriate skills are sent here and impressed into service to the Protectorate, mining the system for materials."

"And those in the slaveholding pens?" Steph asked with an ice-cold sensation forming in the pit of his stomach as he began to make the connections.

"Their families, of course," Gurenn said, as though it were obvious. "To keep any attempt at revolt in line."

Well. Fuck. Me.

Steph was honestly starting to *detest* the "Free Stars."

Archangel Two

Commander Black was looking over the numbers in preparation for taking the operation live when her comm came to life.

"*Two, One* Actual."

She frowned, recognizing the voice. "Go for *Two.*"

"Hey Alex," Stephanos said, his image appearing on her primary display a moment later. "Have some last-minute updates for you. Just got a bit of an intel bomb. Not sure how, or if, it affects our operation."

"Now is a fine time," Alexandra Black said as she looked for, and quickly found, the incoming files and opened them. "What am I looking at?"

"You know that the workers here are indentured slaves, right?" he asked.

"Of course, it was in the briefing," Alex said, frowning as she read some of the descriptions. "I thought we'd already identified their locations."

"We did. Apparently we didn't know enough to ask about where their *families* were being held, however."

Alex grimaced. "Oh, damn it."

Steph nodded. "Theoretically, this doesn't affect us if we go with the official plan. We're strictly on a hit-and-git op here, and none of those facilities are within our operational zone."

She nodded, knowing that.

However, they'd made a lot of *unofficial* plans that this intelligence was going to seriously screw with.

"If we go with plan L, do we have the lift?" she asked.

"Not even close."

Alex sighed. "No, I didn't expect we would. What are you thinking?"

"The smart move is to do the op as planned, worry about the rest at a later date."

"I've never known you to do the smart move, Stephanos," Alex said dryly.

Steph put his hand over his heart, a patently fake look of hurt on his face. "How could you *possibly* say such a thing, Noire? After all we've been through."

"That would be how I can say it."

"You are such a party pooper," Steph said, rolling his eyes. "Must have been a real pill in your sorority days."

"How did . . ." Alex clamped her mouth shut.

Steph snorted. "Seriously? You *were* in a sorority? Wow, I did not see that coming. Of course, I didn't go to college, so what do I know."

"You didn't?" Alex couldn't help but ask, fighting to keep her face from reddening. "I know you have degrees."

"Mostly mail and teleconference stuff," Steph said offhandedly. "I was a kid when the war started, and a bit of a delinquent at that . . ."

"So . . . no change?"

He chuckled. "Eric and the rest, well, they adopted me, I guess you could say. Made sure I got an education, though it was pretty pointed at the time. After the war I picked up the course credits I needed to fill out the degrees in my own time. No one really cared by that point."

"Or before I expect," Alex said.

"Or before," Steph replied agreeably. "For a while, it looked like we were going to lose before the war even really got started. The USA's debt was so deep that when China and India started selling off their shares in it at cut-rate prices . . . Well, military spending went the way of the dodo, but not before everything else."

Alex had heard the stories, but she'd been a kid herself then. And not the precocious teenage hellion that Stephanos was rumored to be in legend; she'd literally still been in diapers.

"Hard to explain just how bad things were then," he said pensively. "You'd have to have experienced it to really understand. There were more people on the streets than in homes, and the US Navy literally abandoned ships where they floated because they couldn't get enough people to crew them home.

"Inflation, well it was a thing," he went on. "Let's just say that. It was shocking, really, just how *fast* things went in the shitter. We'd been living above our means for decades, and the debtors yanked the rug out from under us. When things were at their worst, that's when the Block began to move."

Alex knew most of this, basic world history, but she just nodded. She knew Steph well enough by this point to be confident that he was going somewhere with his words.

"We ignored them, at first. Taiwan wasn't *our* problem. Someone else could help them as the people there were put into labor camps." He sighed. "Korea? Well, maybe it was time for North and South to be united again, right? Never mind that North Korea was a Goddamned hellhole and South Korea was an ally. Wasn't our business. Eastern Europe? Let the Russians have that headache. NATO was in tatters anyway. Couple presidents earlier saw to that."

He laughed bitterly. "We didn't start to pay attention until Okinawa was overrun. I still have no idea why there were any Marines *left* there. No one can seem to tell me, even though I've checked. The base was slated to be shut down at least fifteen times in less than a year, but somehow never quite got the axe."

He shook his head. "I don't know why the Block did it. Maybe they got sick of waiting for us to abandon Japan like we'd abandoned everywhere else. Maybe they thought we *had* shut it down. There weren't many left there after all. But they screwed up. They did the one thing that saved us. They invaded territory that people finally considered *ours* enough to care."

He shook himself visibly, taking his mind out of the memories.

"When we liberated Japan, Taiwan, Korea . . . other places," he said, "it wasn't pretty. Work camps were the norm for political prisoners, which meant anyone the enemy felt they needed to control, plus their families, sometimes their close friends."

Steph looked away from the screen for a moment, his face a little pale and drawn, but Alex thought that might be from the lights of the screens in front of him.

Maybe.

"A lot of people, they said it wasn't our job to care, to police the world. They're probably right," Steph admitted. "But I was never able to answer the question for myself. If I could do something about those sorts of evils, and I didn't . . . how was I any better than the monsters who actually inflicted those evils onto people. I can't look away, Alex."

She took a breath, uncertain.

"This is going to change a lot of plans, sir."

"Yeah. I know. Let's get to work."

Chapter 3

Eric Weston looked out at the black beyond his ship, only vaguely not-ing the running lights of the remaining vessels in his squadron as they blinked in the darkness.

The *Odysseus* had been running patrols almost nonstop since they'd been refitted after the throwdown with the Empire, and it was begin-ning to wear on the crew. Space was filled with long hours of boredom, something that had been a relief at first after the fighting but was now growing wearisome.

We'll need to schedule leave soon. It'll be another few weeks before the Earth's next squadron can take over our patrols, and even that leaves the frontier far too badly unguarded.

On the other side of the coin, the new crewmembers of the *Odysseus* and her sister ships were shaping up well. After a rocky start, as such things went, he was confident that they could handle anything thrown at them just as well as they had before the expansion of the fleet.

Of course, that just means that I'll soon lose more crew to the new squadrons to help spread the experience around.

Eric hoped that the plan wasn't to "spread" the experience so thin that it tore like wrapping paper upon a major challenge, but he also understood the problems that the Earth's government(s) was/were dealing with.

He grimaced, taking a sip of his coffee.

Which, of course, was the *other* problem.

The Confederation controlled the Americas, more or less, with only a few holdouts not having joined up by this point. It was largely led by former US, Canadian, and Mexican members still, but that was slowly changing to a more even representation. The rest of the planet was sliced up into sections controlled by the Block, the Russian Federation, the European Union, and a few unaffiliated groups here and there that really didn't count, aside from Australia and New Zealand. The latter two were quasi-affiliated with both the EU through their ties with the UK and the Confederation through their ties with Canada.

Somehow, because of the existence of former treaties such as the Commonwealth Freedom of Movement, or CANZUK, any citizen of the European Nations or the Confederation had full freedom of travel without passport between any member nation of the two, using Australia or New Zealand as a "bridge" of sorts.

That had to have been a nightmare for security to figure out, he supposed, but it had been a massive boon for the allied nations involved, as it basically turned them into a three-state governing body that controlled better than half the planet. The Russians and the Block weren't happy about it, but no one in the Big Three gave a damn.

That gave them a lot of power, both politically and with the world economy, and had kept the Big Three on top so far.

The problem was, more than *two-thirds* of the world population were still under the control of the Block and the Russian Federation, and manpower was beginning to be the stumbling block as the space forces continued to expand.

New squadrons coming online, each requiring tens of thousands of trained people, were the least of the issues. The Forge needed even more people, highly trained workers, to build those squadrons, and the

Earth's Kardashev Net might have been an automated build platform but maintaining it still took the attention of thousands more, requiring a demand for brains that was damn near exponential.

Combined with the Rogues, their ongoing cooperative missions with the Priminae, and the new demand for fighting forces in case of ground warfare with the Empire, even the total population of the Big Three was starting to become strained by demand.

Eric just hoped that the admiral had a few more tricks to pull out of her sleeve, because if the Empire decided to push this anytime soon, he didn't think things would go well.

So far, thankfully, the bluff he'd pulled during their last encounter seemed to be holding as well as, or better than, he could have reasonably hoped. The Empire had withdrawn their expeditionary force entirely and limited themselves to a probing fleet clearly commanded by someone of a different caliber than the one he'd met in battle.

That was Eric's current problem, and the reason he was staring out at the black and thinking about all that could go wrong.

He reached out and picked up a display from a pedestal near him, bringing up the numbers he'd been thinking about when he came out to the observation deck.

So far, the probing fleet had been content to quietly pick around the edges of Priminae space, leaving Earth well alone. That didn't help much, in some ways, given how ruthless they appeared to be in the manner they conducted their probing runs.

Every time the Imperial force had chosen to engage with others, whether it be ships or planets, they'd left no witnesses to speak of. A few survivors on a bombed-out world spoke of the nightmare they'd lived through, but no one who'd been in a position to witness the attack. Similarly, they'd found the occasional survivor on a derelict, if they got there in time, but it was rare, as the Imperials generally made certain that the computer core of any ship they destroyed was well and truly eliminated before moving on. That pretty much took out any people on board as well.

This enemy was ruthless, efficient, and *cautious.*

The last time Eric had them close enough to set a trap, the enemy had refused to take the bait, even though they clearly had a superiority of forces.

He dropped the tablet back down, irritated.

"You're frustrated."

Eric didn't even glance to the side. He could feel the slight shift as the entity appeared beside him.

Entity.

Perhaps that was the wrong word.

Odysseus.

Avatar.

The soul of the ship, perhaps.

"And now you're poetic, it's a nice change," Odysseus said lightly. "We will find the enemy, Captain, you know that."

"Do I?" Eric asked, tired. "They're wary, these ones. Careful. Forcing an engagement with them will be almost impossible, even if we do find them. I should know, since I've undoubtedly driven many of my own opponents mad with similar frustrations in the past. Space is just too big, and for all the speed our vessels have, there's too much room to hide in."

"Perhaps, but you know the answer to that as well as I do."

Eric glanced over now, taking in the figure that stood beside him. Odysseus had grown up some. He still wore his ancient Greek–inspired armor, but now the attire looked more like it was made of carbon fiber. His makeup was more tasteful—the garish hot-pink eyeshadow the entity had insisted on rarely made an appearance now—but he took care to present an androgynous look to those he interacted with. His body leaned a little to the male side, his face clearly more to the female, but both just close enough to the center that the entity could pass for either gender.

A ship with gender-identity issues was not in the manual, Eric thought wryly, not for the first time, before he turned back to the black and to the actual issue he had to deal with.

"I do," he said.

There was really only one thing he could do, as much as he despised it. If the enemy wouldn't let him force an engagement, he would have to make *them* force the fight.

Convincing them that the battlefield was to their advantage would be a problem, however, because the only way to really sell that point would be to effectively *make* the battlefield to their advantage.

And that was something he was *not* eager to do.

Damn it. Needs must, I suppose.

Eric turned, nodding briefly to Odysseus before the entity faded away.

"I suppose we have some work to do," he said to the empty observation deck as he walked out. He keyed open a channel. "Command, Weston."

"Go for Command, Commodore," Miram Heath's voice came back almost instantly.

"Contact the Priminae," he ordered. "If I remember correctly, they have a few operations on the go that I want a look at. Tell Admiral Tanner that it's about time we turn the tables on our ghost problem."

"Aye Commodore. Are you coming up?"

"I'll be along shortly, I need to check the archives for something first," he said.

"Very well. I'll have the information you asked for waiting when you arrive."

Eric let the channel close off. It was time to stop trying to react to the enemy and start making *them* react to him. It was a game of hide-and-seek, perhaps, but maybe they were due for a little change in the rules.

Ready or not . . . here we come.

———

Sol System

"Admiral, reports on the materials delivered from the Archangel expeditionary force were just sent to your system."

Amanda Gracen half turned before she nodded. "Thank you, Lieutenant."

Her aide nodded in response before stepping back out of her office, leaving Gracen to bring her terminal out of sleep mode and call up the files in question.

Interesting, she noted a few moments later as she read the summary.

The intelligence they'd gleaned from the computer dump of the captured destroyer already made the entire operation worth what they'd put into it, but apparently the crystals themselves were of some interest as well.

She flipped past the summary, reading the rest with more focus.

A few things jumped out to her and certainly had caught the eye of some of the researchers. The crystals didn't belong to the expected isotopes, and if they hadn't come with some basic instructions, the researchers wouldn't have known what to do with the damn things.

Still, they'd been able to determine a few bits of interest that hadn't been included in the brief provided by Stephanos.

Interesting. Very interesting.

The crystals had a quantum flux that made them ideal for a quantum computing core. Their capacity was, in fact, superior to the respectively unique base designs used by Earth and the Priminae.

That explains where the Empire got the changes in their tech from the common base we'd calculated for, she decided.

For the moment, those crystals were being seconded to making a new cluster that would hopefully serve as the fastest and most powerful supercomputer in the solar system. As a benefit, it appeared that some of the crystals had trackable quantum linked elements. If the research was correct, they could compute in real time, no matter where in the star system they were located.

Gracen made a note, requesting that they test the range on the crystals to see if they really would be good across light-minutes, or farther.

She wasn't completely certain of what benefits that would hold, though it seemed like faster and more effective communications might be one of the big advantages.

The admiral frowned, thinking hard about that for a moment.

She quickly sent off another missive.

Need to see if that means the Empire currently has a major communications advantage over us, strategically, or if they haven't noticed what they have yet.

Normally, Gracen wasn't one to underestimate a *clearly* dangerous enemy, but she'd learned the hard way that it was almost impossible to judge alien technical abilities based on human tech development. There was just no comparing across the board.

Sometimes what seemed obvious to her was complete magic to the Priminae, and some of the matters they considered simplicity itself still made her bug out.

———

Imperial Eighth Fleet Command Vessel

Birch examined the data from their long-range scouts, uncertain whether she was entirely happy with the progress of the mission to date or not. On the one hand, they'd had no major setbacks, but there hadn't been a lot of major advances either.

They'd tested the enemy defenses, which were apparently nonexistent, but learned nothing they didn't already know . . . That is, the enemy had *nothing* significant protecting their colonies.

She supposed, if she were being generous, she might concede that defending young colonies was rarely a big priority, even in the Empire. Still, even considering that, the lack of early warning pickets, defensive fleets, and even stationary platforms were enough to make her just a little paranoid.

If not for the fact that they'd utterly decimated an Imperial Fleet and then gone on to make their point by putting an entire Imperial shipyard facility to the torch—something she'd not even realized *possible* in the vacuum of space—Birch would have made the decision by this point that they were dealing with a soft target.

And then, no doubt, proceeded to get destroyed by the enemy and have my title removed by the empress as punishment.

"Fleet Commander?"

"Yes?" she asked, glancing over.

"We just received new intelligence from a few of our scouts. You may be interested in some of it."

"Send it here."

"Yes, Fleet Commander."

The files were delivered a moment later. Birch opened them up reflexively. She examined the numbers and telemetry for a moment before she understood what she was looking at.

"Sub-Commander," she said. "Look at this, tell me what you think."

Robe made his way over, leaning against her console as he looked over the data briefly.

"Is that a Colony convoy?" he asked.

"That is what it appears to be," she confirmed. "Look to the vectors."

Robe examined the numbers again. "It's away from our border with the Oathers. Do you think they're looking to avoid our probes?"

Birch nodded. "That would be my guess, Sub-Commander. Based on what I'm seeing, I think we can get ahead of them as well."

"The cargo ships do seem to have a relatively low maximum speed, based on the power curve and their sheer mass," Robe confirmed. "Shall I issue the orders?"

Birch nodded. "Do it. I want to make them fear us, in every corner of their space."

"As you command."

Chapter 4

Dutchman, *Hele Protectorate Space*

"Sir, system scans are complete, as best they can be using passive scanners only."

"Understood." Steph acknowledged the report, opening the appropriate files so he could see in better detail what they were dealing with.

Grabbing data on anything hot was easy. Ships and facilities transmitting pretty much on any level were basically calling out their position for all to hear. Once you knew where they were, then it was just a matter of focusing the scanner on that location and you could snap up tons of information, from visual to magnetic and plenty more.

The big issue was finding everything that was currently in a mostly powered-down or passive mode.

Ships could be out there, waiting. They couldn't power down *forever*, of course. Eventually life support would lose the battle of keeping the ship from radiating heat, even with the most efficient reclamation systems, but for hours? Sure. Even days with a properly designed vessel was possible.

However, he was more concerned with unmanned defensive drones.

So far the Empire hadn't used the tech, and the Priminae barely had any inkling of what weapons were it sometimes seemed, let alone unmanned weapon platforms, but the intelligence they'd been given by the Kingdom indicated that at least some degree of automated defenses existed here. That was a new development that Steph found both inter-esting and somewhat irritating.

Not really a surprise, he had to admit. If you were going to defend anywhere, the materials mine that kept your civilization ahead of the pack was the place to do it. *And you sure as hell don't pull any punches on those defenses either.*

Unfortunately, drones didn't radiate *anything* unless they were operative, and they could be sitting almost anywhere, listening for a signal to activate.

Almost anywhere was the key, though, a limitation he could work with.

Unless they built a Kardashev Net.

Steph *really* didn't want to think about that side of things at the moment. There was no evidence that anyone in the Empire or the Free Stars had begun playing with that level of technology. Technically, this was beyond the scope of their technology, but then again it was *techni-cally* beyond the scope of *Earth's* technology and Admiral Gracen had still pulled the application off.

Mostly.

There was no sign of any of that on the scans, however.

That's what the Imperials thought when they came barreling into Sol, his mind told him treacherously.

The Imperials hadn't been *looking* for anything like the system, though, and that counted. There *were* defensive points floating around, guarding the mining operations and administrative stations. There were even a few guarding the slave pens, he noted with some rancor.

Those had their weapon ports pointed *inward.*

We'll have to eliminate those first, before we announce ourselves, Steph noted on the file.

He checked the telemetry with the rest of the Archangels, noting that they'd tightened their formation as planned, and were close enough for a conference call to go out live.

"Put me on with the squadron," he ordered.

"Aye sir!"

———

Archangel Three

Jennifer "Cardsharp" Samuels settled into the main command area, letting the virtual and augmented displays fill her field of view as the microgravity harness kept her in place. One by one the other pilot commanders of the fighter-gunboat squadron appeared around her, with the only odd man out being the commander himself.

Stephanos appeared as a two-dimensional screen at the center of her view, a counterpoint to the near perfect virtual representations of her other flight mates.

"Data from the passive scans has been completed, as much as we're going to get, anyway," Steph said once everyone was present. "We have a full system-wide base scan, and we've of course taken the time to focus in on closer trouble spots. I'd like to bring the automated defensive platforms to your attention, if you'd open the detailed file please."

The files opened in front of each of them, floating in their view.

Jennifer idly flipped through the specs, eyes mostly looking for specific details.

"Is this right?" she asked. "They don't seem large enough to handle the containment system for a singularity core."

Steph nodded. "Good eye. They're not. These are magazine limited, a compromise on the part of the designers I have no doubt. If they had a core, they'd be able to fire effectively forever, at least in tactical terms. However, if they had a core, we'd have found *all* of them by now, and let's not pretend we didn't miss any, because it's a deadlock certainty that we did."

"Do we know how *big* a magazine we're talking about?" Tyke asked from the control room of the *Revenge*, or *Archangel One*.

"Intelligence wasn't clear on that, but we do have power specifications for Imperial capacitors," Steph said. "And assuming they match both the best in Imperial power storage and generation, then we're looking at a ten-round box at the outside. Based on observations of Free Stars technology so far, I'm saying maybe as much as fifteen pulses, but at significantly lower power levels than Imperial combat lasers."

"That's still more than enough to torch us," Tyke said, frowning.

"If they hit us," Jennifer countered. "And that's a big if."

"Don't get cocky, kid."

Steph stepped in to silence the conversation.

"We've spotted over a thousand of these drones so far, which makes them a concern," he said firmly. "However, most of them are not in position to target our primary points of interest."

"I believe I recognize this system."

Everyone turned, noting that a new image had appeared in their augmented displays. Similar to Steph, Milla was in her office and had been listening in while the pilot commanders had begun their strategy session.

"This network is very similar to a mining system in use in Colonial Space," she said, perusing the numbers and information. "I believe that it was adapted from those plans."

"Or those plans were adapted from this weapon system," Steph said. "I can see how this would be useful for mining, but no one designs a multi-terawatt laser grid with mining in mind, Milla."

"Perhaps." She shrugged. "Honestly, I do not know. The plans I have worked with were old long before I was born, and they made no mention of weapons technology. However, if the grid is based on the same concepts, I believe we may have an option."

"I'll be glad to hear it," Steph said seriously. "But I think no matter what, we're going to need to do some more prep work, however. Too much new data overriding the old intelligence."

42

Milla nodded. "I would agree, Stephan. The Kingdom's priorities were quite different than ours, and that alone has rendered much of their information . . . questionable."

"No kidding," Steph said. "Okay. We take a step back, gather more intelligence. Milla, give me your plan so I can see what can be worked out."

"Of course, Stephan."

Hele Protectorate Command Station

"All blue, Commander."

Geth nodded, not bothering to say anything else. Another shift, another confirmation that everything was running as it was intended. All was right with the universe.

He settled in to look over his documentation for the shift, noting that the mine productions were down somewhat, but not too much. Still, if he allowed that to go on he would inevitably run into questions, and worse, from the homeworld.

He sent down an order to increase production by whatever means required and made a note to the supervisors that they would be held accountable if they failed. One way or another, production would increase or someone would be made an example of, and it would not be him.

The deep matter being mined was vital to the economy and defense of the Protectorate, one of the few things that they could trade with the Empire that was of real value and important enough to buy Imperial protection with. Not that the Empire provided protection from anyone other *than* the Empire, sadly, but even that was worth a lot.

Archangel Three

Sergeant Kiran quietly examined the signals intercepted from his small station, noting the orders being shifted back and forth as well as the production numbers.

The squadron was on intel-gathering duty for the foreseeable future. New developments mid-mission *sucked* generally, but at least the boss had the authority out here to deal with them as they came. Back home, on Earth, Kiran had no doubt that they'd still be in a holding pattern, waiting for orders from command on *what* to do rather than just being able to alter the plan and do it.

The locals, some Protectorate or something, were pretty lax in their information network, which made his current job easier.

He was gathering information about the disposition of assets around the system, or at least that was his primary assignment. Beyond that, well, he was getting pretty much everything else.

This place churns out a lot of strange-matter production, he noted with interest.

Strange matter was vital to the gravity cores that powered larger vessels like Earth's own cruisers. The *Odysseus* herself was powered by a twin core system that couldn't exist without a small starter block of strange matter.

Kiran wondered briefly where they'd gotten theirs because he doubted it was something that could easily be mined around the Sol System. But then maybe he was wrong and it could. His knowledge on the subject ended shortly after the more commonly known uses of the material, and he knew basically nothing about how the resource was acquired, either by Earth or the Priminae.

Though, we probably get it from them at this point.

Likely, though not certain.

Here, however, the material was clearly immensely valuable, a point driven home when a small notation crossed his display. His eyes widened and he tagged the section immediately, reaching for the controls to the ship's comms.

"Yes?" A soft voice responded almost immediately to his comm request.

"Ma'am," he said. "Sergeant Kiran here."

"Yes Sergeant," Lieutenant Commander Samuels said. "What is it?"

"I've tagged an interesting bit of intel you might want to check out," he said. "It seems like the protectors, or whatever they call themselves . . ."

"Protectorate," she said, amused.

"Right, them," Kiran said, going on. "It seems they have a rather important client for the material they mine here."

"Oh? Someone we know, I assume?"

"You assume correctly, ma'am," he confirmed. "The Empire."

Samuels was quiet for a moment. "*The* Empire, Sergeant? Not one of the little pocket pretenders around these parts?"

"No ma'am, the Empire itself. If I'm reading this right, it sounds like they're talking about a periodic tribute made to the Empire in exchange for 'protection,'" Kiran said firmly.

"That's . . . *very* interesting," she responded. "Very interesting indeed. Good work, Sergeant. I think you may have just bumped the value of this mission significantly, and possibly made Stephanos a soon-to-be very happy man."

"Thank you, ma'am?" Kiran said, uncertain how exactly to take that. He hoped that was a good thing, though sometimes it wasn't all that great when you made your boss happy.

Sometimes pleasing the boss meant more work, usually the worst kind.

"I'll pass the intel along, Sergeant," Samuels said. "See what else you can dig up."

"Wilco, ma'am," he said before the comm went dead.

Well, that was interesting.

This is very interesting, oh yes . . .

Cardsharp was a pilot at heart, so a lot of what they were doing here wasn't really to her personal taste, so to speak, but she'd known from the start that her ambitions to join the Archangels would mean pushing boundaries and her comfort zone. Perhaps not quite so much as she was currently doing, but it was an experience.

The information that the sergeant had brought to her attention was an example of why it could be *very* good to push those boundaries. If they hadn't dropped into an intelligence-gathering stance due to what Stephanos had found out from one of their . . . new crewmates, well, they likely would have missed this entirely.

And this isn't something to be missed.

She read over the tagged section of the intelligence file first, then went back and read the entire document just to be sure. Only when she was done did she make her way to the command deck of the small fighter-gunboat in order to access the secure comm.

The squadron was split up a little, moving in three groups to gather as much data as they could, while the *Dutchman* was holding back well out of detection range a little farther out in the system. That meant she couldn't establish a real time link with the commander, but they knew where each other would be and had carefully plotted their course to prevent any accidental oversplash from lasers comm.

"Secure laser to *Dutchman*," she ordered, slipping into the command chair that was the centerpiece of the room when not in tactical combat mode.

A tone beeped, confirming that the laser had been targeted to the appropriate section of space.

"Send to *Dutchman*, Commander's Eyes Only," Cardsharp ordered. "Intelligence packet Niner Four Three Bravo. Append personal notations, Cardsharp Alpha One Bravo. Transmit when ready."

The system responded shortly after with a "transmission sent" confirmation.

Dutchman

"Captain," Dumora said from her station. "Signal from *Archangel Three*."

"To my station," Stephanos ordered, already bringing the system display closer so he was ready when the file was linked to his account.

He opened it quickly, reading the brief that was in Cardsharp's notes before looking at the file. His eyes widened as he recognized the implications almost instantly.

The Empire acquires strange matter from here? That's . . .

Honestly, he didn't *know* what that was. Steph knew it was important, likely damned important, but he was missing a few key data points to be sure just *how* important.

"Huh." He half turned, calling up all the star charts of the region that covered both the Free Stars and the section of space they'd attributed to the Empire.

It was a significant amount of space, encompassing a chunk of the galaxy a few hundred light-years across and containing *thousands* of stars. More, probably, but he didn't need a count on how many *stars* there were. No, he needed something more specific.

Interesting. There are no known neutron stars in the region at all . . . Steph grimaced. *Well, that's a worthless load of nothing.*

He then had been forced to go and read up on the nature of neutron stars, as well as estimates of stellar density in the galaxy, and was left more or less where he started from.

There were an estimated *billion* neutron stars in the galaxy; however, less than three thousand had been located by Earth observers to date. The files he had from the Priminae didn't seem to cover that information, though he wasn't sure he was reading them correctly. The main issue he could see up front was that the majority of neutron stars were like the one they were currently orbiting, which was to say quiet in stellar terms and rather stealthy due to very low emissions rate.

The vast majority were estimated to be billions of years old and had been in their collapsed state long enough to lose energy and go quiescent. That made them devilishly difficult to locate, even from close range.

That could be good for us, but it could also be bad. Damn it, we need more data and I don't know how to get it.

Steph shot off a note through the system directed to the *Revenge*, and Milla, as soon as they had a secure link with his ship. He still considered the *Revenge* to be his ship, far more than the *Dutchman*, but that was an entirely different matter than what he was currently dealing with.

Steph sighed.

He much preferred direct actions over all this skulking around.

Hele Protectorate Command Station

Geth noted a mild alert come past his station and opened it reflexively.

The system had flagged an unusual gravity anomaly for further inspection and had automatically directed scanner platforms to intercept. So far there was nothing from those systems, he noted, which likely meant it was just a stray planetoid drifting by somewhere and messing with the detection grid.

An annoyingly common problem.

They could account for almost all of the local gravity sources, which was really just a matter of running the gravity scanners long enough and mapping all the subtle interactions that existed within the system. After enough time, you would have a model that was within the ninety-ninth percentile for accuracy, more than sufficient for most tasks.

Rogue planetoids, however, were effectively impossible to map out, and they were unfortunately common in the vicinity of a superdense neutron star, tending to be sucked into the gravity field or, more likely, sucked *back*.

The entire region was a littered mess of such chunks of material, likely blown out of the system when the star had exploded billions of years ago. Some had stayed close enough to occasionally be drawn back in, and that was sheer hell on maintaining an accurate gravity map of the system.

He jotted down his authorization, signing off on the decision to have the system further investigated. Probably a waste of time, but they had little else but time this far out from the Protectorate, and if it was one of the other polities making one of their infrequent raids . . . They might get away, but he'd enjoy making them cut and run without the material they'd come for.

Parasites that they are, it's a surprise they haven't been properly eliminated by the Empire a long time ago.

Geth knew better than most that the Empire did *not* take kindly to interruptions in their deep matter supply.

Chapter 5

Dutchman

No plan survives contact with the enemy. Great, already knew that, but the plan isn't supposed to be scrapped twice even before contact is made. This is nuts.

Steph glowered at the display as he looked over the new intel and began reformulating strategy on the fly.

They now had new multiple mission objectives. Luckily, none were exactly contradictory. Less luckily, some were exceedingly complicated.

The Kingdom wanted a supply of strange matter, or what they referred to as deep matter. Understandable, doable. The initial mission was plotted as a hit-and-get: come in, mess things up, grab a stash, and get the hell out.

Easy.

The presence of labor camps and families being held as slaves and insurance changed things for him, made it personal. Arranging for them to be lifted out was more complex, requiring capturing local ships and neutralizing defenses quite a bit more than the original plan called for, but all was still doable.

Now, however, they had another wrinkle.

The Empire was running a protection scheme on this particular system, taking a chunk of their production in exchange for a promise not to raid the place.

That was priority-one intelligence.

He just needed to figure out what the hell to do with it.

It was a problem that required considerable thought, he was quickly realizing. During the war, if they'd come across something like this, the answer would have been pretty obvious.

If you can't hold it, *destroy* it.

Steph wasn't sure he could do that to a star system.

"Particularly not a neutron star system," he said, now talking to himself as he examined the scans. "Damn thing was destroyed several billion years ago. Nothing we have could do much better of a job."

He *could* maybe create a runaway singularity if he wanted to sacrifice the *Dutchman*, but he was far from certain that would actually do anything significant in the system, and the very idea scared the *hell* out of him.

Not ever doing that.

His name wasn't Doohan, after all. He'd heard about that crazy bastard, and that Eric flat out refused to let the man set foot on the *Odysseus* after hearing about what he did with an antimatter cannister. Steph didn't blame Eric one bit; he'd not be inviting the man on board any of his ships either, especially not the *Revenge*.

There was antimatter on the *Revenge*.

No one in the fleet was going to willingly let Doohan anywhere near antimatter other than Morgan, and that guy had to be as crazy as his engineer was.

Steph grumbled, "This is getting me nowhere."

He was going around and around and off on stray tangents while he should be focusing on the current problem. The Empire was pulling war materials from the system, and he needed to figure out how he could best use that. Unfortunately, destroying the materials was pretty much impossible. He wasn't sure if anything, short of a singularity, could do much to neutronium, let alone strange matter. The most he could pull off, realistically, would be to delay shipments to the Empire.

Maybe cause them to take over the site from the Protectorate themselves, expend some resources and effort, but nothing . . .

Steph trailed off, a thought sparking in his head.

He called up his display, checking some of the data he'd gotten, then began to quickly schedule secure laser comm pulses to the rest of the squadron.

"Ensign," he called out.

"Yes Captain?" Dumora turned, looking at him.

"Make certain the crew knows to be ready for action," Steph said firmly, knowing that he couldn't trust them entirely to respond properly to the general quarters alarm.

He had dealt with all sorts of soldiers during his tenure with the Archangels, some elite and some decidedly not, but Steph was certain that he would take the absolute worst examples of soldiers from any allied force on Earth over the examples he'd found here in the Free Stars. Worse, he was nearly certain that he'd gotten some of the better ones. Certainly he'd gotten people who were actually willing to work, the ones who'd volunteered.

The people who'd left had been a mix.

A few were good, mostly among the officers. The sort who were what you'd expect from an officers' corps from a third-world, but competent, force. Patriots in their own way, they opted to return to their worlds when he offered.

The people he got were barely trained, mostly not the brightest bunch, but ready to get their hands dirty.

Not a despairing situation, but they would need a lot to get them up to shape, which was why he was sitting his ass in the chair he had and not back on his Archangel where he was *supposed* to be.

"Yes Captain. I will issue the commands."

"Make sure they're followed," he said, expression serious. "I don't want to hear of anyone ignoring this. There will be consequences."

She nodded fervently. "Yes Captain. I will see to it."

Steph nodded curtly, hating that he had to give such a command. The crew knew their jobs, but they had no real pride in their work, and that was a problem.

———

Archangel One, Gaia's Revenge

Milla looked up from her work when her system chimed, signalling the arrival of a priority message. She set aside the panel she was working on and immediately went to the computer, opening the new file. She read through the first half, eyes widening with almost every passing sentence. By the time she was halfway through, she was convinced that Stephanos had lost what little remained of his mind.

Terrans are all insane, I knew this, but something special must have bitten Stephan for him to come up with this.

She was reaching for the comm panel, intent on speaking with Tyke, only for it to chime before she could touch it.

"Yes?" she asked hesitantly.

"Milla, Tyke," the pilot's warm voice said, sounding concerned. "Have you received the message from the *Dutchman*?"

"Yes," Milla responded. "I was about to call you."

"Decided that Steph lost his gourd too?"

"I am . . . not certain I would have used those words," she offered uncertainly.

"No doubt. Alright, come on to the command deck," he said. "We need to talk. This is going to mean a major change in our approach."

"Yes, that is quite evident," Milla said, acknowledging the request and signing off.

She surveyed her office, deciding she didn't need anything, and headed out for the command deck.

If nothing else, serving with the Terrans was always interesting. Rarely safe, but always interesting.

———

Tyke looked up from the *Revenge*'s system control displays as Milla stepped into the open command deck.

"Hello. Thank you for coming up," he said. "I believe we have a few things to discuss."

"I believe I can agree with that," she responded in a remarkably dry tone for someone with her soft voice.

Tyke chuckled. "You remind me of Jack when you sound like that, just don't mention that to her."

Milla rarely had the opportunity to interact much with the young pilot who mostly kept to herself. "If you wish."

"Steph's putting us in a tight spot," he went on, "not that I don't understand why. The new intelligence Cardsharp's crew snagged is lightning in a bottle. We almost have to use it somehow, and the options for how we can leverage it are depressingly slim."

"Perhaps, but what he is suggesting is . . ."

"Ambitious." Tyke nodded. "And that's if we're being very, very polite about things. I know. Still, it's likely the best of several bad options and we've been given our marching orders, so we're going to make it happen, come hell or high water. Right?"

Milla took a deep breath before setting her jaw and nodding firmly.

"Right."

"That's the spirit," Tyke said, chuckling. "Alright, the first part of the mission holds the same, no real modifications. Where are you on that?"

"We are ready," she said confidently. "The defensive network is crude, but clearly based on archival technical diagrams. If we were dealing with Imperial Systems, I would not be so sure, but what I have found here is quite simply . . . inadequate."

"Well, that's good for us," Tyke said. "Alright, we'll be ready to execute the opening move in three hours. Can you make it happen?"

"Certainly."

"Good. That leaves the follow-up," Tyke said, blowing out a deep breath. "That is mostly going to be on Steph, though. If he can't pull off his part of all this, we're blown."

Milla could certainly agree with that, though she had become used to the Terrans pulling off stranger things, she supposed. Still, there almost had to be something wrong with them, in her opinion, that he kept on trying the craziest ideas.

They were fascinating to observe, if nothing else.

———

Archangel Three

Cardsharp examined the new orders with a raised eyebrow.

"I think I heard the clank all the way over here," she said.

"What clank?" her young second in command asked.

"Stephanos' balls coming together when he got up to write this piece of shit," she said, handing the tablet back to where Jack was waiting.

The young woman frowned, taking the small system and reading the summary quickly. Her eyes widened and she looked up sharply, then back and forth between her CO and the new orders.

"Clank? How'd they not *explode*?" she asked, disbelieving. "This isn't gutsy, Jen, this is *nuts*."

Cardsharp gestured idly. "The difference between the two is often only determined by the outcome. I suppose we can revisit the point after we see whether he can pull it off."

"We're all gonna die," Jack moaned.

"Yes we are," Cardsharp agreed cheerfully. "It only remains to be seen if today is the day."

"Worse, the crazy is spreading."

"The crazy spread a long time ago, girl." Cardsharp laughed. "You don't join a squad like the Double A without at least a *little* crazy in you. So imagine what it takes to actually *lead* it."

Jack just groaned.

———

One by one the Archangel squadron received their latest orders via secure laser comm, with varying degrees of incredulity expressed. Each immediately set about implementing them without hesitation as they'd been trained to do, though with grumbling roughly matching their incredulity.

The Protectorate System had several key points, spread over a fairly large section of space.

Stellar mining operations tended to be far-flung, at least by planet-side definitions, which was both a weakness and a strength when looked at from the side of defense.

On the one hand, actual assets were spread thin, making any single area one might strike at relatively worthless in terms of expenditure. Destroying one mining machine among thousands was a waste of time and resources, and with them being spread out so far as to be literally *light-minutes* from one another at even some of the closer ranges, not even a determined fleet could cause serious damage in a quick strike.

On the other hand, it also meant that providing security for those same resources was effectively impossible as well. No reasonable number of ships could respond across the entire swath of the mining operations in anything resembling a reasonable time. That was so self-evident, in fact, that the Protectorate didn't even bother to try.

The mining resources themselves were entirely unprotected, and simply left to their own devices. To the mind of those in charge, it was an obvious thing really. After all, who cared about the lives of the slaves running them. They couldn't actually *go* anywhere even if they got it in their heads to try.

At the fastest speed any of their mining rigs could manage, they'd die of old age before they got too far out of the system.

Their families would die well before that from other causes.

Workers had literally nowhere to go but right back to their captors, and while they had no particular defense against attack, they had no value to any prospective attackers either.

This was a weakness in the system that could be exploited.

Miner 4389135

Corin Del wiped the sweat from his face as he finished the last few steps to locking up the cargo section of the small mining ship, checking to ensure that the entire system was showing secure locks, then began plotting the return trajectory to the central processing area of the Protectorate facilities. He'd been doing the job for longer than he cared to remember and was something of an old hand at it. Many of those who'd been *recruited* at the same time as he had been were no longer around for various reasons, none of them good. It wasn't a safe job, not even by the standards of his homeworld.

"That took longer than it should have," he said, slumping back in the slightly beaten seat, letting the computer handle the calculations.

He'd check them, twice, when the process was completed, but there would be no rush to doing that. They had hours before there was likely to be anything they might crash into, and in the meantime the computer could be trusted to at least get them started.

"This chunk is running low," his companion said tiredly.

Corin nodded. "Get some rest, Hil. You look like frozen waste."

Hil Tharn laughed sharply. "You're one to talk. You planning on racking any time soon?"

"Going to get some rest once I'm sure the computer's course won't kill us while I'm sleeping," Corin said. "You know these things glitch too much once you get in close to anything significant, and central processing is *crowded*."

Hil nodded. "Yeah. Alright. I'm going to—"

He was cut off when an alarm sounded, causing both to bolt upright and temporarily forget any fatigue they'd been working with.

"What's that?" Hil asked, coming forward and sliding into the side seat.

"Proximity alarm, I think," Corin said, focused on the console in front of him. "Something must have come close enough to trip it."

"Threat?"

"Doubt it," Corin grumbled. "If it were, we'd probably already be dead. The Protectorate only puts a fraction of a light-range detection system on these things, not enough to actually get out of the way of anything coming at us at speed."

Hil snorted. "That just figures. Why put them on at all?"

"Honestly? Probably because we use the same rig to track ore rocks and stay in range while working," Corin said as he kept trying to figure out what had set off the alarm. "Otherwise, they probably wouldn't have bothered."

"Oh. Yeah, that would explain it. Any idea what set it off?"

"No clue," Corin admitted. "Which is worrying, 'cause it's still reporting a contact."

"It is?" Hil leaned forward.

"Yeah, I just killed the audio. Something is pacing us, and getting closer," Corin said. "Hold on, I'm going to alter course so we're not on an intercept vector anymore."

He tapped the controls, thrust pushing them to one side as the ship moved under his command. A few seconds later they returned to normal gravity. Corin checked the instrumentation again.

"We clear?"

"I think so," Corin said. "There's still something out there, but I can't quite pin it down—"

He was interrupted when the ship suddenly slammed hard to one side, throwing the men out of their seats and to the floor. Corin scrambled back to his feet, eyes wide as he lunged for the controls.

"What the hell was that?!" Hil demanded, just behind him.

"I don't know!"

Nothing in the system indicated an impact, but then the system was pretty uncooperative in revealing what had set the thing off in the first place. He ran system diagnosis first, slumping in relief as everything returned intact and functional.

"Whatever hit us didn't do any damage," he said, testing the controls. "I'm going to get us moving back on course . . . Huh. That's strange."

"What's strange?" Hil asked, climbing fully back into the seat and tying the belt around his waist.

"It's not responding," Corin said.

"Engines check out," Hil frowned.

"They do, and they're firing. We just aren't moving."

He hit the thrust again, bracing to be thrown around the cabin when the engines overrode the internal gravity, but nothing happened other than a distant whine that he recognized as the thrust system straining. It made no sense, almost as if they were caught by . . .

Corin scowled, opening a short-range communication system. "Perra, Jusda, if this is one of you imbeciles, I'll call for punishment duty *myself*."

"What?" Hil looked over, confused.

"Something is gripping us," he explained. "And the only thing I know of out this far that can do that is a mining rig."

"Those filth-ridden pieces of—" Hil's swearing was cut off by a bang and a sound of metal being strained that made the two twist and stare at the back of the rig.

The lock built into the system to keep the cabin pressurized at all times seemed normal for a moment, but neither relaxed as Corin felt a prickling run up the back of his neck. Lights suddenly lit up alongside the air lock, and then the entire system *hissed* as pressure was equalized.

The lock swung heavily open, condensate billowing away, and the pair swallowed hard as a hulking figure was framed in the door.

"Do not move," it said in heavily accented Imperial.

"Not a problem," Corin croaked, carefully not making *any* motions as the massive figure stomped in.

This day just kept getting *worse*.

Chapter 6

Odysseus

Eric stood looking over the command deck, letting Miram handle the command of the *Odysseus* while he kept an eye on squadron coherence.

The running lights of the squadron were all visible, along with those of the Priminae convoy they were traveling with, the lights moving against the starfield in occasionally peculiar ways.

Of course, they were actually flying *very* close to one another by most space-based reference points. Hundreds of kilometers away instead of millions, close enough to maintain a secure real time communications network that allowed Eric to use augmented projections to keep a personal eye on each of the ships in his little squadron in ways that normally would have required a shuttle and several hours' transit time.

At the moment he was projecting to the *Bellerophon*, his image looking down on the command deck below with an approving eye. The general precision and well-oiled action of the crew was what he'd come to expect from his former XO.

"Commodore," Jason Roberts said, noting his presence with a nod.

"Captain," Eric returned formally, before smiling. "You've done good work here, Jason."

"I have a good crew," he said, only Eric's knowledge of the man letting him hear the satisfaction behind the formality.

"You do indeed," Eric said. "I've seen your reports, so I won't ask for a status update, but how are you feeling about the operation?"

Jason considered that for a moment. "It feels like a long shot, I have to admit."

"Wrong play, do you think?"

He shook his head. "Not necessarily. We were not having the greatest of luck with more standard approaches. I can't say I like using the Priminae as bait . . ."

Eric tilted his head slightly. "I agree, but we didn't ask them to send out the convoy. We merely asked to tag along."

Jason gestured in agreement. "I am aware. If the enemy takes the bait, however, we won't be able to protect them all."

"I know, as does Rael," Eric said, referring to the Priminae's top admiral. "And so do the people in those ships."

"Then there's really little else to talk about," Jason said. "It is a long shot, yes, but we are out of the more conventional approaches. We've done our due diligence, informed everyone involved of the limits of our abilities in the event the worst happens. All we can do now is prepare for the worst."

"And hope for the best?" Eric asked, amused.

"I'm not certain if that's precisely what we want," Jason admitted. "We're actively hoping for an attack, aren't we?"

"I suppose you have a point there," Eric said ruefully. "Prepare for the worst, hope for . . . something better but not too good? Doesn't have the same ring."

"We don't deal with best-case scenarios," Jason said. "You know that as well as I do. If we did, we'd be working some civilian job."

"And making actual money," Eric said.

"That too."

Eric smiled. "Alright, I'm doing my rounds but keep up the good work."

"Always, Commodore."

Eric didn't doubt him and silently shifted his projection, moving to the next ship.

Imperial Eighth Fleet Command Vessel

Birch quietly regarded the signals they were tracking, waiting for further intelligence to be obtained before she made any true decisions concerning the future of her current operations.

Robe had located the Colonial convoy easily enough. As with many of the Oather elements they made little, if any, attempts at hiding. This was an aspect of the Oathers that she both appreciated and found rather disturbing. It was, after all, always nice to have your enemy be willing to so easily share key information with you . . . However, it sent a consistent crawling sensation down her spine, and the persistent worry that the entire situation was a trap.

There was no sign of that for the moment, at least.

The Colonial convoy was as expected, if a little larger than they'd calculated. Undoubtedly at least some of that size was additional security. They had analyzed that the overall power curve being scanned in the cluster of ships was somewhat more powerful than the mere numbers themselves would indicate.

That likely means combat cruisers, at the very least, Birch knew.

Still, nothing that the Eighth couldn't handle based on the raw data. More importantly, here was an opportunity to gain vital intelligence, whittle down enemy forces, *and* make an important point concerning the power of the Empire.

All in a single move.

Just the sort of operation that she preferred.

"Robe."

Her second in command looked up, then carefully extricated himself from his current task and made his way over.

"Yes, My Lady?"

"Move the fleet to an intercept point ahead of the enemy convoy and position us to observe their approach," Birch ordered. "Be sure that we are in a position that affords the choice to intercept or merely observe them in passing. I will not be dictated to, either by the enemy or by some whims of fate."

"As you command it, it will be done, My Lady."

She nodded curtly, dismissing him to his task, and immediately moved her attentions elsewhere.

The maps of known Oather worlds were spread out by her, along with known locations where the enemy squadrons had been located with the times of their passage.

Something was there, she was sure. Birch simply couldn't put her finger on it.

Yet.

―――

Odysseus *Task Group, NACS Boudicca*

Captain Hyatt examined the telemetry readings that were coming in from the long-range probes they had running out ahead of their path, as well as covering the port flank of the convoy. Gravimetric readings were within expected ranges, which unfortunately meant very little.

Within any given range of space of significant size, the sheer number of planet-sized objects was startling. Despite common misconceptions, space wasn't very empty at all.

They were currently outside the gravity field of any stellar objects, but within the several light-day scanning range of the *Bo*, there were no fewer than hundreds of planetoid-sized objects and countless asteroids, not to mention the almost innumerable objects smaller than the planetoid classification.

If they'd been within a star system, that result would have been many degrees of magnitude larger.

Space was an incredibly crowded locale, no matter how empty it seemed due to the sheer vastness of distances between objects.

That, unfortunately, made detecting potential enemies rather difficult. This was a basic fact that the commodore had used to his advantage more than once in the past, but was now being turned on them as they were forced into the defender role rather than playing hunter-killer.

It would be bad enough if they knew for certain someone was out there, but they didn't even have *that* to their side of things. Maybe someone was watching them right now, or maybe the enemy was already making their move on some other poor sap a hundred light-years away.

No one could tell, not until it was likely too late.

Hyatt sighed, closing the telemetry display, and rose from her station to cross the command deck to better observe the real time imagery coming through the primary scanners to the main displays.

The system was not holographic—that technology had only recently been cleared for use on combat vessels—but it was a shift adjusted perspective screen. Three-dimensional, in the common usage, based on parallax technology combined with eye tracking. The system would automatically note every single set of eyes focused on the screen and individually project parallax images intended for their position and angle.

Impressive technology mostly wasted in its application here, much to her amusement.

She wasn't entirely certain who decided to include it on starships, but they'd obviously forgotten to take into account the sheer breadth of range that would be the norm, and that humans only viewed parallax over a relatively short distance. At a certain range, the human eye gave up and focused to infinity.

Still, the computer could occasionally do some interesting things with the technology as an augmentation on human vision, so as she looked over the enhanced scans of the Priminae Fleet, she could see vessels floating in relative distances from one another.

As she swept her gaze across the fleet, however, something caused her to pause and backtrack.

It wasn't a ship—not one of the Priminae, or their own at least. Too far out, she realized, but there was a glint of light that was moving all wrong to be a star.

"Adelaide," she said softly.

"Aye Skipper?" Lieutenant Brooke Adelaide replied.

"Grid square . . . Gamma Nine by Bravo Twelve," she said. "Enhance and identify."

"Aye ma'am."

The young lieutenant turned to the work and the image flickered from the main screen to one of the side displays, causing Hyatt to half turn to focus on it as the square in question was magnified.

"Passive telemetry indicates possible planetoid mass," Adelaide said. "Full-spectrum analysis shows no sign of atmosphere. Temperature is . . ."

She trailed off, eyes rising from her screen to the enhanced image that was really only a larger, fuzzier dot of light.

"Target is radiating heat above fifty degrees centigrade."

Hyatt turned around, striding to her console, and opened a channel to the squadron.

"Sound general quarters," she ordered. "Likely enemy vessel has been detected."

Odysseus

Soft alarms brought everyone to full focus as Eric made his way calmly through the halls, heading back for the bridge with a coffee in his hands.

Why does this always happen when I go to grab something to eat?

He wasn't hurrying. There was no combat alert at the moment, but he was making sure that his strides ate up the ground at a good pace.

Eric stepped out onto the admiralty deck, overlooking the command deck below where everyone was hopping quite nicely, and set his drink down on a table as he passed. He didn't interrupt, just looked at the main focus of their attentions, and recognized the contact as being not naturally occurring.

Not this far out from any star, at least.

It wasn't entirely impossible for it to be a natural contact, of course. A rogue planet with large enough moons could easily generate its own heat through geothermal tidal forces, but he'd have hit the alert if he spotted a contact like that too. If this turned out to be a false alarm, well fine, he was sure the science boys would enjoy checking it out.

For the moment, however, they would assume the phenomenon was something . . . other than natural.

"Commodore," Miram said, noting his arrival. "Captain Hyatt spotted the contact and is asking whether we should actively pulse the area?"

"Negative," Eric said. "I don't want to alert them, if they are the enemy. Let them think they're still undetected, remain with passives, but reposition the ships so we can function as a distributed array scope."

"Aye, aye, issuing those orders now, sir."

A lot could be determined from passive scans, particularly once full-spectrum imaging was on the table. Light that bounced off the target would be absorbed by the material it was reflecting from, and thus would direct specific wavelengths back depending entirely on the elemental makeup of the surface.

Granted, the process wouldn't tell you much about anything below the surface, but starships didn't tend to be painted, not for long. Solar and cosmic radiation burnished the surface almost as fast as a constant peppering of dust and other materials did, leaving the exposed armor as the only thing that really lasted.

That tended to be a very specific sort of material from species to species or culture to culture.

Terran humans liked hardened steel, or did until recently, while Priminae tended to use ceramics. The Empire used a hyper-alloy with high titanium and steel content that Terran scientists had been chomping at the bit to study. But despite capturing many samples, there hadn't been much advancement in determining how the material was made, and the secret wasn't disseminated among the rank and file of Imperial soldiers.

The crew of the *Odysseus* knew exactly what it looked like on a spectrograph, however.

"Spectrograph confirms Imperial armor, Commodore," Miram stated after running the scans through the system.

Eric smiled thinly. "Well, then it would appear we have guests."

"Aye sir."

He opened a channel to the *Boudicca*. "My compliments, Alexandra. Good eye."

Captain Hyatt took a moment to return. "I got lucky, sir. Just happened to move against the stars the wrong way as I was looking. I would never have noticed it otherwise."

"Some people say better lucky than good, Captain," he said. "But I firmly believe it's better to be good enough to capitalize on your luck. I do believe you just proved that you were. Most people wouldn't have thought twice about it, even having seen the ship. Take the compliment."

"Aye, aye, Commodore."

"Orders will be forthcoming, Captain," Eric said firmly. "For now, previous orders stand. We're running security, so continue as you were."

"Yes sir."

Eric closed the channel and moved across the admiralty deck, waving over his aide.

"Sir?"

"Coordinate with the destroyer screen," he said. "Make sure our Rogues are ready to move on my order. I don't want any hesitation."

"Yes sir."

He opened up the squadron tactical map, noting the current orientation didn't quite match the position of the enemy ship. Eric didn't know if the vessel was just a scout or if the location was indicative of the main body of the enemy forces, so he didn't alter the orientation, but he did set in a secondary plane that crossed the current one along the line the enemy rested at. This allowed him to picture the orientation of the contacts better in three-dimensional space, which could quickly become a difficult feat when dealing with multiple contacts at the ranges involved in space combat.

"What are you going to do?"

Eric shivered slightly at the words coming from beside him.

"We're going to close the trap," he said. "Since you've decided to interject here, class is in. What do you see?"

Odysseus peered at the displayed tactical map, something Eric was amused by. The entity didn't need to look at the image; he was fully aware of all things within his domain, so what the ship knew, he knew.

"An enemy scout," Odysseus said after a moment's thought. "Imperial armor, mass indicates a cruiser most likely, perhaps a small squadron of destroyers. They're in position to observe our passage but aren't preparing to intercept. Yet."

Eric nodded slightly. "Very good. Now tell me what you see, not what you think the rest of us see."

Odysseus looked up, confusion on his face.

"I don't understand."

"You have the knowledge of what the crew is thinking at any given moment. You pulled the scout information from my head. I know what I was thinking. I want you to analyze it yourself," Eric said firmly.

"I . . . don't know how."

"Excellent." Eric smiled. "An honest answer. Now, look here, see the position of the vessel compared to our course?"

Odysseus nodded, leaning in closer. "Yes."

"At our closest passage, we won't cross their engagement range. They could conduct an intercept, if you assume maximum Imperial acceleration versus the hardest pull of our slowest ships, but they'd only have us in their range for under an hour, and it wouldn't be close range either. Thus, they're not plotting an interception, right?"

Odysseus nodded, then paused and looked sharply at Eric, who was smirking at him.

"Wrong," Eric said firmly. "Your analysis made an assumption because you were relying on our immediate thoughts and didn't think about how many missing factors we're currently dealing with. If these are scouts, then the analysis is probably correct. However, what if they're not scouts?"

Eric gestured quickly, adding new dots to the map. "What if they're not here to look at us, but rather to ensure that they can slam the door on us if we try to run?"

"A trap?" the entity asked, now intently staring at the map.

"Possibly," Eric said. "Reverse engineer the trap, assuming the ship we've spotted is waiting to shut off that escape route. Where would the main body of the enemy force be?"

Odysseus examined the map again, walking around it slowly as he made the calculations. Finally, he pointed to a blank section.

"There. They would be there."

"Excellent," Eric said.

"What now?" Odysseus asked.

"Now we start passive scans of the area you pointed out," Eric said, then indicated the other points. "Plus these areas as well, adding some room for error . . . Just in case our visitors aren't as good at the math as you are."

Chapter 7

Hele Protectorate Command Station

The shift was almost over, and Geth was pleased to see that reports of production had increased sufficiently to cover the earlier slips. He would ensure that the overseers were rewarded for that, but would also have to take the time to review the current resource predictions.

They were likely reaching the end of ideal production in too many of their work areas. It was fine to have a few on the downswing—pulling lower production numbers was acceptable in order to properly clean out an area—but doing that with too many sections at once would lead to a censure for sure.

That was something he had no intention of enduring, particularly as it was one of the first of disturbingly few steps that would end with him becoming one of the miners rather than system supervisor. Something else he had no intention of enduring.

That particular fate was a fair ways off, however, not something he needed to worry about too much for the moment.

The shift miners were all on their way back, a few lagging behind as usual, but none so far that he needed to comment.

All in all, a successful shift, one he was well pleased with.

"Have the miners swept for issues and turned around as quickly as possible," he ordered.

"Yes Commander."

Getting those machines and crews back out was vital to keeping the success rolling, and while he wasn't the shift commander for the next group, he'd make certain that there was nothing on the record that could besmirch his command. Geth was well aware that other shift commanders would be more than happy to leave him sucking the airless void if it got them even a single step ahead.

——

Miner 4389135

"Miner 4389135 requesting clearance along Docking Arm Seven."

Corin sweated as he waited for the response, twitching as he felt the presence of the hulking figure looming over his shoulder.

Neither he nor Hil had any idea what the hell the armored people were, if they even were people for that matter. There were stories about things that lurked out in neutron systems, but he'd always believed the tales to be pure fantasy. He'd been working in this system for three full cycles back home and seen nothing unusual at all.

Even now, he knew it was far more likely that he was dealing with a simple enemy of the Hele Protectorate, and more power to them in his opinion, but the looming alien presence of the armor was difficult to ignore.

"Clearance granted, 4389135, proceed at station speed to dock."

He breathed a sigh of relief, though Corin was still a little worried that the armored men would kill both him and Hil once they were no longer of value. Still, there was nothing he could do about that and right now he just wanted the situation *over* with. The miner needed to be docked.

"Go ahead," the alien voice in accented Imperial said, sending a shiver down his spine. "Take us in."

Corin nodded, nudging the controls and moving the ship in at station speed. It was torturously slow, barely moving even by the standards of the miner, and the last thing he wanted was to spend any more time with the armored figures than he absolutely had to, but there was little choice. Corin knew instinctively that attracting the wrong sort of attention would end up with him dead.

So he kept the speed to station standard and eased the miner into the receiving port for the large cargo section where they would dump off the deep matter and be relieved by the next crew.

Poor bastards.

They didn't know what they were about to come face-to-face with.

———

Master Sergeant Buckler looked down at the terrified man who was handling the controls and kept a close eye to make sure he didn't do anything to get them caught. Not that he expected the man to try anything intentionally, but as wound up as he was, it would be all too easy for him to make a simple mistake and bring the ire of the station traffic controllers down on their heads.

That wouldn't end well for anyone.

Not that Buckler particularly cared much for most of the people it would be bad for, but since his people were also on that list, he'd make certain a slipup didn't happen.

His squad had picked this one, Miner 4389135 apparently, as their vehicle of choice mostly due to proximity. The vessel had the bad luck of happening by just after the orders had come in from the boss. More's the pity for the two-man crew, he supposed, though if things went reasonably well they shouldn't wind up in too bad a condition once the mission was over.

If things went badly, they'd be the least of anyone's concerns, Buckler imagined.

War sucks, especially for bystanders.

He leaned over the man to get a better view out the miner's screens, the long arms of the station slowly sliding past as they moved in closer.

The station was an ugly, workaday sort of structure. It wouldn't have been out of place in any of the old city ports back on Earth, at least in terms of how badly battered it looked to be. He could see pitted plates, sections of hull that were corroded by exposure to some of the nastier dusts brought in by the miners, and large sections burnished to a bright shine by regular radiation and debris.

All in all, it looked like a place where people worked and the bosses didn't care much for upkeep beyond the bare minimum.

Feels like home.

He'd grown up in the ports of New York before the war, his dad a dockworker before everything went in the crapper and the docks wound up mostly abandoned. Buckler had signed up with the Marines when they began recruiting again, after Japan, but he'd spent his formative years working somewhere that felt a lot like this station.

Weird.

There were a billion and one ways that the place was *nothing* like the docks, of course. It was a freaking space station, after all. The feel, though, the station had a feeling that was intimately familiar.

Buckler found it fascinating.

Dutchman

The six Archangel-class fighter-gunboats each carried a small deployment of Marines for the sorts of duties that were expected to be encountered during the various types of light combat the squadron was intended for.

Steph suspected that if the people who'd originally drawn up mission profiles for the new class of vessel had any idea what he'd *actually* wind up using them for, well, more than a few minds would have been blown and his career would have been over. At the very least, he was certain that there was *no* chance they'd have offered him the command slot in the newly reformed squadron.

Sucks to be them, he thought with a slightly feral grin tracing itself out on his lips.

Well, in honesty, under conventional circumstances, he'd have agreed with his colleagues. The six Double A fighter-gunboats he had were *wholly* insufficient to the task that he'd assigned them, if you assumed a conventional battle on either side. Steph was certain, however, that the opposing force had no idea what conventional even was, and he had no intention of playing by rules the enemy wasn't aware of, let alone followed.

Of course, that didn't make the whole problem any *easier* to solve exactly. It just opened up a host of different options he could pick and choose from in his attempt to find the solution he was seeking. Options he desperately needed, given the relative dearth of conventional ones available.

When in doubt, make the enemy doubt even harder, Steph thought wryly, remembering something Eric had told him a long time ago.

Early in the war, they'd been used to fighting on the wrong side of every number you could imagine. So they got good at being *creative* with the assets they had in hand, not something the military liked to encourage as things normalized, mostly because being creative only worked if you had a lot of skill, brilliant thinkers, and a fair mix of luck. A rare combo.

Most military commanders would rather not take the risks and lose all their resources in the inevitable times when you *didn't* have that exact mix.

Too bad for them that we're all alone out here, I guess, Steph thought with a grin as he watched the timer count down.

—

Miner 4389135

The mining rig thumped, hard, as the system locked it into place, and then shook violently enough that Buckler and the other Marines had to hold on to keep from being pitched to the ground.

"What is that?" Buckler growled in Imperial, wishing he could curse but honestly not knowing the right words.

The poor bastard at the conn swallowed, eyes wide as he looked back.

"Just pulling the container and dropping a new one on," he answered. "It's normal."

Buckler just grunted, gesturing to have his squad lower their weapons.

Slightly.

The Marine didn't much like this assignment. There wasn't nearly enough support following normal protocols. Buckler was starting to realize, however, that normal protocols didn't have much of a place in his life anymore.

Act like a pirate, Buckler thought with some disgust.

He was a Marine, Goddamn it. He wasn't supposed to act like a pirate. Marines were *death* on pirates. The two were natural enemies. Yet here he was . . .

The rattling and thumping of machinery around them eased to a stop after some time, then the miner jolted and moved again, leaving Buckler and his team hanging on to whatever they could grab to keep from being thrown to the deck.

"We're just being pulled along to the vehicle bay," the man in the control seat explained with panicky quickness.

Buckler didn't say anything in response. He'd already guessed as much, and it wasn't like he was about to shoot the poor guy for what the automated system wanted to do. He might *want* to shoot someone over it, but it wouldn't be some other sap just along for the ride.

He did have a related question, however.

"How long until we're inside?" he demanded.

"Soon, very soon," the man said. "The time frame could change, however, depending on what else is in the system. Won't be long, though, I promise."

Buckler grunted but didn't say anything else.

It would have to do.

Dutchman

Steph watched as the icons for his squadron all began to diverge according to plan. The Archangels were moving into position to execute their part of the operations, his own *Dutchman* already waiting silently within striking range of his own target while the Marines were slowly inching into position aboard their *borrowed* rides.

So far so good.

The Protectorate mining operation was a far-flung setup, no question, but logistics were the universal language of any large organization, whether military or civilian. If you couldn't get the things your people needed to do their job into their hands, you couldn't get the job done.

End of story.

Organizations loved to do everything possible to make logistics easier and cheaper. For the military this often meant lots of redundancy, beefy supply lines, and massive investments in people, supplies, transport, storage . . . you name it.

Civilian groups were judged on profit, however, in whatever form they might exist. If your entire existence revolved around producing something with tangible value, then the effort made to facilitate that production had to, by definition, cost less than the value of what you were producing.

A military victory didn't have a tangible value, it was just something that happened. Putting a dollar value on achieving victory was difficult, if not impossible.

Putting a dollar value on, let's say, strange matter mined from a neutron star system was not only easier but a requirement of mounting the operation in the first place.

For groups that knew the value of what they were doing, the obsession with producing more value for the effort was overwhelming. That meant that they would do damn near anything to lower costs, even to the point of cutting vital corners like logistics.

That was why the Protectorate facilities were actually far closer than necessary, with a great deal of centralization. The design made it cheaper to get things into the hands of the people who needed them.

However, it also created a single point of failure for someone like him to exploit.

"Set the countdown clock," he ordered. "Synchronize to squadron standard, and initiate on my mark . . ."

"Yes Captain. Waiting for your mark."

Steph watched the timer on his personal system, eyes flicking to the icons that showed where the Marines would be at that moment. As the time got closer, he tensed slightly.

"Mark."

"Countdown clock set, we are now counting down," the ensign responded.

Steph smiled, slightly indulgently at how she'd said that. Almost professional. The crew of the *Dutchman* had a ways to go, but they were learning. Wasn't the *Odysseus* yet, of course, but it was starting to feel like home.

His hands twitched slightly. He could almost feel an itch.

Now I just need to get back in my damn Archangel! Tyke is having all the fun. Just not fair.

———

Archangel One, Gaia's Revenge

Tyke examined the scene around him as he floated in the tactical control system of the Archangel. The newly designed interface had been put together by Milla Chans, leading a team of ship designers from Earth and the Priminae worlds, combining bleeding-edge technology from both cultures into a masterpiece he felt privileged to fly.

At the moment, though, he was too focused on the situation to fully appreciate the scene around him. The *Revenge* was drifting in low-power mode, not far from one of the clusters of point defense weapons floating around the system.

It wasn't really accurate to call them point *defense*, in his opinion. He sure as hell wouldn't call a SeaWiz a point defense weapon if it was constantly targeted at the ship it was *mounted on*. These powerful laser satellites were all oriented to fire at the Protectorate facility they'd identified as housing the families of the slaves working the mines.

Unsporting, to his mind, but he'd never really thought all that highly of the sportsmanship of slavers, genocidal nutcases, or, oddly enough, most sportsman hunters for that matter.

That was a totally different discussion than what he was currently having with himself, however.

Never let the voices in your head distract you from the discussions you have with the other voices in your head, Tyke thought. *They're probably trying to get you in trouble.*

His eyes flickered to the right and up slightly as an icon lit up in the three-dimensional environment surrounding him. One of the weapon platforms was adjusting its position slightly, which had triggered a warning check in his system.

No big deal, he decided a moment later as the alignment showed that the weapon was merely being adjusted to maintain its current target, apparently one of the local barracks.

It was messed up, in his opinion, but no big deal as far as the operation was concerned.

Thousands of icons were steadily moving in toward the central collection area, all of them miners returning with full loads. That was something that hadn't changed over the period he'd been waiting. Thousands coming in, thousands going out, a steady stream of motion.

Likely made keeping proper track of everything a nightmare and a half if you were trying to run the place, he supposed, but the hubbub made hiding among the constantly shifting environment a lot easier.

Tyke checked the clock.

Almost time.

———

Miner 4389135

The rugged little craft jolted hard underfoot, like a hammer had struck them with the force of a good-sized wrecking ball, then settled quickly as the sound faded away.

"We're in," the pilot said, looking nervously over his shoulder to where Buckler and his squad were still standing.

Buckler outwardly paid the man little attention, but within the armor the Marine was busy giving orders.

"Alright, leathernecks," he growled. "We're on the clock from this point on. No screwups, or you'll *wish* I shot you myself. Clear?"

"Oorah, Sergeant!"

He nodded crisply in his armor. "The boss wants this to go off like clockwork, and I don't want to disappoint him. You all know your tasks. Don't fuck up."

They all responded in the affirmative, getting ready as they waited for the doors to the craft to unseal.

"Sergeant?" PFC Jerome Kinny ventured hesitantly.

"What is it, Private?"

"Just thinking, Sergeant . . ."

"That's not your job, Kinny," Buckler growled.

"No sir, I know, but the boss . . . Did he really want us to act like pirates, sir?" The Marine sounded like he was dealing with an unusual mix of eagerness and foreboding.

Buckler didn't blame him. He understood the strange mix all too well by this point.

Still, he sighed over the comms. "Yes and no, Kinny. Yes, the boss wants us to play it up, even have fun with it . . . But let me be *clear*. I catch any of you lot doing the darker shit that comes from piracy, and I'll make a damn yardarm to hang you from. Oorah?"

"Oorah, Sergeant!"

"Good," Buckler said firmly, pausing as a deep *thunk* sounded around them and they could hear a hiss of air as the pressure equalized. "Lock and load, ladies. Time to get your pirate on."

"Oorah," they called as the doors ground slowly open.

Chapter 8

Hele Protectorate Command Station

The alarm suddenly whining to life was a good indicator to Geth that inquiring about the status of the mining wouldn't be greeted with a standard response this time.

He made do with a single, sharp word instead. "Report."

The panic and confusion in the room did nothing to make him any happier about the situation, particularly as his order went unnoticed.

Geth immediately strode over to the communications control station, shaking the man there by the shoulder. "I said report!"

The man looked up at him, eyes wide as he shook his head. "We don't know what's going on, sir . . ."

"What?"

His tone was so disbelieving that the man flinched away, which was fine with Geth as he shoved the subordinate out of the chair and took a seat himself, patching into the system and listening. Reports were flying through the system, almost too fast for him to follow.

"Unknown soldiers have breached the slave pens . . . !"

"We just lost power across Section Twenty-Eight! Reports of weapon fire from same section!"

"Damage control to Section Nineteen! Damage control to Section Twenty-Four! Damage control to Section Twenty-Eight!"

"System defenses are under attack! Point defenses down in multiple sections! Updates to the live map!"

Geth snarled, tapping in the command to bring up the live map so he could see *those* reports at the very least.

They were clearly under assault, likely one of the other empires of the Free Stars, if only because the Empire itself would never have bothered with an attack this subtle. The enemy was foolish, in his opinion, and was certainly going to bring the might and wrath of the Empire down on themselves, though by the time that happened it wouldn't be of much value to him.

It doesn't make sense, Geth thought desperately, trying to figure out who would do this. *The Free Stars should know that they're going to bring the Empire down on them for this! Interrupting the supply of deep matter to Imperial coffers is suicide! The Empire will glaze a planet in retaliation for this. We pay protection to them for a reason!*

Again, however, he realized that such retribution would currently serve him no good at all.

He examined the map, noting a pattern.

They're isolating the slaveholdings on the station, he realized with some surprise.

A bizarre choice. The slaves had no power to speak of, no influence on the controls of the system despite doing most all of the work. He might almost think it was a rescue attempt, except there were no prisoners present that would remotely warrant such an expensive action.

If the Protectorate had captured anyone with that level of importance, they'd have ransomed them back long ago, or *someone* would have approached them. It wasn't like the Hele Protectorate were unwilling to bargain. They weren't barbarians, after all.

Still, if they're after the slaves, there's little choice, I suppose.

"All defenses, this is Commander Geth," he ordered calmly over the system. "Initiate defense plan Omer Ki."

The alarm instantly changed as the order was processed. Geth scowled as he got up from the station, grabbing the previous occupant and shoving him back into the position.

"Do your job," he ordered. "And next time I want a report, you'd better have it ready for me."

Dutchman

"Sick bastards. They actually gave the order," Steph said softly as he watched the weapon platforms power up, energy building to their capacitors as they readied themselves to blast into the slaveholding facilities.

None of his current crew were surprised in the slightest by the turn of events as best he could tell, but Steph hadn't expected them to be. They were all from cultures that would have given and executed the same order in similar situations. He'd just hoped that he'd been wrong in his estimation of the culture.

Fat chance.

"Alright." Steph leaned forward. "Let's make this happen. Full power to engines, take us in on the programmed attack run. I want every platform that charges capacitors taken out of my sky."

"Yes Captain."

The *Dutchman* vibrated softly underfoot as power was redirected to every system they'd been keeping dark to remain hidden, a distant whine as their own capacitors fast charged from the reactor.

"Signal the squadron in the open, wide cast," he ordered. "Execute. Execute. Execute."

"Yes Captain."

The destroyer began to warp space on his orders, diving in toward the space platform that they'd identified as slave pens.

"Targets have been locked, Captain."

Steph smiled thinly, his right hand slowly clenching into a fist as he watched the screens.

"Fire."

———

The *Dutchman* slashed through the Protectorate defenses like an arrow loosed from a bow, flares of light erupting in the passing of the ship as it engaged the weapon platforms so close that it was already gone by the time the vessel's lasers fully impacted the targets.

In the first pass, they incinerated dozens of platforms before sweeping around the curve of the station and bringing the force of their weapons against the remaining platforms before they could open fire. The strike was swift, brutally effective, and clearly a surprise to the defenders, who barely had any time to react.

Using the velocity of their attack as a jumping-off point, the *Dutchman* swept away from the slave pens on a reciprocal arc that brought them around to the main target.

Small local strike vessels, larger than the new Archangels but still far smaller than destroyers, were in the middle of scrambling from the rapid deployment bays as the *Dutchman* loomed back around and came nose to nose with the open and vulnerable bays.

The massive gun ports of the destroyer glowed with residual heat as the *Dutchman* hard warped to a standstill relative to the station. The pilots and work crews rushing to get their ships into space froze as they found themselves staring at death incarnate looming over them.

No one moved, all waiting for the brief flash that would be the last thing any of them saw. For a long stretch of time, nothing happened.

The pilots and workmen looked at one another, a few wondering if they could escape by running or just gunning the engines of their craft.

Then the destroyer moved, the silence caused by the vacuum between them only making the situation all the more terrifying, and they saw the lander detach and breach their shield before they could react. It was a standard model with a decidedly nonstandard exterior design, garish green-and-red imagery surrounding a female silhouette printed across the front.

None of the denizens of the bay had any idea what was coming next, and that hesitation sealed their fates.

———

The shuttle lander thumped down on the landing bay floor solidly as Steph shifted his armor and looked over the men he was taking with him.

This part, he didn't like.

He wished he had a team of Marines with him, men and women who were trained to fight to standards he approved of, but all his Marines were handling the details that *couldn't* go wrong in this operation.

That left him with some of the more physical and confrontational members of the *Dutchman*'s crew. Reliable wasn't exactly how Steph would describe any of them, though he knew they tried.

"Is everyone ready?" Steph asked, checking his weapon one last time before sliding it smoothly into the holster.

"Yes Captain," his second in command for the landing responded for the group.

The man was a former officer of the *Dutchman*'s previous owners, one of very few of her officers' corps who had elected to stay on after the capture.

Thankfully, he was also one of the few *useful* officers of that same group. Most had been the equivalent of minor nobles as he understood things, assigned to the ship because it was unimportant enough that they couldn't fuck things up badly in that position. *Those* crewmembers couldn't have run faster for home when given the chance, and Steph had been glad to see the ass end of each of them.

"Question?" he asked, noting a hint of hesitance in the man's stance.

"Apologies, Captain." Geoff Skirm bowed his head, seemingly expecting more of a chastisement.

"Don't apologize," Steph said curtly, walking to the landing doors as the hiss of air pressure equalizing was accompanied by the sensation of his eardrums popping. He swallowed to equalize the pressure before going on. "Just ask."

"Yes Captain. This is not something we train for," Geoff said honestly. "Normally, assaults are managed from larger ships."

"I'm not hearing a question."

"Apologies again," Geoff said, irritating Steph with his insistence of bowing and scraping. "Should we not be striking at strategic targets? We were not briefed and . . ."

"No," Steph said with a shake. "I dispatched Marines to handle those missions. Our job is simpler. We keep them looking at us."

"I do not understand."

The door lit up, signifying that it was ready to open. Steph put a hand on his weapon, eyes sweeping the group.

"Follow my lead and try not to kill anyone unless you have to," he said. "But don't take risks either. Just remember one thing . . ."

He looked them over, his voice lifting slightly. "You're the crew of the *Flying Dutchman*. No one else here is your equal. This is *your* time! This station belongs to *us* now. Your job is just to go out there and let everyone know it. Ready?"

The men nodded, making Steph roll his eyes.

"A little more enthusiasm," he ordered. "Are you *ready?!*"

This time they answered vocally in the affirmative, with enough energy that he gave them a pass. Barely.

"That'll do." Steph nodded before gesturing to the pilot. "Open the doors."

———

Laran Jon had been working on interceptor craft for the Protectorate for most of his life by the point he'd stared down the beam emitters of a destroyer, something he'd never realized he should hope to avoid. Those red glowing emitters, heat still bleeding off them from combat use, had been truly *evil* staring at him against the black backdrop of space that sat just beyond the force screens that kept him and his colleagues alive and breathing. In that moment, he knew he was dead. And yet, somehow, his heart continued to beat.

Pound was more accurate.

The ship backed away from the bay hold that was *far* too small for it, angling slightly as a lander detached and came in.

He still breathed slightly easier, scrambling for cover now that the big warship beam emitters weren't threatening to turn everything in the bay into expanding plasma.

The people in the bay weren't security, and despite working on the small warships housed within, not even the pilots were armed. So most of them either followed his example, trying to find a place to hide, or just stared in shock and horror as the lander deployed its ramp and the figures on board charged out.

Most were, more or less, what he'd been expecting.

An armed party, armored, looking eager to shoot things, though for some reason they were holding back.

Eyes were drawn to the man in the back, though, who didn't charge down the ramp.

He walked.

Slowly. Deliberately. And somehow he managed to look more dangerous on his own than all the rest combined, even with no weapon in his hand.

"Spread out," Laran heard the man order in accented Imperial. "Secure the bay."

His men were enthusiastic in their task, quickly finding everyone, including Laran, and herding them off away from the attack craft. In moments he and his fellow workers were being held under the guns of the boarders, yet somehow no one had been shot yet. Laran hoped that trend continued, though he couldn't imagine it would.

While he had time, he focused on the man in command, wondering slightly at how different he was from any officer he'd met in the past.

The man was tall but covered in armor, so it was hard to tell how much of the difference was the man's own and how much was a function of what he was wearing. The build was similarly disguised, but he was certainly imposing there as he stood. The image was topped by the neat featureless helmet he wore, making him an impersonal force as he looked over the captured techs and pilots.

"No weapons?" he asked, his tone uncaring.

"No Captain," one of the men responded, *very* respectfully, Laran noted. "The Protectorate wouldn't trust such as these with arms."

That caught the man's attention, his featureless helmet turning slightly as his stance shifted.

"Really?" he asked, looking back to where the attack craft were parked. "And they don't mind letting them out in *those*?"

"Those all likely have self-destruct systems wired directly to command here," the same man answered.

The commander in black snorted, sounding amused.

"I do so love a stupid enemy," he said. "Finish securing the bay. We have more work to do."

"Yes, Captain Teach!"

Teach? I've never heard that name before, Laran noted.

Teach turned to look at the pilots and tech personnel. "Do as you're told and no one needs to be harmed. Resist, and I'll take no responsibility for your continued health. What happens from here . . . is on *you*."

With that, he turned and walked away.

Laran very carefully sat down and put his hands in the open as much as he could. He didn't know anything about this man, but he knew he stood no chance against the boarders and, frankly, wasn't paid to fight anyway. He wasn't going to test this Teach, not without far better reason than he currently had.

———

Steph put his back to the captured men, noting that there was a distinct lack of fight in all of them.

None of them give a damn what we do here, as long as we're not shooting them up, he realized with disgust.

It wasn't aimed at the men, though, but at the Protectorate in particular and the Free Stars in general. No one present had the urge to fight in the defense of their commanding officers and organization they belonged to. He'd fought some of the worst his planet had to offer, and even the very *worst* of them had the loyalty of their men.

Wasn't always perfect, of course. Hell, the loyalty of the Confederation was far from perfect for that matter, but the grunts *cared*. They fought for their homes, for their leaders, and for each other.

Here, in the Free Stars, he was seeing a true scarcity of that most valuable of commodities.

Some of the Kingdom had shown loyalty to their homes, which was the foundation all loyalty was built on, but precious little beyond that. The crews of the ships they'd captured, including the *Dutchman*, hadn't even really shown that for the most part. They didn't know where their home *was*, as best he could tell.

Many had been captured young from various worlds and polities. Most would apparently be unwelcome to return even when he offered to grant them passage to their homes.

There was something sick about any culture that couldn't manage to scrounge up a *minimal* quality of loyalty, to his mind at least.

Steph strode across the deck to where his men were getting ready to breach the station beyond the bay.

"Are we prepared?" he asked as he stepped up behind them.

"Yes, Captain Teach."

"Very well," he said in Imperial. "Breach."

"Enemy is preparing to breach the inner doors of the interceptor bay, Commander."

Geth seethed, glowering at the displays as he took in the overflow of information that just kept flooding in.

"How long until they breach?" he demanded.

"Moments now, Commander."

He nodded, lips curling back.

Such a waste.

Still, he had no other options now.

"Disrupt power to the bay's fields."

The tech half turned, eyes wide, but Geth didn't give him a chance to object. He dropped his hand to his sidearm and just glared.

"Yes Commander."

The orders went out then, and again the distant alarm changed subtly, this time to warn of potential hull breaches.

Steph heard one of his specialists swear, and immediately turned in the man's direction. "What is it?"

"Command has authorized a disruption to the fields here," the man said. "We're going to be in hard vacuum in moments."

Steph's eyes widened under his helm. "Seriously? They have to know we're in hardened armor with environmental gear."

"Of course they do," the specialist said as he worked. "But it'll delay our attempts to break this door significantly."

"Their own *men* are in here!" Steph looked over at the completely unarmored and unprotected prisoners.

"So?"

Steph swore under his breath.

Fucking so-called Free Stars.

He spun on his heel, marching back to the prisoners at double time.

"Everyone onto the landing shuttle!" he ordered. "We're about to lose atmosphere in here! Move!"

Alarms started blaring, and suddenly the prisoners were looking *motivated* to move. He knew he had to get a lock on that, fast, or one way or another they'd end up with a lot of dead people in the bay with them in the next few seconds.

"Be *CALM!*" he ordered, modulating his armor's broadcast system to a higher volume and dropping his hand to his holstered weapon, keeping his own tone as calm as he could manage. "Follow orders, move quickly but *calmly*, otherwise I promise you the lack of air won't be what kills you. Now march!"

He stayed on them as they started moving, quickly, heading for the shuttle that had dropped its ramp again. With a little goading, he pushed them to a jog, motioning to his men to keep up. Steph wasn't worried about the prisoners taking over the shuttle. Where would they take it, really? There were only two possible ultimate destinations in the system, and in short order he was going to control both.

The field began to fail as they reached the halfway point, air making it through the energetic membrane enough to raise a howling sound that drowned out everything around them. The prisoners began to run flat out, and he signalled to his men to let them.

Men were scrambling up the ramp into the shuttle as the field failed completely and the air in the bay rushed out.

"Close the ramp," Steph ordered, picking up a straggler who'd tripped, physically *throwing* him up over the closing ramp and into the shuttle even as others were dragged in.

The human body could endure a short time in hard vacuum, especially here in the bay that was shielded from radiation for the most part, but he doubted any of the prisoners were going to be feeling all that great for a while.

That wasn't his problem, however.

Steph turned back and marched to the door.

"I want *in*," he growled over the radio link to the assault team he'd brought with him. "I want in there, with the person who gave that order, and I want in there *now*."

The men looked nervous to him, though he couldn't see their faces as they shifted around uncertainly.

"Yes Captain."

Chapter 9

Imperial Eighth Fleet Command Vessel

Birch eyed the disposition of her ships as they paced the Oather convoy.

Everything appeared to be running to plan, which was good, but the likely presence of the anomalous species had her on edge. Something about how they operated that simply didn't sit well with her.

That made her cautious.

Perhaps overly so.

She was second-guessing her decision not to engage the enemy the first time she'd had them in her sights. The moment had seemed like a perfect opportunity then, too, aside from that one detail.

Why did they slow their velocity?

She still hadn't been able to answer that question, which was the only reason she didn't entirely regret her decision.

Did they know her fleet was there and opt to lay a trap?

If so, they had to have something up their sleeve. She was well aware of that.

The unknown superweapon, perhaps?

They hadn't brought that back into play as far as she knew, which likely spoke of some sort of limitation they hadn't been able to work out. The weapon was almost certainly located in their home system, and while it clearly *could* target across stellar ranges, she expected that it required reasonably up-to-date coordinates and almost certainly a real time link to the weapon itself in order to make that happen.

Both of those requirements would be difficult, if not impossible, to manage from a forward deployed area, she expected. Hoped?

Somewhere between the two.

Birch actually rather hated the current situation.

She was an intelligence specialist.

She shouldn't be forced to fight half-blind like this. It was *not* the way of things.

"No changes in projected course, Commander."

Birch just nodded at the report. She could see that, but procedures were procedures.

"Stay back," she ordered. "We'll take them on my order, not one moment sooner, and certainly *not* because we screwed up and exposed our location."

"Yes Commander."

Odysseus

"No change, Commodore," Miram said as she came over beside Eric where he was observing from the admiralty deck.

He just nodded. "I'm not surprised. This commander is . . . an ambush predator. We already knew that. He's not going to move until he feels everything is exactly where it needs to be."

"I would prefer if everything were *not* where *he* needs it to be, sir."

Eric chuckled. "Agreed. Our job is to make him think he's got us right where he wants us while making sure that he really has us right where we want to be."

"Yes sir," Miram said, sounding rather unhappy about the whole deal.

Eric wasn't surprised. There was nothing to be happy about when you were staring down the barrel of a loaded ambush, especially when the enemy likely had you outgunned.

Still, the only military strategy more effective than a good ambush is a good counter-ambush.

He just hoped he could pull it off.

There was a lot less environment to leverage to his advantage in space, and the benefit of surprise would only carry the day for so long. Still, he was confident they could tear a heavy chunk out of the enemy when they made their move. Probably wouldn't be able to defeat them in a single action, but all they really had to do was inflict enough damage to make them think twice about running operations in Priminae space or, failing that, hold them off long enough for the convoy to escape before the squadron made their own run.

He was hoping for the first option, but realistically counting more on the second.

It was clear that the current fleet commander, whatever else they were intent on, was a planner and information gatherer. Eric had met the type before, had *fought* the type before at various times. They were irritating by nature, whether you were tangling with them or fighting by their side. That said, if you knew who you were dealing with, it was possible to generally mess with them in ways that most others wouldn't even notice.

Eric walked over to the squadron display and casually observed it for a while before he opened a link to the *Bellerophon*.

"Yes Commodore?"

"Jason, I want you to take your ship forward about three thousand klicks, three degrees up bubble to the system plane, assume standard defensive stance there."

"Aye Commodore . . ." Jason paused before coming back. "Might I inquire as to why?"

"Call it a personal . . . whim, Captain."

Jason snorted. "I might have bought that when we first met, Commodore. I trust you'll tell me about it sometime."

Eric smiled agreeably, promising. "Sometime."

"Very well, I'll see to it then."

Eric chuckled as the communication ended, noting that the *Bell* had already been in motion halfway through their conversation. He returned his focus to the squadron display, eyeing how that move would alter their signature on passive scanners, then went on to issue similar orders to some of the destroyers as well as requesting that the Priminae move one of their larger ships slightly in the formation.

During the exercise, Odysseus had appeared silently beside him. The entity said nothing, quietly observing with a curious intelligence sparkling behind his eyes. Eric finished up before he looked over at the entity.

"Did you follow all that?"

Odysseus nodded. "Yes Commodore. I'm not sure I understand the why, however?"

Eric raised an eyebrow, knowing that wasn't possible.

The entity shook his head. "Not that way. I know why you took this action. I mean I'm not sure I understand why you believe it will have an impact."

"Ah," Eric nodded. "You haven't paid much attention to human psychology at this point, have you? We don't really have a counselor on board, or even a chaplain . . . which, now that I think of it, is a tragic loss. I'd love to have seen how some of the more fundamentalist chaplains I've known would have dealt with you."

He shrugged, though, thinking it through a little more.

"Of course, those types were rare, so we'd probably have a very reasonable one who'd be extremely interested in you and absolutely no fun at all." Eric smiled thinly.

Odysseus stared at him blankly, clearly having no idea what he was talking about despite being able to effectively read his mind. Eric's smile became a full-bodied grin as he shook his head in amusement.

The young Odysseus was a fascinating being, he found, far more so than his fellow entities, the more knowledgeable and experienced Gaia or Central. They exuded an air of near omniscience that he now saw was less all-knowing and more knowing *enough* while having shockingly accurate intuition derived from millennia of existence. Combined, that knowledge and intuition allowed the elder entities to truly seem like the gods of the old stories.

With Odysseus, his youth made the odd holes between knowing and understanding more visible, and fundamentally more humanizing.

"Don't worry about it," Eric said. "I expect you'll run into both types sooner or later, anyway. For now, let's deal with your original question, shall we?"

Odysseus pouted slightly, but quickly straightened his face into a professional mask that was almost up to standards. To Eric it was like looking at a child doing a good imitation of a professional.

He pushed his amusement down, though he knew that Odysseus was well aware of it, and went on.

"Our opponent out there," Eric said, gesturing to the display that was tracking the ship they'd spotted, "is a detail-oriented thinker. They don't like to move unless they already know the outcome. They watch, they carefully note *everything* they see, and they analyze it over and over until they know how their enemies will react in any given scenario. Only then do they make their move."

Odysseus frowned. "Is that possible?"

"No," Eric said, laughing softly. "It's really not, but you can get close enough to fool most people despite that."

"I believe I can understand that," Odysseus said seriously. "I know what everyone on board this ship is thinking, even as they think it, but

I'm fairly certain that I could not predict how even half would react to something they don't have procedures to handle."

"True enough," Eric said, "but don't forget, they *do* have procedures to handle most things. Groups are easier to predict than individuals. Groups with rules to follow are easier again than that. That's what allows someone like our dear friend out there to fool everyone, maybe even themselves, that they know what their adversaries will do in a given situation."

"Then it isn't about psychology, it's about . . . sociology."

Eric tilted his head. "Not a bad way of analyzing it. Yes, our squadron is a society of sorts, one with its own rules, programmed to react to incidents in specific ways. If you understand the program . . ."

"You can predict the outcome based on specific inputs you control, such as mounting an assault."

"Exactly," Eric congratulated the entity. "So now tell me why I did what I did, and why it will have an effect."

———

Imperial Eighth Fleet Command Vessel

"Enemy formation is shifting, Commander."

Birch frowned, walking over to the tactical display.

Why would they change formation now? she wondered. A few reasons came to mind, but honestly only one rang true off the top of her head. Some of her forces had been spotted.

"What was the change?" she asked, eyes on the display.

"These power sources shifted speed and relative position from here"—the tech gestured—"to here."

Birch stared, then stared for a while longer.

"That . . . makes no sense whatsoever," she said finally.

"It appears to be a defensive perimeter adjustment," the technician said curiously.

"Yes, but against *what?*" she asked. "They actually opened up a hole in their flank that's *directly* in line with one of our pincer detachments, and shored up a section of their formation that has no threat to it."

The technician didn't have any response to that, so Birch leaned in and glared at the display some more.

If they'd spotted us, they wouldn't have opened up that hole in their defense. But what are they defending against, then?

"Have squadrons three through six shift their passive scans," she ordered. "Look for anything at all along vector . . . Prim Four Three Vanir, origin point the enemy fleet's current position."

"Yes Commander."

Birch stepped back, irritated by the change. Now she had to find out what the enemy was reacting to before she made any moves of her own. The last thing she needed was to accidentally get caught between one enemy and an unknown threat. For all she knew, the Oathers had made other enemies out here . . .

Or . . . And Birch paled slightly at the thought. *Some of the rogue Drasin are in the region.*

That would be bad in ways she didn't even want to think about at the moment. Hopefully, she was merely being paranoid, but only time would tell.

———

Odysseus

"You are intentionally . . . making more work for the enemy?" Odysseus seemed confused by the concept.

"I am," Eric said. "It's not a tactic that works on most people, honestly. A lot of battlefield commanders would have looked at the formation change, noted how it affected them, and then moved on with their plan, adding only minor changes."

He grew serious. "However, we're not dealing with most people here. This one is *careful*. He doesn't like unknown variables. He has a need to be in control, a driving need to understand his enemy before he commits. This sort of enemy is a *nightmare* to face across any battlefield, trust me, but they have vulnerabilities just the same as anyone else."

Odysseus nodded, expression pensive.

"So another lesson for you," Eric went on. "Know your enemy, know yourself, and you need not fear the outcome of a hundred battles."

Odysseus recognized that phrase.

"Sun Tzu," he said, smiling.

Eric nodded, amused. "Somewhat overrated, to my mind at least, but he wasn't wrong. If you know even only those two things, you're a *very* dangerous opponent to tangle with."

"Knowing your enemy would seem to often be . . . difficult."

"Knowing yourself is sometimes harder, but yes. We can often only infer our enemy's personality from their actions. Here, now, we're even more limited than we would be on Earth, fighting a conventional war. We have no spies delivering intelligence back, profiles, stolen letters to lovers, and so forth . . ."

"Steph—"

Eric tilted his head, interrupting. "Yes, we're working on it, but the Archangels are on a long-term infiltration. The intelligence they're able to deliver right *now* is more general and limited than what we'd need to properly flesh out a profile on our adversary here."

"Oh."

"That's also an advantage, though," Eric said, eyes sweeping the scanners to be sure that they weren't showing anything untoward. "It also means no false positives."

"False positives?"

"Information that looks good, but isn't," Eric said. "Maybe your spy has been flipped, or just identified, and is now feeding you bad intel. Maybe he just got something wrong, for that matter. More information is a good thing, don't misunderstand me, but more information also means more mistakes."

He held up a hand to make Odysseus pause, before leaning in and opening a line to the *Boudicca*.

"Hyatt, take the *Bo* and two escorts up to reinforce the *Bell's* position."

"Sir?" Captain Hyatt sounded confused. "We'll be opening a large segment on this flank if we do that."

"I'm aware," Eric said warmly. "Don't worry."

"Yes . . . sir. *Boudicca* moving out."

Eric closed the connection, turning back to Odysseus. "It's a trade-off, you see. More intelligence means more *bad* intelligence too."

Odysseus frowned. "Would it not be better to limit yourself, then?"

"Well, it would if we could guarantee that the limited intelligence would be uniformly accurate, I suppose," Eric said with a laugh. "But when you limit yourself like that, every piece of intelligence becomes vastly more valuable and important . . . including the inevitable bits of *bad* intelligence."

He gestured to the black beyond the ship. "In this situation, for example, I'm acting on intelligence I gathered personally through experience. How the Empire acted versus how this officer acts. If I'm *wrong*, then I'm making a rather serious mistake . . . all because I trusted *one* piece of intelligence. When you have a thousand pieces, you can find ways to vet them individually and then average them out. It makes it far less likely that you'll make any truly unrecoverable decisions . . . but also less likely that you'll make *brilliant* ones."

Odysseus frowned, looking confused.

"But . . . which option is better?"

Eric laughed. He couldn't help it. He wasn't laughing at the entity, of course, but more at the thrust of the question. One of the commonalities of modern culture.

Which is better.

The individual, or the collective?

"That," he said, "is a loaded question, my friend. People will point to various geniuses and say that they prove that the individual is better. There are hundreds of names, thousands or more probably, through history that support this. Men who made hard calls, risked everything, and came out on top."

He sighed. "But there are uncountably more men who made hard calls, risked everything . . . and lost *everything*. We don't know their names, history doesn't record them most of the time. Were the ones who failed all fools and the precious few who succeeded uniformly brilliant?" Eric shook his head. "No. Most of them were just average for their positions, give or take. Some were lucky, some were not."

Odysseus was silent for a moment.

"What about you?" he asked finally. "Were you lucky?"

"I was *incredibly* lucky," Eric said firmly. "Many more times than I deserved to be."

"Then some people are . . . lucky?" Odysseus scowled. "That seems . . . wrong. The math says that's not possible. Lucky is just probability."

"True," Eric said lightly. "And statistically, some people will have things fall in their favor more often than not. It's a bell curve, I suppose."

Odysseus nodded slowly. "I think I understand. I wonder, can it be quantified? Can we tell who is, or will be, lucky?"

"I doubt it," Eric replied. "I suspect that it's only possible to see in retrospect."

"That . . ." Odysseus looked vaguely horrified and oddly sick to his stomach, which Eric found amusing since the entity didn't actually *have* a stomach. "That is insanity."

"I suppose." Eric laughed lightly. "But from a human perspective, the universe seems to run on insanity sometimes."

He left Odysseus there, thinking about that while he checked the deployment of the ships and casually dispatched another few Rogue Class destroyers to support the *Bell* and *Bo.*

Horrifying Odysseus and messing with the enemy's head. Not a bad day.

Chapter 10

Hele Protectorate

Steph had no more patience with the bullshit at this point. He had a landing shuttle full of *prisoners* he'd been forced to rescue from their own damn side and a sealed door stopping him from moving on to the next objective in the mission. One of those two things wasn't going to be an issue for much longer.

"Blow the door."

His men looked at him in shock.

"Captain . . ." One of them hesitated as he spoke, looking around nervously. "That will decompress the entire section, at *least*. It could destroy parts of the objective."

"I'm having a hard time caring right now. Blow the door."

He would have cursed there, but honestly there weren't many really good ones in the Imperial language as he'd learned it so far.

Downside of learning most of it from the Priminae, I suppose, Steph thought as he watched his men setting the breaching charges.

He looked up at the cameras that were watching, casually bringing his hands together in front of his face and then pushing them rapidly apart while splaying his fingers.

Toss me into a vacuum? Let's see what you do about this.

———

"Commander, they're laying charges."

Geth was pale, could feel the sweat forming on his skin.

"They wouldn't *dare*." He swallowed. "They'll destroy valuable parts of the station. They can't capture it like that. They . . . they wouldn't *dare*."

On the display, the biggest one in the center, the armored figure who was standing apart from his men, looked right at Geth and his crew as though he could see through the screen, and then pantomimed an explosion with his hands.

He's actually going to do it, Geth realized.

He swallowed, thinking about how much damage would be caused, trying to map it out.

If the systems were all in good repair, only that section would be evacuated. Minimal damage. Unfortunately, he couldn't remember the last time the systems were all in good repair. Geth raced through the files, trying to find the maintenance report for the relevant sector, but there was *nothing* in any of the recent files, which meant a long while had passed since work had been done there.

If containment fails, the problem could cascade, Geth thought in horror.

He took a deep breath.

He's not going to do it. The explosion will destroy too much that he undoubtedly wants to take intact. They need this facility to coordinate and handle shipping for the deep matter.

The men on the screen finished up and moved quickly away from the doors.

He's not going to do it.

Geth wasn't sure if he was making a statement or a plea.

He's not going . . .

The men on-screen took cover except for the one in the open. The one in the black armor. He stood, holding up his hand with fingers splayed. One finger was folded into his palm.

No way.

Two fingers.

Geth shook his head.

The thumb.

He's not going to do it. He's not.

Only one finger left.

Geth swallowed, his hand frozen over the controls.

He's NOT going to do—The last finger folded into a fist.

He jerked back as the explosion blinded the cameras, sending smoke everywhere.

In a near panic, Geth slammed a hand down on the controls, activating the fields that sealed off the ship bay. On the display, the smoke was funneled away from the explosion, sweeping around the man in black armor as the air was pulled into the evacuated bay through the breaching hole. In a few moments, the rush stopped.

He stared as the man looked back up at the camera, then drew his sidearm and started walking toward the breach. His men scrambled to catch up a moment later.

Geth collapsed back into his station, unable to believe what had just happened.

———

Steph didn't slow his pace as he strode through the breach, ducking just a bit so the still glowing-hot border didn't touch his armor. He didn't need cooling bits of armor-steel sticking to his head.

It would ruin the image.

There were shocked men and women on the other side, staring in horror as he stood there. Still no one with anything resembling a weapon, let alone something that was actually a *threat* to him in armor. He lowered the pistol he was wielding, letting it casually sort of point at the floor as he stepped farther in to make room for his own men to move through the breach.

The corridors looked familiar, clearly reminiscent of Priminae and Imperial tech, but they were also in pretty bad shape. The station felt like a place that had once been impressive but had been slowly worn away to nothing by a negligent owner more concerned with immediate profits than the future.

He'd walked many halls just like this in the past. He remembered an almost identical feeling back when he first entered the facilities where the Archangels were built. It had been such a waste of potential, he had felt at the time, right up until he saw what was being done.

I wonder if that could be recaptured?

It was an interesting thought. Steph heard his men coming through the breach behind him and gestured them forward.

"Secure the noncombatants," he ordered. "Do *not* harm anyone unless they attack you first."

"Yes Captain!"

He casually walked the hall himself, eyes falling on the cowering people who were looking up at him in unmasked shock. They were all slaves, he noted with growing irritation. The whole place was just one twisted work camp and he wasn't particularly pleased to be walking the grounds.

He stopped.

A man was pressing himself back into the wall, like he was trying to literally escape through the bulkhead into the next room.

Good luck with that, buddy.

"What's your name?" Steph asked.

"Wh-what?" the man asked, looking up at him, confused.

"Your name."

"I . . . I'm . . ." The man hesitated a bit before spitting it out. "I'm Denn, master."

"Don't call me that," Steph growled, making the man shrink away. He took a breath, calming himself, reaching out to offer him a hand. "Tell me something, Denn, if you would."

Denn looked at the hand, clad in black armor, like it was a snake threatening to bite him. Steph didn't move, leaving it there and letting the silence hang until Denn finally seemed to decide that if he didn't respond he might be insulting the man leaning over him. He reached up and took the hand, letting Steph pull him to his feet.

"Wh . . ." Denn swallowed. "What do you want to know?"

"So many things, my friend, so many things," Steph said cheerfully. "Why don't we start with the fastest route to the command deck, however?"

Denn's eyes flickered to the left, and Steph followed his gaze without moving. His armor was useful for that sort of thing, with a heads-up display and full-circle scanners working constantly. He didn't say anything, though, as he was more interested in the man himself than the answer.

"I—I can't," Denn said, shaking as he spoke. "My family . . ."

He looked up, sharply, eyes wide with fear.

"Our families. They'll open fire in case this is a breakout . . ."

"They did try," Steph said. "I admit, I didn't believe they'd actually do it until the weapon platforms powered up."

"Try?"

"Try. They gave the order, so *I* gave an order of my own," Steph said. "Now, the command deck?"

Denn hesitated again, but this time his hand came up and he pointed. "Through there. Three sections in, then all the way up the central pillar to the top."

"Excellent," Steph said, turning now to the corridor that Denn had pointed out. "Geoff?"

"Yes, Captain Teach?"

"Gather the men. We're going to pay a visit to the command deck."

"Yes sir."

"Oh, and Geoff?"

The man turned around. "Captain?"

"Let's make it impressive, shall we? Have a little fun."

"Yes Captain."

"Just a little now, don't get carried away." Steph waved a finger at him.

"Understood, Captain."

Steph laughed softly as he looked back to Denn. "Take a seat. You may as well just relax and wait it out. Nothing more for you to do I'm afraid."

Denn nodded shakily, slumping against the wall and sliding slowly back down to the floor.

Steph walked away, aware of the eyes on him as he headed for the corridor, deeply enjoying himself as he led the team along.

Yo ho, yo ho, a pirate's life for me. Steph considered humming the tune, but it didn't fit the image he wanted in their minds at the moment. *Perhaps the "Imperial March"? Nah, I'm not messing with those lawyers, not even this far from Earth.*

He came to the door and paused, sending a quick message through the network. A moment later, the door opened as if on command . . . mostly because it *was*, and he stepped through.

"Come," Steph ordered. "We have an appointment to keep with the commander of this facility."

———

Buckler looked around carefully, noting the security had thinned out considerably. He wasn't terribly surprised at that, given what they were monitoring over the tactical network.

Someone had to have soiled their pants when the *Dutchman* swung around like that, pointing her beam emitters right into the launch bay.

He knew he probably would have had to make a special laundry day if it had happened to him, which he wasn't remotely ashamed to admit.

The boss had capitalized on that entrance and seemed to have gathered all the attention for himself.

Such a show stealer, Buckler thought.

"Alright, find the security room," he ordered. "It'll be on the innermost spiral, near the core."

"Oorah."

The squad of Marines moved in, through the connecting corridors that branched the spiral habitats of the facility. A fairly conventional design, Buckler supposed, but practical as far as he could tell. The workers here had little need for spin gravity, but the concentric design did improve security considerably.

Unless you were dealing with determined Marines willing to deploy breaching charges.

Still, it was certainly an effective defense against slave revolts, he had no doubt.

So far they'd breached three security doors, but only the first had been somewhat of a challenge. That one had been a lock, while the next two were primarily intended to secure against atmosphere loss. Since the atmosphere was still intact on both sides, the doors didn't have the added force of atmospheric pressure behind them to help keep them shut.

"Watch the gunfire," he reminded his team. "I don't want to put holes in places that shouldn't have them."

"You got it, Sergeant."

"No problem, Sarge."

"How about a really small hole, Sarge?"

"Watch your mouth, Timmy," Buckler growled, shooting a glare over the team's secure network.

"Don't worry. Just kidding, Sarge."

"Kid somewhere we don't have to worry about explosive decompression, Tim."

Buckler didn't need any of the squad getting ideas like that, not even in jest. Working in space was no joke, and while they'd been spoiled of late with the types of ships they generally got to work from, places like this station were evidence that not every space-born environment was near as good as an Archangel or the *Odysseus*.

"Intel from the locals puts the security room for this sector just ahead," Buckler said. "So look sharp, we're likely to run into resistance soon."

"Not much, if they're using those peashooters we've seen."

"Don't count on that, Tim."

"Yeah, yeah, staying frosty, Sarge, I got you."

Buckler shook his head but gestured to the squad as they continued to leapfrog up the corridor, covering each other forward and back. Security was total crap, but he'd be damned if he let his team get sloppy just because the enemy were idiots.

If the Empire is the Block, then these Free Star jokers are Muj at best, Buckler thought darkly.

Not that he wanted the enemy to be competent per se; it certainly made things easier on the ground when you were dealing with idiots. However, it was also his experience that while it was far easier to just roll over the idiots, they were also the ones who constantly made trouble just because they were too stupid to realize that they would get their ass kicked.

The Block didn't start a war until they thought they could win, and they'd been damn well close on the money. If you wanted to avoid a war with intelligent enemies, that was a simple thing, show them that it would cost them more than such a war was worth. A smart person wouldn't start trouble when he knew it would actually set him back.

An idiot, on the other hand, always thought they could win, and were lousy at actually understanding the threat matrix they were facing.

Irritatingly, that same stupidity often made it more costly to kick their ass because the pricks were too stupid to realize they'd lost. Often it wasn't even worth fighting them in the first place, because their stupidity would translate into increased costs for you, making the whole effort a losing proposition.

Yes, sometimes being stupid was a survival trait in the most utterly inane way possible.

He wasn't sure if that would hold true with the Free Stars. He'd like to think that a spacefaring civilization wouldn't be quite that foolish. Unfortunately, Buckler had seen too much to have even that much faith left.

"Corzky, you're up," he said as they approached the security room.

Anton Corzky shuffled forward, pulling an intercept system from the gear hanging from his armor. The local cultures in the Free Stars all used Imperial tech, likely millennia out of date, but that didn't matter as much as it might on Earth. Since Imperial tech was almost identical, with a few exceptions, to Priminae systems, hacking it was possible, if not actually easy.

Corzky got his gear linked into the local system, using some method that went completely over Buckler's head. No actual wires or connections were involved but the process seemed to work somehow, so he just dubbed it Alien-WiFi™.

"System has reasonable security, Sarge. This will take a minute."

Buckler held back his reaction. Reasonable security shouldn't be cracked in a minute, but he wasn't going to bitch.

Much.

"Codes have been cracked. We have control of the local security functions, Sarge."

"Only the local ones?"

Corzky nodded. "Yeah, they were at least smart enough to isolate sections. If we want control over everything, we're going to need to take the main control deck."

"Alright. The boss plans on that anyway," Buckler said. "Speaking of, has he made his entrance yet?"

"Boy howdy."

Buckler groaned. "How bad?"

"They tried to blow him back into space and he responded by threatening to blow us all back into hard vacuum. They called his bluff," Corzky replied. "Only one problem . . ."

"The boss wasn't bluffing."

Corzky pouted. Actually pouted. Made Buckler want to groan, but he managed to resist.

"Don't steal the punch line like that, Sarge."

"Show me the boss," Buckler said, ignoring the gripe.

In a moment Buckler was looking at a corridor pretty much like the one they were in at the moment. The boss was there in armor, not much different than what his Marines wore, aside from the blacker-than-black color scheme, of course.

Captain Teach in black armor. *He has a weird sense of humor, but at least it's not dull.*

He was talking to a man on the floor, even going so far as to help the man to his feet while they chatted. Buckler brought up the network feed from the tactical net and put it side by side with the security feed they were hijacking from the station itself. Stephanos was putting on a nice show, he decided, being very casual while everyone around him was losing their shit.

Nice play.

Buckler listened in on the conversation and noted the directions to the main command deck. Good intel. They'd needed that. When the boss left the man and walked over to the door blocking the way, he was ready for the request that came through.

"Open the doors for him, Corzky. Clear the road."

"Oorah, Sarge."

Chapter 11

Hele Protectorate

Geth glared at the display, fuming as he watched the black-armored figure just walking through checkpoint after checkpoint as though he had clearance.

"How is he doing that?!" Geth demanded, leaning over the master security console, and making the tech there shy slightly away.

"We don't know," the man admitted fearfully. "Something is opening the doors for him, but we haven't worked out who or what, or even where they've gained access to our system."

"Find them," Geth ordered.

He started to pace angrily, each step getting more and more frenetic as he watched the man lead a boarding crew through *his* station with near impunity.

"Security is holding them in section five on the inner circle for the moment, Commander."

"About time. Put them on display, now!"

"Yes Commander."

The display flickered, then turned to show a scene from different angles, his security personnel lining up using whatever cover they could manage while being limited to the corridors of the station. The invaders moved forward with seemingly implacable intent.

Geth seethed. Just a glance across his boards showed that while many of the system defenses were still intact, none that *mattered* appeared to be. A destroyer was out there, plus whatever the others were, and they had gotten so damn close before they revealed themselves that he was certain betrayal was the only explanation.

That was proven by the fact that the first thing the destroyer had done was eliminate the weapon platforms put into place to keep the slaves in line.

Someone sold me out, Geth thought with certainty.

"Kill them," he growled over the system's communications channels.

When they'd dealt with the boarders and pushed off the infernal ships, he'd have every slave in position to have remotely accessed the communications systems killed.

———

I need a theme playing in the background, Steph thought, his head going to strange places as he tried to focus on the situation at hand without cackling.

"Captain." One of the men came jogging back to his position. "Security teams have secured a junction ahead. They have cover. We'll have to charge right into their guns if we want to push them out."

Steph nodded. "What are they armed with?"

"Someone must have authorized heavier weapons, Captain." The man grimaced. "They're using combat-grade equipment now."

Well, the game was fun while it lasted.

Normally, the Free Stars didn't seem to do much face-to-face fighting. They generally carried very light fléchette weapons as a rule, at least on ships and stations from what he could tell. Useless against even basic armor, the light weapons were very good at one thing—threatening people who were unarmored.

Catching a burst from them without some sort of protection would be ugly, but they were otherwise safe to use within even the lightest of ships and unarmed civilian-type crafts with little to no worry of causing damage that you might regret.

Not that I'm going to regret what I do with this, Steph thought as he idly hefted his sidearm.

The Alliance pistol was more of a hand cannon designed to defeat military body armor up to and including light-powered suits. The designers of the big pistol had never intended to see the weapon used on a space-going vessel, but his current persona wouldn't care about that, and frankly, he didn't particularly either.

It was a pain that the enemy was finally doing away with such caution, as it left his men vulnerable to injury or worse.

Steph's own armor was a tougher grade, though short of the full-power suits they'd equipped the ground forces with on the *Odyssey*. That stuff was expensive and had been at a premium since the Drasin invasion unfortunately. He didn't even have suits like that for his Marines.

Still, he was confident enough in his current kit that he could take a couple chances.

"Hold back a moment," he ordered. "I want to take a look."

Steph stepped over to the corridor wall, moving smoothly to the edge of the corner and slipping a camera from his belt. The device was a small thing, half the size of his palm, with a set of eight ducted fans that counter-rotated, tuned to emit canceling frequencies. The camera whirred almost silently to life and he tossed it out into the corridor.

Steph immediately received a drone's-eye view of the corridor. No one had apparently spotted the small device, or at least they weren't pointing and yelling or shooting at it. He guided the drone down the hall, getting a good look at the defensive positions the enemy had taken, and deliberated on his next action.

Grenades would be the tactical option the situation called for, but he was leery of using anything quite that explosive inside a pressurized environment. Even if he didn't pop the seal on the whole place and kill a bunch of folk that probably didn't have it coming, the dangers of fire in an enclosed oxygen-rich environment didn't require contemplation.

He instead drew his sidearm and haloed a target with the drone, setting his weapon to automatic fire control in the process. Then he simply squeezed the trigger down and swung out to point it in the right direction. The computer took over from there, discharging the round only when the muzzle crossed the target he'd chosen.

A roar filled the air, and over the drone footage he saw a man go down.

The security detail opened fire in a panic, their heavier weapons gouging out holes and furrows in the wall as he swung back to cover and watched the scene through the drone's camera.

"Touchy, aren't they, Geoff?" Steph asked lightly.

"Did you get him?" Geoff asked.

Steph turned to look at the man, tilting his helmet to one side, and stared silently.

"Sorry, boss." Geoff ducked his head, wincing in the expectation of coming punishment.

Steph moved back around to the corridor, noting the new position of the security men. He opened the battle network he had with his Marines.

"Squad Three," he said after a moment. "You're up."

Sergeant McKenzie was the senior non-com assigned to *Archangel Three* for the mission, and she found that she was enjoying the more relaxed nature of this particular deployment. The ships were too small to properly maintain full discipline, especially over the periods they had been deployed already. That didn't mean she let her girls and boys *slack*, of course; that would be a recipe for disaster. It just meant that she treated the scenario more like an extended patrol mission than a shipboard assignment.

When the skipper let them off the leash, though, things got even better.

"Hold the position," Jane "Mac" McKenzie ordered the two handling the drag position, causing them to stop, nod, and drop to a knee on either side of the corridor, covering the rear position. She looked over to the others. "Boss needs an obstruction cleared just up ahead. You know the brief."

"Oorah, Sergeant."

She took the remaining members of the fireteam forward now that their six was covered, being cautious as they moved. There was a distinctive sound of weapon fire from ahead, but nothing she was really concerned about. It sounded panicked and wasn't aimed in her direction.

"Boss man has them jumping at shadows," Mac said, amused. "Move in quietly, don't engage until I give the go ahead or they look like they're about to engage first."

The men acknowledged the order as they jogged easily around the slightly curving corridor and got themselves into position. Mac spotted the first of the enemy security team, and a fist in the air brought the fireteam to a stop as she dropped to one knee and rested her rifle against her leg.

"Amateurs," she mumbled, wishing she wasn't wearing a helmet so she could spit on the ground while she said the word.

Modern gear was effective, she had to admit, but it took some of the romance out of things. Marines should have a cigar in their teeth, like they did in the movies she grew up on, giving orders and laughing in the face of certain death. But no, she had to have a full environmental armored helmet. Great for stopping bullets, but the damn thing was so sanitized it smelled like a hospital.

She liked to think of herself as an old-school Marine, someone who'd cut their teeth out in the sun with saltwater beating at her face. She knew she was a spoiled brat compared to many who came before her, but that was the hand she'd been dealt.

Time marches on and sweeps us all up whether we like it or not, Mac thought as she sighted the enemy and opened up a channel to the boss.

"Squad Three, in position."

"Roger," Steph replied over the communications channel. "Stand by. Engage on my mark."

"Oorah," Mac said while inwardly frowning. *His mark? We have them in our sights. What the hell is the boss up to?*

———

Steph extended his hand, catching the drone as it came to a smooth landing on his palm, then tucked it back into the pouch he'd pulled it from. He reviewed the imagery from the Marines' cameras instead, taking note of the enemy from their point of view before he psyched himself up.

"Mark in three," Steph said as he began walking. "Two . . ."

He stepped out around the corner, turning casually, and started walking toward the enemy right up the center of the corridor in full view.

"One. Fire."

Steph never broke step as a few stray shots ricocheted down around him. A blare of fire from ahead told him that the Marines had started the job proper while the enemy was focused on him. He glanced back, noting his men were fearfully looking around the corner in disbelief.

"Well?" Steph snapped. "Are you coming or not?"

They were taken aback momentarily until a brave soul stepped out into the open behind him. When they weren't shot, the rest followed suit and Steph continued walking as he dispatched new orders to the Marines, who fell back along the corridor as Steph reached the bodies.

He stepped over the remains of the security detail, idly kicking a few of their weapons away from twitching hands as he looked around.

The Marines were thorough, he had to admit with detached admiration.

The security team hadn't really seen the strike coming, and while some might consider shooting them from the back . . . well, the side really . . . to be unsporting, Steph figured that even if you did ascribe to that unrealistic image of warfare, the fact that they were firing at him in the first place neatly invalidated the argument.

His recruits gingerly followed him and stared wide-eyed down at the bodies before looking back at him in shock.

Steph just gestured casually as his men looked at him with those fearful eyes. "It seems they angered someone. Probably for the best that you lot stay on your best behavior, don't you think?"

He had to kill the audio to his external speaker to keep his cackling laughter from slipping out when he saw how fast the men rushed to agree. That suited him just fine, though, because he was well aware that he couldn't entirely trust any of his Free Stars recruits, not yet anyway.

He needed the extra help to continue with his plans, but he couldn't afford to let any of them think for a *second* that he wasn't the man in command. That might start giving them ideas, and it would be better all around if no one started down that road.

"Geoff," he said casually, standing in the middle of a scattered pile of corpses.

"Sir! Captain! Sir?" Geoff stammered.

Steph ignored him, nodding up ahead. "There's a security office at the end of this corridor, I believe?"

Geoff nodded slowly. "That was what we were told."

"I believe we should pick up a visitors map to the facility," Steph said, his tone light, though he wasn't sure if Geoff was getting that or not. "Wouldn't do to be wandering around, lost, don't you agree?"

Geoff didn't look like he had any clue what Steph was talking about, but he nodded furiously.

"Good. Let's be off then, this way."

"Boss is moving in this direction with his daycare class."

Buckler acknowledged the report, turning to the rest of the squad. "You heard the man, pack it up and clear the area. Boss wants the kiddies to feel like they accomplished something here."

The Marines quickly closed out the tap they had on the area's security, having already exhausted the greater part of its value anyway, and got their gear packed up so they were moving within sixty seconds of the order.

Buckler nodded with approval, though in his armor no one would have seen it and really that was how he liked it anyway, the motion just felt right to him. The team was moving like pros, reward enough in itself.

They cleared the area just as they heard the rhythmic tapping of the boss' armored boots on the metal of the station floors from a few turns of the station away.

Just in time and right on schedule.

———

Steph reached the security station, eyes spotting almost by instinct alone some of the telltales that the Marines had been there.

Scuffs on the floor where their armor had left a few flecks of paint. A twist to an access panel that had likely happened when someone forced it open with leverage. Those sorts of things would mean everything to someone with the right context.

Luckily, his men didn't have that.

"Search the station," he ordered. "Get me a map of this place."

Geoff nodded. "Yes Captain."

Steph left him to it, though he surreptitiously kept an eye on the man. Thankfully that was made easier by being in armor.

Geoff returned quickly with an Imperial slate, a portable system that wasn't much different than what the Priminae utilized. Steph accepted the tablet and found that it did, indeed, have a station schematic on the display.

"Good work," he said, not bothering to look closer. He already had the map on his heads-up display provided by his Marines. "Looks like we need to head down this way."

He gestured, then nodded to Geoff. "Take three men, Lieutenant, and secure the path."

Geoff was startled, recognizing that the moment meant something. Then he seemed to register the change in ranking and nodded firmly.

"Pirro, Ger, and Mirrin." He pointed. "Follow me."

Steph smiled slightly, letting the four move on ahead a bit before he followed suit, with the rest going along with him.

It would take a bit of time, he knew, but he'd get them to where he needed them to be.

In the meantime, his Marines would have to take up the slack.

There was something downright heretical, however, in using Marines to train up pirates to a decent standard. Somewhere out there, Steph had no doubt, Eric was resisting an urge to kick his ass for all of this.

The things we do in the name of protecting our world, he thought with a mix of ironic humor and honest horror.

Steph resolved to do his best to ensure that the whole damn thing didn't get away from him. He'd seen that more than once, during the war and since. It was all too easy to lose control of a situation, and when that happened, with military weapons mixed in, things tended to go sideways in a hurry.

For now, he had a mission to complete.

———

Geth stared in horror at the scenes on his primary displays.

The boarders were wading through his security like threshers through a harvest, barely even slowing when they encountered defenses, and if they did slow, it often seemed to be more out of some bizarre form of personal amusement than anything else.

"They've reached the central lifts, Commander."

"Lock them down," Geth ordered.

The lifts were the only way to the command deck, a sometimes inconvenient thing but done with intent for specifically this situation. With the lifts locked down entirely, nothing was coming up just as nothing was going down.

He knew he couldn't hold the station, not as things stood, but Geth would delay the enemy as best he could. The station was due to receive a shift change and transshipment of materials within a short time, and if he could hold that long, then the Protectorate destroyers escorting the freighters would be able to put down this attack.

What it would do to his career was now a secondary concern.

———

Archangel One, Gaia's Revenge

Tyke floated in the suspension field, eyes flicking around the augmented display that surrounded him, feeling a level of satisfaction he hadn't entertained since the war.

The combined arms strike had gone off as close to flawlessly as one might hope for, particularly given the inclusion of the *Dutchman* in the operation. They needed the firepower, to be sure, but he didn't like leaning so hard on that many unknown factors, not even with Crown sitting in the hot seat.

Tyke couldn't help but smile a little fondly, thinking about the snot-nosed punk he'd helped train up after they caught him sneaking into their facility one too many times. It was either turn him into something useful or call the cops and probably get him a record that put him on a bad road. He and Eric had made a call back then that their investors weren't happy with, but neither had ever looked back.

Kid turned out pretty damn good too.

"Sir." Milla's voice came over the communications system. "I believe there is something on the long-range scans you should be aware of."

Tyke flicked his fingers in a quick motion, swiping from tactical scans to the overview that included information from the long-range systems. It took only a moment to find himself looking in the appropriate place, a number of contacts lighting up his system as he tried to separate the initial contacts into more refined results.

"Damn. How many are inbound?"

"Uncertain," Milla responded as they both examined the gravity anomalies approaching at high speed. "The contacts are not in the system as of yet and are decelerating from hyperlight velocities. I believe I have spotted multiple destroyer-class cores, but they're mixed up at this range, and there are others that I am not certain about."

"Best guess?" he asked tersely.

"Given our location combined with the data I have available? I would say a freighter convoy."

"Huh, right. I suppose that does make sense," Tyke said. "Well, that isn't as bad as I was envisioning."

"No, I imagine you were thinking cruisers, likely Imperial," Milla said. "We have not yet drawn that level of notice."

"Yeah, yet. Alright, thanks for the heads-up. Need to alert the boss."

"You are welcome."

Hele Protectorate Command Station

"You're sure?" Steph asked, listening intently to Tyke as he detailed the situation. "No, I have no reason to doubt you. We knew they'd have some sort of traffic through here, just would have been nicer if they gave us a little more time. Okay, you know what to do. I'll get things in place over here."

He closed the connection and examined the locked-down lifts with a little more urgency.

"Force the doors," Steph ordered.

"Yes Captain," Geoff responded, but looked confused. "But the lifts will not respond."

"We'll have to go up the hard way," Steph answered. "I hope no one here is afraid of heights."

Geoff swallowed, but nodded in his armor as he turned back to his work.

The clock was ticking now.

Chapter 12

Odysseus

"This one likes to play games," Eric said to himself.

Nothing he hadn't already been aware of, of course, but somehow he kept reminding himself of it at the most frustrating times.

There was the better part of an Imperial Fleet pacing them, but Eric couldn't tell if the Imperials knew they were being tracked or not.

Might be their standard operating procedure, he supposed.

This would make sense, playing with expectations just on the off chance you were detected. He'd done similar things in the past, playing with his adversaries' minds. He just didn't much like it when *his* mind was being played with.

After spotting the first ship, they'd immediately begun looking for others. It wasn't hard to find most of the vessels, or they hoped it was most of them anyway. As Eric had informed Odysseus, there were certain sectors of space that the fleet would have to control if they were plotting an ambush.

Direct the passive scanners in those directions, then lo and behold, there they were.

Mostly.

The enemy commander was a bit sneakier than Eric would prefer to deal with. They moved their ships around, sometimes backing them out of range or in some other way vanishing from the scans.

That wasn't something that should happen, not once they had a lock on the location.

Space was *huge*, and it made hiding very easy, but it was also *empty* . . . So once something was found, it damn well should *stay* found.

The *Odysseus*, like the *Odyssey* before her, could pull off the stealth thing by using the cam-plate modifications to absorb all radiation. Wasn't exactly a perfectly safe thing to do, even when you weren't being fired on by terawatt scale lasers, but for limited periods it was a feasible tactic.

The Imperials hadn't shown any sign of that technology in any of their previous encounters, however, and Eric didn't know of any other methods that could be used to hide in plain sight.

So how the hell are they doing this?

It was frustrating, but whatever the technique, it didn't seem to be something they could maintain for long since they weren't *staying* hidden, which made him believe they were using something similar to the cam-plates. He was intimately familiar with the problems those had, even with ships designed for their use. For Imperial ships, who wouldn't have the necessary cooling apparatus inherently built into their hulls . . . it fit what he was seeing.

This was a new capability, however, and that meant it was going to mess with his tactics, especially until he figured out how the damn thing was being done.

Imperial Eighth Fleet Command Vessel

"They've refocused their formation once more, Commander."

Birch scowled in annoyance. "Where are they defending against this time?"

She was growing irritated with the enemy commander, in part because she was almost certain now that he knew the Eighth Fleet was in the vicinity, and was actively playing games with her. She didn't have proof of this; none of his actions were aimed *at* the fleet, but that alone was almost proof enough of his knowledge to her mind.

Her aide dispatched the new data to her displays, and she looked it over while viciously suppressing the urge to sigh from the frustration.

Are they actually detecting something out there that we can't?

Nothing she'd done had shown any sign of other targets, yet the enemy kept making tactical moves that made no sense if something wasn't out there. Somewhere.

Unless they know we're here, in which case every move they've made has been calculated to drive me insane.

It wasn't the usual sort of play her enemies made, but it was certainly a valid one. Birch herself had been known to play with enemy expectations more than a few times in her career and had even gained the praise of the emperor for such tactics before his passing.

He was a man who was very frugal with praise, so she had counted it as one of her greater accomplishments despite having grown up with his daughter, who had gone on to follow in his path.

Such experience was telling her that the enemy *was* in fact messing with her, playing games to keep her jumping. Maybe they didn't even know for certain she was out here, but she was almost certain that they were playing games anyway.

Almost.

Therein lay the crux of her current headache.

She couldn't be entirely certain that it was just games. If the enemy vessels were, in fact, detecting a potential threat that she had missed, then the Eighth Fleet had to identify it. That meant constantly pulling ships from formations and sending them off to investigate the vectors the enemy seemed to be guarding against.

This was hard on the crews in more ways than one, and managing the stressors on the ships was becoming an irritation beyond the mind games themselves.

The captured technology that the Empire had taken from the anomaly and Oather vessels was quite good at hiding ships from even intense scans, but it had come with a problem that they'd not anticipated.

Engaging the stealth aspect of the coating caused the ship's armor to absorb *all* radiation. In space, even out in the black void itself, that was a dangerous proposition. Lethal levels of radiation could be absorbed quite quickly and, since the ships were not insulated to the degree needed, provide quite the health risk for the crews.

Birch was going to have *personal* words with the research division who'd jumped so quickly on the new armor technology without looking at the rest of the hull composition, such that they'd *missed* that the captured ships had far denser internal insulation than was normally deemed necessary.

Imperial arrogance was such that it apparently never occurred to them that maybe the Oathers and the anomalies had made those design choices for a *reason*.

For the moment, it meant that her ships couldn't really utilize the stealth technology to the highest degree it was capable, but they would do the best they could with what they had.

"Dispatch ships from squadron nine to investigate under stealth," Birch ordered. "See to it that none exceed the limits we've posted, otherwise I will be . . . irate."

"Yes Commander. Orders dispatched."

So far none of the checks have found anything. If this too comes back negative, then I will assume that we are dealing with a psyops campaign and adjust my strategy accordingly, she decided.

The necessary delays in action were dragging on everyone, and she wondered if this was how her enemies had felt in the past.

For the first time, she felt a degree of pity for those she had been hunting, if so.

Bellerophon

Jason Roberts examined the results of their long-range scans again, wondering what the hell he was looking at.

"The ships keep disappearing and then showing up again," he growled. "Are they using cam-plates?"

"It appears so, Captain," Janice Sheen, his chief scanner specialist, said. "The signature is close, at least."

"Close?" Roberts asked sharply.

"We're still collating data with the rest of the squadron, but if I'm reading the numbers correctly," she said hesitantly, "I would say that they've implemented a variation of the technology, but they've not done it properly."

"Oh? How so?"

"We're scanning an increase in radiation in some of the vessels," she said. "I've cross-referenced our scans with the *Odysseus* and other ships, and while we can't be certain yet, I believe they haven't adjusted their hull structure to compensate for the black hole radiation issues."

Jason sat back, thinking about that for a moment.

"You can scan that this far out?" he asked after a moment.

"Radiation leaves a signature," Janice confirmed. "If they are using cam-plates and not something new, they didn't properly shield the hulls."

Jason nodded. "That's . . . very interesting. Have you sent the speculation to the commodore?"

"Yes sir."

"Good work."

"Thank you, sir."

———

Odysseus

Eric found himself looking at the screens more and more, thinking about the enemy commander.

He wondered what they were thinking, if they were doing the same thing as he was. He assumed they probably were, in some way or another. The tension on the *Odysseus* had been slowly increasing since the first moment the enemy had been spotted.

Everyone in the squadron knew they were out there, watching, by this point. Everyone was expecting a fight, that was in the nature of the Imperials. What no one could predict was when that fight would kick off.

That was what made these Imperials different than previous contacts.

The more they waited, the more the ship felt like everyone was walking on eggshells.

It might be wishful thinking on his part, in a twisted way of sorts, but Eric had the feeling that the waiting was going to be coming to an end shortly.

The new information was looking more and more like the Empire had acquired, at the very least, cam-plate technology from the ships they'd destroyed while fighting the Priminae and Earth forces.

Likely several other technologies as well, he thought grimly.

It was only a matter of time, he expected, before all of their tech was in the open more or less.

He knew that sharing the transition drive with the Priminae had been necessary, but Eric was regretting that more than he could say at the moment.

I'm going to have to submit a recommendation that we don't share too openly with our allies going forward, not that I honestly expect that will be a problem.

The admiral had almost been chastised for sharing transition tech, and that was despite it being a requirement for saving the solar system from the Drasin plague. No one was happy with their most strategically vital technology even being in the hands of the Priminae, and now it was clear that the Empire was investigating and implementing technical developments from captured ships.

That was going to be a problem in the future, but it was one he would deal with as it came, he supposed.

"Priminae Fleet captain for you, Commodore."

Eric looked over, surprised, but quickly recovered. "Put him through, Lieutenant."

"Aye sir."

He turned to the display that flickered to life, nodding to the Priminae captain who appeared on the screen.

"Captain Goran," Eric said. "How can I be of service?"

Elnan Goran gestured politely. "We have been monitoring your fleet actions, of course, Commodore Weston."

"Of course," Eric said. He'd have been surprised otherwise.

"Your actions have been confusing, we are not certain how to respond," the Priminae captain said.

"Hopefully the Imperial forces feel the same," Eric said with some amusement. "We've largely been playing games with the enemy, Captain. My thanks to you for playing along, incidentally."

Goran nodded, though he looked slightly confused. "Do you expect an attack?"

"Most certainly, Captain," Eric said firmly. "Likely soon. When are we expected to arrive at our first destination?"

Goran glanced aside, checking the numbers Eric assumed, then looked back.

"Shortly," he answered. "We are due to begin deceleration within twelve hours."

Eric considered that. "Then yes, the attack will come soon. You remember the plan in case of this event?"

"Yes, we have been preparing, though you'll pardon me for admitting that we had wished not to require the implementation of the plan."

Eric chuckled. "No doubt, Captain, no doubt. I would have preferred a boring cruise myself, but the reason we made our plans was because it was inevitable that the enemy was going to begin striking deeper into Priminae territory. Pickings had gotten too slim in the sectors of space close to Imperial territory. Just follow the plan and you'll be fine, Captain."

Goran nodded. "Thank you, Commodore."

"I have to return to my duties," Eric said. "However, I will warn you if the situation changes."

"Very well, until then, I suppose."

"Until then, Captain."

The signal cut off, leaving Eric considering his options carefully.

The game was afoot, as the old saying went, and that meant he had to seriously consider his endgame plans.

The first priority was to give the civilians cover to escape, but only shortly behind that was finding a way to permanently discourage Imperial aggression within Priminae or Earth space. That was probably being optimistic, of course, but Eric had always believed in aiming high.

He began laying down plans, and plans, and more plans. Putting them into the computer to be shared among the squadron, then making variations that he could have people shift to quickly without being forced to explain what he was trying to accomplish.

The clock was now ticking, and it was just a matter of who set the final action into play . . . and when.

Imperial Eighth Fleet Command Vessel

Birch made the call, finally.

The enemy was conducting psyops, toying with her and her fleet. It was annoying that it had taken this long to make that decision, but such was the problem of dealing with unprofiled enemies, she supposed. The empress knew her foes must have felt the same dealing with her, more than once.

The enemy convoy was slowing, apparently aiming for a nearby system. She was unsurprised. Her forces had listed it as a high likelihood of being the destination some time ago and made appropriate plans.

"Issue the order to the fleet," she said finally. "Close on the enemy, block their escape, and engage with the full force of the Eighth."

"Yes Commander!"

She smiled thinly at the eagerness she heard in her subordinate's voice.

It was one that she felt echoed in her own blood.

Intelligence specialists or not, one did not achieve the rank she had in the Imperial forces without having a certain fondness for direct combat.

The Empire grew on the blood of its enemies and citizens.

It is time to grow the Empire once more.

Chapter 13

Destroyer Mirran's Bane, _Hele Protectorate_

Commander Jorra walked across the command deck of his destroyer, bored near to death but happy that the assignment was almost half over. Protection had to be assigned, of course. The transport of deep matter was too valuable to the Protectorate to do otherwise, but it was an easy job and effectively never had surprises.

No one was foolish enough to attack an armed convoy, particularly not when they knew that the Protectorate had Imperial backing in exchange for a tithe of their material.

Tithe. Jorra snorted. That was a nice way of saying that the Imperials took more than _half_ of the mined material, but it was still a far better deal than the Protectorate would have without them. Even if one assumed the Empire wouldn't get involved personally, which was a laughably optimistic assumption in his opinion, the other polities of the Free Stars would certainly make themselves well-known in their efforts to acquire control of the mines for themselves.

It was why the Protectorate was even willing to sell some of the material to other polities, despite it being a vital strategic resource. Better to appease them with a trickle of material than force the entire region into self-immolation that would inevitably bring the Empire down on _all_ of them.

Practical, but it did make for rather dull assignments.

"We've crossed the stellar boundary, Commander," his second offered.

Jorra nodded. "Thank you, Brekka. Let the station know we're coming. I'd like to have everything ready for a quick load-up so we can get out of this abyssal system as quickly as possible."

"Yes Commander. We're expecting a system challenge anytime now. Should we transmit first?"

Jorra frowned. "They haven't challenged yet?"

"No Commander."

"That's . . . odd. We should have been on the long-range scans some time ago, and they knew we were coming."

He walked over to the repeater display that was linked to the long-range systems, checking the telltales from the neutron star system they'd just entered. Nothing seemed particularly out of the ordinary. The station and mining facilities were all as expected, though the broadcast traffic was rather low.

"Transceiver failure," he grunted. "Send the signal. They should have receivers operating, but either way I doubt we'll be able to turn this around as quickly as I had hoped. Pity."

"Yes Commander."

———

Hele Protectorate Command Station

Geth found himself sweating as he stared at the displays, watching the boarders forcing their way through the lift doors. He had hoped they would be stopped for a little longer, perhaps trying to override the system. That would have been a vain attempt, since the lifts were hardware locked at the moment, and the only way to reactivate them was in the room with him.

Instead they hardly paused at all, immediately opting to force the doors and prepare to climb the remaining floors to the secure decks.

These are not normal forces, he decided. *However, which of the Free Star systems would risk this much to send their elite on a mission this fringe?*

Certainly, the potential reward was high, but the costs were certain to match if not exceed those rewards. The Protectorate had maintained control here for as long as it had by virtue of simply making it cost too much to be *worth* the risks, even if you succeeded.

Of course, the Protectorate defenses somewhat assumed a direct assault by a small fleet, not what amounted to a squadron sneaking in and *boarding* the station as they had.

He still wasn't sure how they'd managed that.

His security teams were scrambling all over the station, responding to emergency calls from areas that didn't even seem to have any intruders. The main body of enemy forces had zeroed right for the command deck, but beyond them, Geth was realizing that several small squads had cleared the way for them with a skill he'd not even recognized when he saw it originally.

"They've accessed the lift passages, Commander. First teams are climbing the emergency access points now."

"Dispatch security to the lift doors," Geth ordered. "When they breach the doors, I want them *dead*."

"Yes Commander!"

He sat back.

Come on then, walk into my kill zone.

———

Steph examined the shaft of the lift system with a critical eye. It really didn't look much different than an elevator in any building at home. Okay, it was circular, but that wasn't a surprise. Round constructs didn't have shearing weaknesses the way a square one did. He'd read about how commuter aircraft used to have square windows, back in the day, until one accident too many caused people to realize that the fuselage was shearing at the corners where the metal was weakest.

An elevator on a stationary building didn't encounter those sorts of forces, but something on a space station, particularly in a neutron star system? Shear forces had to be taken into account, and that was before you started thinking about starships with singularity cores flying around.

Another difference was the lack of cables, but he'd seen a few even on Earth that used alternative locomotion systems. Not much of a change when all things were considered.

One thing every lift shaft *ever* had in common: they all had a way for maintenance to access the length just in case something needed fixing.

"Captain . . ."

Steph glanced back at Geoff, taking his eyes off the slatted inserts he was willing to bet functioned as a ladder. "What is it, Lieutenant?"

"You do know they will be waiting for us above?"

Steph smiled under his armor.

Smart man.

"Of course they will. Is that everything?"

Geoff swallowed, but nodded firmly.

"Okay, follow me up." Steph swung into the shaft and hooked his fingers into the cutouts.

The gravity inside the shaft was lower than outside, he noticed quickly. It wasn't something he needed, but he wasn't going to complain about his job being easier, especially not while he was in the middle of climbing. The secure command deck wasn't high above, only a few levels.

Easy climb.

What was waiting for them at the top might be another issue, of course, but that was to be dealt with as part of the job. Steph made it up to the command deck level easily, then pulled a cable from his armor and used a carabiner to latch onto a handy section of piping after he tested it for strength.

"Marines," he called out. "Status on operation."

"Squad One here," Buckler said. "Quadrant One is secure, security has been neutralized."

"Squad Three," Mac reported. "We've got Quad Two secured. Security is bunkered down but unable to move at the current time. Should we neutralize?"

"Negative," Steph said. "Just keep them locked up."

"Roger that, boss."

"Squad Two," Sergeant Bean said after a moment. "We're securing Quadrant Three. Minimal resistance encountered. No significance to report."

"Squad Four, Quad Four is ours," Sergeant Keith said simply.

"Good work. I'm at the command level," Steph said as he worked. "Deploying breaching charges."

"Boss, we can be there in two minutes," Buckler offered.

"Relax, Sarge, I've got this," Steph said confidently.

"Whether you have this or not isn't the point, boss," Buckler practically growled at him, making Steph grin.

"Sergeant Buckler has a point, sir," Mac spoke up, having listened in. "You have Marines for this job."

"No, I have Marines for the job the Confederation assigned us to," Steph said. "I have *pirates* for this particular job."

"Sir, they're amateurs."

"So are the idiots we're taking on," Steph scoffed. "But that's not the point and you know it. We're establishing a legend here, Sergeants. The mission isn't conventional, and you need to get used to that."

"Unconventional, I get," Buckler grumbled. "But a captain doesn't do this."

"A fleet captain doesn't, Marine," Steph said as he finished planting the charges and climbed up above the door where he let himself hang from the cable. "A pirate captain, on the other hand, *does*."

"You enjoy this too much, boss," Mac said, exasperated.

"That, I cannot deny," Steph responded. "Now shush up, would you? I'm about to start this party."

———

The Protectorate security force was arrayed along the length of the corridor that the lift opened up onto. Unlike many of the other parts of the station, this length had been designed specifically for this situation. The security had layered cover and a clear line of sight on the lift doors, putting them in a tactically superior position when it came to holding the command deck against a slave uprising.

They didn't know much about what was happening. The commander hadn't informed them of any details, but that was what the security team expected was the cause of all the chaos. Slave uprisings weren't exactly a regular occurrence, but they happened with some frequency. It was rare for them to get this far, but not unheard of.

None had ever made it past this point.

With resupply due in short order, the security force knew they didn't have to hold for long either, so no one was particularly concerned.

That began to change when the doors blew in, flying down the corridor and only missing some of them because they'd all automatically ducked back behind their cover as the heavy metal slabs ricocheted off the walls.

The sound of metal bouncing on metal caused them to look up again, just in time to spot cannisters rolling merrily in their direction, hissing and spewing smoke in thick clouds that filled the corridor quickly. Several panicked, fearing that a fire was the cause.

"EVLs on!" Taya, the security chief, called as she dropped her enhanced-vision lens over her eyes, recognizing the smoke for what it was. In a moment the color of the world became less, but she could again see down the corridor to where the lift door opened on a dark, empty shaft.

Another pair of cannisters bounced in, but she ignored them, expecting more smoke to pour forth. Instead, Taya and the others who'd followed her order were suddenly assaulted by blinding flashes of light and concussive sound.

Clutching at their eyes and ears, they missed the black-clad man swinging down through the door and into the corridor, landing with practiced ease as he cut himself loose from a cable and drew his weapon.

———

"Lieutenant, bring them up," Steph ordered as he started walking up the middle of the corridor.

"Yes sir! On our way!"

He knew it would be a few seconds before the others made their entrance. That was fine. He took the moment to examine the layout and had to admit it wasn't bad.

Definitely a kill box, and a decently designed one.

It was, however, clearly designed to be used against a mutiny or troubles with the slave population in his estimation, and certainly *not* against a military force.

Dealing with barely armed slaves is one thing. Let's see how you lot like a trained combatant with a budget for the good stuff.

A couple of fragmentation grenades would have taken the wind right out of their sails, he knew, but Steph would prefer *not* to leave nothing but corpses in his wake if at all possible. Probably the wrong call, especially given his limitations, but he'd never in his life considered himself so weak that mercy wasn't an option.

Geoff and the others were climbing through the gaping doors, pouring into the smoke-filled corridor behind him, so Steph waved them forward.

"Secure them," he ordered. "Don't kill anyone unless they give you no choice, but feel free to rough them up as needed."

"Yes sir!"

That sounded a little too eager, but Steph really didn't care much. Slavers weren't high on his list of people to feel overly sorry for. But most of his own people could be counted among the ranks of slavers themselves, if they hadn't *been* slaves that was, which kept him from being too high and mighty about it.

His men rushed past him as he strode up the center of the hall, grabbing the stunned security detail and trussing them up with zip-cuffs and taking their weapons. Steph couldn't help but smile a little as he saw multiple Imperial-style weapons being shoved roughly into waistbands.

It's feeling more and more like the Barbary Coast every day, out here in the stars.

He was focused on the prize, however, and right at that moment, the prize was the command deck of the station itself.

Steph strode on.

Geth stared at the screen, face white as death.

One man.

One damned man.

Oh, others had come after, certainly, but the screens were quite clear that it had only taken one to practically walk through his men. If the boarder had been inclined to kill, the corridor beyond the security doors would be a charnel house.

It just wasn't possible.

He looked up as he heard a hissing sizzle at the security doors.

It's not possible.

The metal of the door began to change color, turning red, then white, and finally smoking as it melted away. Geth swallowed and walked stiffly over to his station, where he retrieved his personal sidearm before turning to face the door. The metal screeched as it was forced, the now-melted lock providing no resistance as the doors were pushed open to reveal the man in black.

He lifted his weapon, drawing an immediate response as the men behind his target pointed theirs at him, only to be stopped.

"Surrender," the man in black said in oddly accented Imperial. "I have no wish to see you dead, and your weapon isn't going to be effective on me anyway. I'm not some slave in chains looking to avoid a beating."

Geth snarled, firing his needler on rapid-fire. Sparks lit off the black armor as the man stepped in, his sidearm coming up.

"Last chance."

Geth reached for his station, fingers stretching out for the command controls. He didn't hear the boom of the weapon that bucked in the man's hand. He felt something hammering him from the side, but nothing other than that until he hit the ground.

He wasn't sure how he got there. Geth tried to get up but found he couldn't. He tried a couple more times before slumping in place and staring up at the ceiling until a shadow fell over him.

"Bad move," the man in black said, towering so high that Geth wondered how someone so large even fit on the station.

As he watched, the man seemed to stretch before him, the world going dark, and then Geth saw nothing more.

———

Steph sighed as the commander died on the ground beside his own station, taking a moment to examine the controls before he grimaced.

Self-destruct? Seriously? Crazy bastards. I didn't think anyone actually used that bullshit.

The Free Stars used Imperial script, thankfully, so he was able to navigate the system using the commander's codes that were already in the software. Without knowing how long they'd be good for, Steph knew he'd need to get a prisoner or two with real access.

"Secure the prisoners," he ordered, not looking back. He could see his men moving to grab everyone else on the deck, most of them apparently shocked into immobility by the sudden violence that had beset them.

He wasn't surprised, really. The station wasn't a military facility, despite the weapon platforms and the like. The people here were miners and administrators; for all the violence they likely visited on others, they weren't used to being on the receiving end.

"Yes, Captain Teach!"

Steph deliberately turned and took a seat in the commander's place, not looking back at the man's body as it cooled on the deck behind him.

The administration staff, officers of the facility, were staring at him with wide eyes, and that suited Steph just fine.

Just fine indeed.

"If you're quite done being all dramatic there, boss," Tyke's voice cut in, "we have a bit of a problem coming our way."

Steph grimaced.

"Couldn't give me just one damn minute, could you?" he asked dryly.

"Of course not, boss. What did you think this was, the chair force?"

Bastard enjoyed that.

"Alright, what crisis is befalling us now?"

"Check the station's long-range scanners."

Oh crap. There was no way that was going to be anything other than a bad thing, Steph knew. He gestured to Geoff.

"Lieutenant, do you know these systems?"

"Yes Captain, they're standard."

"Long-range scans, now."

Geoff turned immediately and brought up the current systems. And there it was.

A destroyer squadron and what looked like a freighter convoy. Coming right at them.

Steph sighed. "When it rains, it pours. Alright, let's get to work."

Chapter 14

Mirran's Bane, *Hele Protectorate*

"Still no contact from the station?"

"No Commander. System communication traffic is almost entirely off as best we can tell," Brekka said. "There is some, but it appears to be from mining craft."

"Some sort of system-wide fault," Jorra grumbled. "Everyone knows that they can't keep underfunding this place and expect it to run properly, but the Protectorate keeps cutting the budget."

"The Imperial tithe cuts heavily into profits," Brekka offered weakly.

Jorra snorted. "Then raise the damn prices on what we do sell."

He shook his head. "Doesn't matter. Alright, standard approach but increase scans. With communications down we might have debris or ships or anything at all in the approach path as we get closer."

"Yes Commander."

It wasn't likely, he knew, but paradoxically if there were going to be any debris floating around in this situation, it was more likely to be in the path of his ships than anywhere else simply because they were using the highly trafficked approach.

Normally this would ensure that the area of space was cleared; that was what standard approaches were for, after all. In this case, however, if an accident had caused the problem . . . or been caused by it, the chances were high that it would have happened on the heavily trafficked sections of space.

All such an annoyance, but it had to be dealt with, he supposed.

———

Archangel Three

"They're coming in, fat, stupid, and lazy from the looks of things," Tyke said over the comm as he was examining the telemetry.

Cardsharp hummed slightly to herself as she followed suit. The freighter convoy certainly wasn't showing any sign of being ready for trouble, which was a nice change as far as such things went. They all knew that they couldn't count on this lasting, but it was fun sometimes when you got to run a nice little ambush.

"What do you want us to do about them, Crown?" Tyke asked.

Steph, joining them from the captured command facilities of the station, looked up from the displays he was examining.

"Well, I'd like to capture some of them if possible," he said. "But at the very least I want them driven out."

"Capture them?" Cardsharp asked, shocked. "All our Marines are currently deployed to the station and slave pens, sir. We're stretched paper-thin at this point. I don't know if it's wise to be taking any more prizes."

"Disabling shots would be fine," Steph said. "Let them drift until we're ready for them. If they get away or are destroyed, that's fine too. I'd just like to keep building the legend."

Cardsharp snorted, shaking her head with some degree of disbelief. She'd known from the start that Steph was the sort with a predisposition toward flashy statements, but she was thinking now that she'd only ever caught the tip of that particular iceberg.

"We can do that," Tyke said over the network, his tone even. "The freighters more easily than the destroyers, but we've got full schematics on the latter now, so disabling some of them won't be difficult."

"I'm sending you their standard approach route," Steph said, tapping out a few commands. "Apparently this system is pretty messy, so they really stick to one path and keep that cleaned of rocks, leaving the rest to the miners."

Tyke nodded, examining the files as they arrived. "We can work with this."

"Good," Steph said. "I'm going to leave some of my men here to keep the station under control while I get back on the *Dutchman*. Start making plans and deploying our forces, Tyke. I'll be back with you shortly."

"You got it, Skipper."

Archangel One, Gaia's Revenge

With the impromptu conference finished, Tyke turned his attentions to deploying the Archangels. He would leave the disposition of the *Dutchman* to Crown, but he could at least get the early placements finished while they were waiting for Steph to retake command of the destroyer.

He contacted the others while sending deployment instructions over the network.

"Maintain stealth to the strongest degree possible," he informed them. "Our advantage is that the enemy has no idea what they're currently traveling toward."

He didn't really need to say that. The others were all more than experienced enough to follow basic instructions even if they weren't aware of the need for stealth, yet somehow he always found himself going over the basics.

"ROE?" Burner asked casually as he looked over the data.

"Disable if possible," Tyke said. "You heard the skipper. Prizes are . . . well, a prize."

He grinned at that, drawing return smiles before he got serious again.

"Do not risk yourselves, however," Tyke ordered firmly. "If the destroyers choose to get rowdy, put them down and move on. Clear?"

"Yes sir," the others murmured.

"We have numbers on the inbound fleet, now," Tyke said. "Light-speed data finally caught up to them after they dropped below the threshold. Half a dozen destroyers. The rest are bulk freighters. Big suckers, but unless someone is playing games, they shouldn't be a factor in this fight."

Cardsharp hummed slightly. "You're not kidding about them being big suckers. They're not showing up much in the mass side of things, though, are they?"

"We expect that they're empty, so the effect they have on local gravity fields is minimal," Tyke explained. "Full, they likely pull an equivalent mass in the multi-tera-ton range, but we're still trying to work that out. If they can fully load with strange matter, frankly, they're going to mass a lot more than that."

Cardsharp whistled. "That's no joke."

"We'd like at least one of those intact," Tyke said. "Or close enough to be repaired. The destroyers would be a good bonus as well, but again, do *not* risk yourselves."

"Roger that."

"You know your jobs and have your assignments. Let's set up for the little surprise party."

"Aye, aye."

Hele Protectorate Command

Steph found himself staring at a load of frightened prisoners, eyes watching him like hawks as he crossed the bay toward the shuttle.

"Got them clear of the lander, I see," he said to the man he'd left in charge.

"Yes, Captain Teach," Ira Honn replied with a firm nod. "Soon as the air was back and it looked like things would be stable. Didn't want them on my ship. Sorry if that was a problem, Captain."

"Not an issue, Ira," Steph said with a firm shake. "Good decision. I need a ride back to the *Dutchman*. Good for a short flight?"

"Always, Captain."

"That's good," Steph said, trying not to pay attention to how the eyes of the prisoners followed him across the bay. He had a foot on the landing ramp before he turned slightly back to Ira. "Attentive lot, aren't they?"

Ira coughed slightly. "We may have been telling them some . . . stories, you see."

"Oh God," Steph scoffed. "Don't you get them going too."

Since he'd taken the *Dutchman*, the stories about how he'd pulled off the heist had gotten more and more outlandish even among the people who'd *been there*. It was well past the point of having gotten out of hand and was now becoming ludicrous.

He'd already experienced that sort of nonsense with the Archangels, but luckily, it had mostly been Eric who got the brunt of the hyperbole back then. He did *not* want to deal with it firsthand without the shelter provided by a nice figurehead.

Maybe I should get one of the men to take over as "Captain" and just give orders from the shadows like a good evil overlord?

Sadly, not really an option.

Not for a while, anyway.

Steph did make a note to start looking for a good Dread Pirate Roberts type to take over as Captain Teach in case he needed to make a run for it or, more likely, was called home on another assignment.

He settled into the VIP seating on the landing shuttle, both weary of and more than a little entertained by his thoughts and the direction they were taking him.

Sometimes the work he did brought him to the *strangest* places and people.

"God, I love my job."

———

While transiting over to the *Dutchman*, Steph examined the deployment plans Tyke had begun. Other than a couple minor tweaks he made on the fly, Steph left them alone as implemented. There was only so much cleverness you could deploy in space, really, and Tyke had that quota nicely capped for the most part.

There was debris in the system to hide around, which would work decently well for the Archangels. They were roughly one-tenth the size of a destroyer, with a much tighter profile due to their construction and design.

The *Dutchman*, on the other hand, was going to be a bit more of an issue.

Hiding in an open system wasn't impossible or even particularly hard. Hiding somewhere close enough to be of any *use*, now that was a far different story.

Space was a massive area to scan, such that it really couldn't be repeated enough to hammer that idea into many a young officer's head. Steph knew well, because he'd once been that young officer, and until he'd tried to actually conduct operations of his own he'd still not managed to really understand the vastness of the area he was working with.

As powerful and detailed as the scans on modern detection gear could be, against the sheer vastness of space they were utterly worthless without some idea of where to look in the first place. That made hiding from an enemy who didn't have some sort of idea of your general location a relatively easy thing to do.

However, once someone knew where to look, there really was nowhere you could *possibly* hide.

A bizarre contradiction, he supposed, but that was the nature of military tactics in space.

Luckily, the mining nature of the system gave his people a few options to work with and Steph took his time, looking over all of them as the shuttle ferried him to the *Dutchman*.

Mirran's Bane, *Hele Protectorate*

Jorra scowled openly, not caring by this point who noticed.

They should have been contacted by *someone* before this point. Even basic electromagnetic frequencies would have sufficed given the range they'd closed to. A laser comm would have also been viable.

"Still nothing?" he demanded, knowing the answer before he even asked.

"No Commander."

He didn't like this. Something was amiss, but other than the bad comms, everything looked normal in the system. Well, the miner traffic was low, true, but that was easily attributable to the lack of communication traffic. If the system was out, coordinating mining efforts would be all but impossible.

How many times have we told the Protectorate that this place needed better maintenance?

Jorra sighed in frustration.

"Continue on course, continue sending requests for contact," he growled. "Have the other destroyers confirmed that they're on alert?"

"Yes Commander. The squadron confirms it has made ready for action."

Well, that is something, I suppose.

He doubted there was anything much for any of them to actually do, but it would be good training if nothing else.

Anything to wake up some of the trash we've been assigned.

Unfortunately, destroyer escorts weren't exactly the top assignment in the Protectorate. The very few cruisers they fielded tended to get the best personnel, and after that the Destroyer Shield Forces. Escorts, especially freighter escorts, were a low-priority dumping ground of people too valuable to toss out into the void yet troublesome enough to not want around.

That made maintaining discipline a rather difficult matter.

"Commander . . . there's something odd on the scanners."

Jorra turned, his scowl softening to more annoyed puzzlement. "Odd how?"

"Mining traffic has altered, Commander."

Mining traffic? Jorra blinked, uncertain what to make of that. He walked over to the console. "Show me."

"Here, this is the traffic pattern earlier . . . I'm speeding up the time of our approach, watch the highlighted sections."

In compressed time, the traffic moved around the system at ridiculous speeds, bouncing from one place to another in what looked to be the normal sort of traffic Jorra had come to expect in the system, if a lot lighter than usual. As the convoy closed, however, it became clear that something odd was, in fact, happening.

The traffic cleared the section of space they were approaching on.

Are they moving out of the way of the convoy? Jorra wondered.

That didn't seem likely. There was no reason for it, and the pattern wasn't quite right for that either. If they were clearing away from the convoy, he would have expected them to depart on diverging courses, but some of them actually came *toward* the convoy before arcing out of their path.

It was more like they were moving to avoid something else. Something that was approaching the convoy's course from the direction of the command station.

There was nothing there, however.

Jorra twitched slightly, feeling paranoid.

"Active scan," he ordered. "Combat threshold. Ring the station like a bell."

"Yes Commander."

———

Archangel One, Gaia's Revenge

"Holy shit."

Tyke twitched uncontrollably for a moment as the energy passed over the fighter-gunboat, sweeping past like a wave. The tingling he felt was the Archangel's neural interface giving him direct feedback so he could react more quickly, but it felt like the damn thing tried to electrocute him.

"Maybe dial back the sensitivity, Lieutenant Chans," he said, "because that was *weird*."

"Apologies, Commander," Milla said. "That was a directed energy detection pulse."

"Did they spot us?" Tyke asked, concerned.

"I do not believe so," Milla said slowly. "The pulse was below detection threshold for our stealth armor. However, it does mean that they are, shall we say . . . looking, yes?"

"Looking definitely," Tyke said. "See if they spotted the *Dutchman*, will you? I'm going to make sure we're ready to respond."

"Yes Commander."

He returned his attention to the approaching convoy, wondering what had them spooked exactly. Of course, there were clearly a few things to pick from, so he supposed the only real question he should be asking was why it took them this long to get suspicious.

Tyke reached forward, toggling several projected hard-light switches to bring the Archangel from "manual" to fully neural-controlled mode. With each switch, he felt his senses expand and the power of the fighter-gunboat thrum deep in his veins.

As the final switch flipped on, the Archangel stopped being a *thing* and became an extension of his body, part of his soul . . . *him.*

Ten thousand tons of power, weapons, thrusters . . .

It was a rush, pouring through him, better than even the original Archangels, and those had been the greatest addiction of his life. Tyke looked up, eyes focusing on the point in space that the scanner pulse had originated from.

Around him, the projected imagery of the system warped slightly and zoomed in on the approaching convoy.

Ten light-minutes and counting. They're technically in range.

Lasers would attenuate at that range, unless he intentionally refocused them, but kinetic weapons would reach, and if Steph gave them clearance to use the transition cannons, they could smoke the whole convoy from a *lot* farther off.

That wasn't the mission profile, however, and their current ROE would keep them fighting at knife range. Dangerous, stupid, but those were the orders.

———

Dutchman

Steph hadn't been settled into the hot seat for very long when the sensor pulse passed by them. Luckily, the *Dutchman* was covered, using a mined-out asteroid as shelter. It was mostly nickel iron and carbonaceous compounds, an odd mix but decent enough at scrambling scanner-signal returns, which was what he needed.

He wasn't surprised that the convoy escorts were getting antsy. They were pretty damn close to the facility by this point and no one had contacted them.

He'd have abandoned the approach a long while back and taken up a high orbit while scanning for anything suspicious, but he was a combat pilot, and from what he knew of the Free Stars, he doubted that the escort crews were exactly the best of the best.

They're still coming, despite being suspicious enough to go active. Stupid.

He wasn't complaining, of course. He had enough problems already and could do with a few things not screwing up on him, especially since he was sure that plenty would go wrong before this whole escapade was over.

"Orders, Captain?"

Steph looked from the display, eyes skimming across the men present on the bridge.

He realized that they were honestly scared, which surprised him slightly. Not the fear itself, as even he was feeling that thrill running through him like an icy wind chilling the blood in his veins. No, it was more the open expression of fear.

Somehow I expected that they'd be better at covering that up, from what I've seen of the Free Stars.

He pushed the thought aside. There were other things to be concerned with for the moment.

"No orders," he said. "Just stand by as you were already told. They're coming to us."

He sat back.

"Never interrupt your enemy when they're making a fatal error."

Chapter 15

Odysseus

"Commodore, looks like they're making their move."

Eric slumped slightly, though even he couldn't have said if it was from regret or relief.

"Show me," he said, pulling his repeater display closer.

The imagery flickered as Miram redirected the passive scanner information to him, and he took a long moment to examine it in detail. The Imperial ships they'd spotted were most certainly on the move, closing in on an interception vector that would close the noose on the convoy he was playing wet nurse to.

Good plan. They've secured against escape vectors, locked us in good and tight.

Eric nodded with approval. A solid move.

"Direct the convoy to accelerate to maximum velocity and redirect to Vector Bravo Zulu," he ordered. "Signal general quarters to the squadron . . . no . . . Hold on general quarters until we're a little closer I think . . . yes."

"Aye Skipper," Miram said firmly. "Convoy has acknowledged orders and are preparing to take evasive actions as commanded. Should we hold with them?"

Eric nodded. "Oh yes. We'll break from the convoy when we engage the enemy, but not before. No sense in letting the enemy pick them off piecemeal."

"Very good, sir. Intercept in . . . six minutes, sir."

Eric winced.

The enemy was *moving*. Fast.

They'd been scanned quite a significant distance out. The first contact had been light-days away, but many of the enemy's forces were weeks out at the pedestrian speed that light was limited to. For them to close the range in six minutes, though, meant that they were hauling ass with serious intent.

"Sound general quarters," he ordered. "Looks like we're skipping coffee this time."

"General quarters, aye Skipper."

The alarms began to wail across the *Odysseus* and the squadron.

Imperial Eighth Fleet Command Vessel

"Enemy have adjusted course and are increasing speed . . . as predicted, Commander."

Birch nodded, a thin smile tracing across her lips.

The prediction system for the anomalous species was rather hit or miss, she knew, so it was good that they'd gotten this one down. Her forces were likely getting closer to a solid model for how the species and its culture would react to various stimuli.

That would cut down significantly on combat losses, at least once they got a better handle on the enemy's strategic weapons.

Those images still haunt me, she had to admit.

The idea of fire just appearing from the empty black abyss, like some angry god scorching the subject of his ire . . . wasn't a pleasant thought.

She was far from certain that it was a good idea to keep poking at this particular nest, but her orders were absolute and from the empress herself.

"Good," she said aloud. "Continue with the planned approach."

The enemy vessels were reorienting their vector along the predicted best escape route that she'd left open for them, something she'd been half uncertain whether they'd take. So far they'd proven good at picking less obvious routes and generally making more trouble for her and her fleet.

"Begin long-range scans, full active pulse."

"Yes Commander!"

The ships of the Eighth alternated firing pulses from their FTL scanners, gaining a near real time image of the enemy convoy as they pushed their approach at high speed.

"Identify and target enemy noncombatant vessels," she ordered. "We'll take them out at range before closing to deal with their escorts."

"Yes Commander, targeting now. We are inside extreme range. Engage?"

Birch nodded. "Yes. Keep their attention on us. Fire when ready."

"Yes Commander. Engaging enemy!"

———

Odysseus

"All ships report drones have been deployed. Holding position at five light-seconds out."

"Thank you, Commander," Eric said, not looking up at Miram's pronouncement. He was picking his way through some of the scans, looking for what he knew had to be there.

"Lasers detected! Automatic response initiated! The *Reliant* intercepted a beam heading for the Priminae convoy," she reported by rote. "Cam-plates held up. Drone-detection net is functioning as designed."

Eric didn't respond this time. He knew they had to trust the beam-detection system, because without it they were just dead men running. But he also knew the system worked.

The drones would pace the squadron at five light-seconds or farther, each with a limited FTL transmitter. Imperial lasers were like those of the Drasin and the Priminae, intensely powerful, more than enough to excite any stray atoms in space as they passed, and that allowed the drones to detect and identify the frequency of the beams as they passed and then pass that on to the squadron.

From there, it was all on automatic, because no human could react that fast, but the computers would maneuver the closest ship into place to intercept or dodge as needed while adjusting the cam-plate mods to reflect that frequency of energy to the highest degree possible.

Not a perfect defense, not even remotely, but it was the best anyone had come up with to this point.

"More lasers, sir. Ships are responding on automatic."

Eric nodded absently, entering orders of his own.

"Squadron orders!" he snapped out, coming to his feet.

"Sir!"

"Cruisers, beams on my command," he ordered. "Targeting data has been sent to your stations."

The ships of the squadron responded quickly, acknowledging the order.

"Rogues," Eric went on. "Full spread of pulse torpedoes on my command, targeting data is on your computers."

The Rogue Class destroyers responded just as quickly.

"Rogues. Fire for effect."

The squadron's thirty Rogue Class destroyers flushed their tubes in a single barrage, the little sparkling chunks of antimatter hell flashing away from the convoy at high speed as Eric watched them go. He counted off the seconds before taking a breath and hitting the transmit switch again.

"Cruisers, beams for effect! Sweep the target area!"

He felt more than heard the whine of the capacitors discharging on the *Odysseus*, knowing that the same was being felt and heard on the six cruisers of the squadron. Hellishly powerful beams in the multi-terawatt range lanced out into space, sweeping a few arc minutes as the ships followed his order.

Three . . . two . . . one . . .

Eric closed his eyes, knowing that he wouldn't know if he'd been right until after the light had time to make it back to the *Odysseus*' sensors, but he had to act right then.

"Dispatch to convoy," he ordered. "Captain Goran, you are clear to leave. Good journeys, Captain."

There was a moment before the captain replied, but he saw the convoy already accelerating harder.

"Thank you, Captain Weston. Good luck."

Eric killed the comm, moving on with the tactical situation.

"All ships," he said over the squadron command network, "come about to new vector, Zero One Niner Mark Negative Three to the bubble. All ships, fly the colors."

As they finished the maneuver, behind the ship now, spheres of light erupted into existence in an apparently empty section of space.

———

Hiding with what the humans would have called full "black hole" camplate settings was a double-edged sword.

The stealth setting on the armor provided a ship with a near perfect radiation dead zone, making the ship all but invisible to almost any practicable scanner system. No light, radio, or transmissions of any sort escaped the surface. Nothing reflected.

That had several drawbacks, all related to the very thing that benefited a ship trying to hide.

The armor absorbed radiation. Without extreme care, it would eventually cook anyone within by taking in all heat, radiation, and so forth, slowly overloading the internal heat sinks until the ship turned into an oven.

A somewhat more pressing issue happened when the ship was in battle, however, and the stealth had been seen through.

For the ships of the Imperial Eighth Fleet that had been hiding in position to close the trap on the escaping convoy, that issue became instantly, blindingly, and lethally obvious as they were hammered by powerful beams and antimatter torpedoes.

Armor that absorbed energy and had nowhere to properly direct it afterward wasn't *really* armor.

Like matchbooks before a blowtorch, the ships flared in the dark . . . and died.

Imperial Eighth Fleet Command Vessel

Birch paled, stricken as she saw lights signifying her third *and* fourth squadrons go out.

"They knew," she whispered harshly. "They knew right where they were hiding."

She didn't know how the enemy had worked it out, but that attack was too precise to be anything but a carefully predetermined precision strike.

"Commander! Enemy fleet is changing formation."

"Show me."

Birch put aside the loss, focusing on the changing battlefield. She would worry about what had happened later. First she had a situation that *needed* her entire focus.

The enemy convoy was breaking up, she noticed immediately.

The combat vessels were peeling off from the core, letting the transports race on ahead as they curved back around. She checked the new trajectories and her lips twisted.

Right for our main body. Of course.

So much for being clever about the situation, she supposed.

Birch didn't like what was happening one bit. The enemy was outnumbered, outgunned, and should be running through the hole they'd just made in her formation for escape. Instead they were turning around for a head-on fight.

She steeled herself. Certainly she wished for more intelligence, but it was clear that this enemy liked to play games, and that made much of the information she could gather from their actions all but worthless.

Still, there was more than one way to gather real intelligence.

"Tighten formation," Birch ordered coldly. "Increase velocity. Let us bring them into our range quite properly."

Sometimes you could get intelligence just by watching. Sometimes you paid for it in blood.

So be it.

Odysseus

"Priminae Colonial convoy is away, Commodore," Miram said as Eric pored over the telemetry feed he was receiving from the ships of the squadron, focusing on the enemy.

166

"Good. Come here and have a look at this," he said, nodding to the screens.

Miram approached, glancing at the display. "They're accelerating."

"Right down our throats," Eric said. "Too bad, really. I was hoping that little show would have put them off a little."

"It was impressive," Miram allowed.

"Not really. Once we knew they were using something like our cam-plate modifications, it was clear *how* they would use them. The commander over there is clever, but I've been devising tactics for that technology for *years* at this point. They've had it, maybe months?"

Heath nodded. "Agreed. Still, knowing they were there and spotting them isn't the same thing. Our scanners couldn't find them, not the automatic systems at least."

"They did fine once I had them look for blotted-out stars," Eric said. "But that still leaves us with the current situation."

"Indeed."

"They've doubled down," Eric said. "I had some hope that the commander would withdraw and regroup, but I suppose it was too much to ask for."

"Most likely, sir," Miram agreed.

Eric straightened up, opening a communications channel to the other ships in the squadron.

"Form up on the *Odysseus*," he ordered. "Tighten our drone screen to one light-second and stand by to engage the enemy at close range."

Miram eyed him nervously.

"Commodore," she said softly. "One light-second is the *minimum* effective range for the drone screen. Any closer and we'll never be able to receive the frequency and adapt in time."

"I am aware," Eric said grimly, "but they're going to push this. We're going to wind up fighting with the enemy *inside* our screen as it stands."

"This will be bloody," she said.

"It will," Eric confirmed. "But it won't all be ours."

He closed the squadron comm and opened up a broadcast frequency, unencrypted, leaning forward as he started to speak.

Imperial Eighth Fleet Command Vessel

"Enemy squadron is accelerating to the attack."

Birch nodded absently, impressed by the gall if nothing else.

Outnumbered, outgunned . . . and they were charging.

It was almost *Imperial* in its nature.

"Secure our formation, stand ready for a passing engagement," she ordered. "Be ready for antimatter weapons as well as beam and kinetic strikes."

"Yes Commander!"

The enemy had a total of six cruisers and thirty escorting destroyers. A respectable force, she had to admit, and they certainly struck above their class by all accounts. There were limits, however, to what a force that size could truly do.

"Commander . . . signal broadcast from the enemy squadron, no encryption."

"Put it through," Birch ordered.

The system crackled slightly as an imperfect signal was routed to her station. Birch noted the video component. She looked into the face of someone she recognized, the man who had commanded the defense fleet that had torched so many Imperial vessels and infrastructure with flame from nowhere.

He leaned forward, eyes focused on the screen and, through it, her, speaking calmly in stilted but very clear Imperial.

"You should have turned back sooner."

Chapter 16

Dutchman

"Enemy convoy is entering our range, Captain."

Steph nodded. "Thank you, Ensign."

He looked over the telemetry, running the numbers in his head. Like many fighter pilots, math was almost second nature to him. He'd learned a long time earlier that while computers were more precise, a good guess was even faster than the fastest machine he'd ever found, and it was damn useful to already be leaning in the right direction when the computer spit out the exact numbers he needed.

"I want the destroyers taken out of play *fast*," he ordered. "The Archangels have their orders, so we just have to do our jobs. We will not be failing that, am I being quite clear?"

"Yes Captain!"

"Good. Halo the primary and secondary targets, stand by for orders to engage."

The Archangel squadron was already in motion, which was fine. They could get in close without being noticed, which made the real trick in this all about the timing. Steph kept one eye bouncing back to the clock as he counted it down in his head.

Then, it was time.

"Engage," he ordered, leaning forward in the command station as the order went through.

The laser capacitors' distinct whine-click sound was like something screaming in his ears on the *Dutchman* compared to the far better insulated nature of the *Odysseus*, but that didn't feel wrong to him just the same.

"Beam out," he said with satisfaction as he settled back.

Those listening to him didn't recognize the significance of the words, and honestly he didn't have time to give them a crash course in artillery fire control codes. Not when there was so much else they needed to be brought up to speed on. For the time, Steph was happy to just keep things from falling apart.

I know I like flying by the seat of my pants, but this mission is pushing even my limits.

Mirran's Bane, *Hele Protectorate*

Jorra shook his head, frustrated.

He didn't like this, didn't like *any* of this.

"Still no response from anyone?" he demanded.

"Nothing, Commander. Routine traffic on mining frequencies, but as you're aware that's almost entirely automated," his communications officer said, looking confused. "I'm not sure that is exactly running smoothly either. I believe there are repeat requests filling the traffic, as if the automation systems aren't getting the responses they expect."

It was a systems failure of unprecedented proportions, Jorra realized, *but what caused it?*

There was no sign of any attack as best he could tell. The station and auxiliary locations were all intact, and even the defense network had been in place when they entered the system. Perhaps an enemy would leave the mining infrastructure in place, but how would they get in past the defenses while leaving those intact?

There are rumors that the Empire has a new stealth technology, Jorra supposed, *but they wouldn't bother with that here. They would just roll over everything and take the system in a show of power.*

His ship, and he assumed his squadron, were on edge as they got closer. Nothing seemed to make sense.

"Continue sending challenge queries," he ordered. "Maintain active scans."

"Yes Commander."

He really should dispatch the convoy back on their own, he thought, but by the time he'd come to that conclusion they'd already been so deep in the system that doing so would just leave them unguarded and unable to warp space effectively for far too long if, indeed, this was the result of some sort of attack.

He was still debating his rapidly diminishing options when an alarm startled him, snapping his head up. He began to ask for details on what tripped the response, but before he could, Jorra and all those around him were roughly thrown about as something hammered into the ship with enough force to make the command deck buck under them.

Barely hanging on to the station beside him, Jorra cast around at the displays showing telemetry of the convoy. "What was—"

Another rough moment of turbulent motion cut him off, and this time damage alarms began to wail.

"We've been fired upon, Commander!"

"I had determined that much!"

Jorra was not in a particularly good mood as he struggled back into the station and got a better grip on what was happening. Damage-control crews were already reacting to the alerts, most of which appeared to be the results of combat lasers as best he, and the computer, could determine.

How did anyone get that close without being detected by active imaging?!

"Find the sources!" he ordered loudly, trying to be heard over the multiple blaring alarms.

What the hell is going on in this damned system?!

"Destroyer detected ahead, Commander!"

———

Archangel One, Gaia's Revenge

Screaming past the destroyer screen, lasers slashing out from their pivoting emitters and burning through the destroyers' armor, the six Archangel fighter-gunboats started shifting course by thrusters only, keeping their positions and existence hidden for as long as possible by avoiding warping space in any noticeable way. They interpenetrated the convoy, cutting between massive freighters at high speed, and opened fire on those as well.

Behind them, fires burned in the vacuum as their targets staggered from the Archangels' blitz.

"Come about, Pattern Three Delta," Tyke ordered, sounding almost bored as he physically twisted himself to bring his fighter about on reaction-thrusters only. "Do *not* warp space. I say again, do not warp space."

The others confirmed the order, and he could see the icons for the squadron begin to turn around him as they made their way through the convoy, wreaking havoc as they did.

It would be a fine line, Tyke knew, judging the right time to drop the stealth they were using here, and opt once more for best general deflection. They couldn't risk using the cam-plate armor often, but at the same time they didn't dare cripple themselves so much that they ignored the advantage entirely.

Ideally, no one would ever see the Archangels utilize the technology, or any other that might be connected back to Earth.

Realistically, well, they'd push it as long as they could.

———

Dutchman

Steph counted down the range, keeping mental tabs even though the computers were tracking it all to the meter and millisecond.

"Full power to warp," he ordered. "Shift perpendicular to present course, port side!"

"Yes Com—Captain," the helmsman stammered out.

The destroyer's drives hummed deeply, enough to be felt more than heard, and the *Dutchman* seemed to pitch slightly to the left as Steph reached out to steady himself while the ship "fell" into the gravity depression the drives had created off the port side.

On the *Odysseus*, he wouldn't have felt a damn thing. The ship was huge, generating space-time warping steep enough so that it really couldn't be felt from any one position. The *Dutchman*, however, didn't have remotely that power, and his guts twisted as the ship seemed to fall into the trough of a wave in response to his command.

Just as well that I don't get motion sick.

An alarm went off, and he checked the system at a glance, noting with a satisfied smile that it was a proximity alarm warning them of a laser that had just cut through space right where they had been a moment earlier.

It was remarkable, sometimes, how simply counting off the seconds and knowing the ranges was enough to dodge *lasers* in a space battle.

Meanwhile, the return signal from *their* initial barrage was now finally showing up on the scanners. Light-speed delay was always a major part of calculating the factors of a space battle.

"Hits to enemy destroyers are recorded. Protectorate destroyer screen is damaged. We're detecting atmosphere being bled into space, Captain."

"Continue firing."

"Yes Captain."

The whine-click of the *Dutchman's* capacitors continued to fill the background noise of the ship while mostly being drowned out by alarms and shouted reports flying back and forth. Steph ignored it all as he worked instead to coordinate the fight as best he could without access to an FTL comm.

What he did have on his side was intimate knowledge of his allies, and the benefit of having issued them their orders before sending them off. The Archangels would be weaving through the enemy convoy at this point, taking shots of opportunity and generally wreaking havoc while he took the *Dutchman* right up the middle with guns blazing in the hopes that the enemy would spend most of the focus on him.

———

The *Dutchman* gleamed in the eyes of everyone in the system, making no attempt to hide its position or its intentions as it fired all forward lasers and charged right into the teeth of a squadron that outmassed and outgunned it six to one.

Somehow such details did little to comfort those staring down the beam emitters blazing nonstop in their direction.

———

Mirran's Bane, *Hele Protectorate*

"Commander! We're losing power from our primary reactor! We'll be on the backup shortly at this rate!"

Jorra swore, knowing what that would mean. The backups weren't intended for anything more than basic survival and barely powering the ship back to a port of call where repairs could be made. If he tried to fight a *battle* with nothing but the backups operative, he'd be condemning himself to . . . at *best* . . . being stranded in this system until repairs could be managed.

If he had any idea what the situation was in the system that might be an option, but without any contact he didn't know who had control of the repair yards, or even if the yards were properly *intact*. They appeared so, but that could easily be a misleading assumption.

"Status of the squadron!"

"*Corrin's Blade* is reporting similar damage, Commander, and *Damaca's Breath* is already disabled!"

Jorra winced.

"The rest?!"

"Still operative, combat ready, Commander!"

Three destroyers fully to fighting trim, he thought grimly. *Against the one we can see, that would be sufficient, but no single destroyer could mount that kind of firepower. There are others here, hiding. Damn them to the abyss!*

"Signal the withdrawal!"

"Commander?"

"I said, signal the withdrawal!"

"Yes Commander." His second swallowed, issuing the orders before he came back. "What of the freighters?"

"What of them? They're empty bulk ships crewed by the filth of the Protectorate," Jorra snorted. "If they can't keep up, we leave them."

"Yes Commander."

———

Archangel One, Gaia's Revenge

Tyke spotted it first, the destroyers' formation breaking up. One was disabled, running on momentum alone, but the rest peeled off from the main body of the convoy.

"They're making a run for it," he called.

"Do we let them go?" Cardsharp asked.

Tyke wasn't actually sure. They had multiple contingencies for that, but they were a little fuzzy with this particular situation.

If they had been able to secure the entire group, then any stragglers were to be hunted down. No witnesses, by preference, at least not in the short-term. However, with five destroyers making a run for it, he'd have to split his team and send a single Archangel after each destroyer, basically.

That was an unacceptable risk, as it vastly increased the odds of the enemy escaping with vital intelligence.

Tyke sighed.

"Negative," he ordered. "We're still cloaked. They never pinged us past the detection threshold, but if we engage them at close range, they'll get a clear shot of us for sure. Orders are to remain undercover as long as possible."

"Yes sir."

"Take a few shots to send them on their way," he advised instead. "Disable them if you can. I'm sending an update to the boss."

"Roger that, *Archangel One.*"

The squadron got down to the work at hand, including Tyke, as he prepped a message to shoot off amid running calculations for his next, and last, attack run.

Dutchman

Steph stood over the jubilant bridge crew as they watched the enemy destroyers running for the hills, considering the message he'd just received from Tyke.

He agreed with the other man's decision, but he would have preferred to keep any of the enemy from escaping if possible. He couldn't keep the occupation of the neutron system under wraps for long, but it would have been nice to have a little bit more lead time.

"Open a channel to the freighters," he ordered.

"Yes Commander. Channel is open."

Steph nodded, facing the screen he knew would be recording.

"This is Captain Teach of the *Dutchman*," he growled. "Your destroyer screen has run, leaving you to my . . . *mercies*. If you want to claim any of that *very* limited resource, I advise that you power down your drives and prepare to be boarded. If you do not, I will burn out your armor, bleed your air, and take your ships after you're dead."

He turned away from the screen, glancing back only for a moment.

"Please, *test* me."

Then he killed the transmission.

The convoy was only a few light-seconds away at this point, so he counted down the time for them to receive the signal, then listen to it, before he nodded firmly.

"Active scan, full power," Steph ordered. "Establish laser lock on the lead freighter."

"Yes Commander."

He waited, eyes on the screen, imagining the chaos on board the ship. They knew that they couldn't outfight him, not with their destroyers running for the edge of the system as fast as their drives would carry them. However, he could also imagine the calculations they would be making at the moment.

Would he really fire? Could some of them escape? They could only see one destroyer.

Best to cut that line of thought entirely, Steph was quite certain. When the convoy didn't change their drive settings, he grimaced.

"Fire."

"Yes Captain!"

Beams lanced out from the *Dutchman*, slicing across the vacuum at three hundred thousand kilometers per second. Enough energy to flash sublimate steel from solid to gaseous form burned into its target in less than three seconds. Gaseous steel exploded, shaking the freighter as part of its mass was blown off in violent reaction.

The previous tension on the convoy, already to the point of breaking, shattered into flat-out panic. Orders were given, countermanded, reissued. In a mad moment of time, no one knew what was going on or, in some cases, who was even in charge.

Finally, however, on each ship, the outcome was the same.

Drives died as their crews realized they had no choice, with no weapons entrusted to them by the Protectorate and now with their escorts fleeing, they had nothing to defend themselves with . . . and honestly little enough reason to bother, even if they did.

The fighting for the now former Protectorate System ended as eight massive bulk freighters surrendered to a single destroyer while their protectors abandoned them.

The battle was all over except for the cleanup, but for the man standing command of the *Flying Dutchman*, the war for the system was only beginning.

Chapter 17

Imperial Eighth Fleet Command Vessel

She'd dealt with all sorts of arrogance in her life, from false bravado to the smug assurance that reality would bend to the will of the imbecile she was facing just because he somehow deserved it to be such. She'd seen fools and geniuses brought low by levels of arrogance that didn't even *approach* what this enemy commander was displaying.

What she had never encountered, not *once* in her entire career with the Empire, was such a smug disregard for the power of an Imperial Fleet. Her Eighth, which was often underestimated by allies and enemies alike, had never been so disregarded.

"Close with the enemy squadron," she ordered through gritted teeth. "I want them burned from my sight."

"Yes, Fleet Commander."

Her Eighth outmassed the enemy squadron by eight to one, outgunned them by a similar degree, and she would be *damned* if her fleet was run off by a jumped-up squadron . . .

Birch closed her eyes.

Slowly she took breaths, her mind catching up to her emotions.

What is his plan? she wondered. The enemy commander had intentionally infuriated her with that statement, she had no doubt. The implication was that his squadron could take her fleet, or at least make any victory second only to defeat itself.

Was it possible he was right? Birch didn't want to think so, but the enemy had shown unknown capacities, the torching of the Fifth and Imperial shipyards coming to mind.

She didn't think that the enemy had that capacity out this far from their home system, however. She'd been probing them for some time, pushing constantly to see how they would react. If they could call down the flames as they had against the Third, surely they would have done so by now?

She believed so, but couldn't be certain.

Birch cast a glance to the disposition of her fleet. For the moment her squadrons were well spread out and unlikely to be caught by a single attack of the nature the reports from the Third described.

Birch dispatched orders to keep it that way as she continued to force herself to calm and examine the situation more closely. The enemy had a plan.

What was it?

Odysseus

"I hope you have a plan, Commodore."

Eric grinned at the tone of resigned exasperation in the commander's voice.

"No faith in me, Miram?" he asked lightly.

She shook her head, eyes rolling at the question.

"I have faith that you'll be you," she said flatly. "But the rest of us may not be quite so lucky."

"Being me is a pretty good gig," Eric admitted cheerfully.

"Too bad being *around you* isn't the same," Miram countered sourly.

"I believe the Block once said something very similar, you know," Eric said with a relaxed casual tone. "A Chinese admiral told me something like it, anyway, right before we faced off over Okinawa."

Eric paused thoughtfully. "Turns out he may have had a point. Certainly it didn't turn out so well for him being that close to me."

Miram knew what he was doing. She couldn't have worked with the man this long and not pick up that aspect of his command style. Knowing that Weston was intentionally masking his tension to project a calming influence on the crew didn't actually help her deal with how damned annoying he was, however.

"I'm sure," she said. "I would, however, like to refer you to my original statement?"

Eric frowned. "Which was what again?"

"I hope you have a plan."

"I always have a plan, Commander," Eric said simply. "What we need to hope is that it's a good one."

Miram pinched the bridge of her nose in an attempt to defuse her annoyance. There was nothing that would keep him from playing his games, she was sure.

Eric, meanwhile, had turned to the strategic display. It showed the converging forces on a two-dimensional plane with vector information as well as intercept times displayed clearly. The Imperial forces were separated into multiple groups while their own force was neatly concentrated.

The problem with that was that each of the Imperial groups was easily a match for them, at least on paper.

It would be different if the t-cannons were reliable against ships with singularity cores, Miram thought sourly.

Unfortunately, what was arguably the single most game-changing weapon at their disposal turned out to be preemptively countered by the *fuel* tanks of the enemy ships. Unless they deployed parasite destroyers, the cannons would be a minimal influence on the fight, at best.

Well, almost.

They did have antimatter shells, or rather, they could put antimatter payloads into transition-cannon shells. It didn't matter much if the payload didn't reintegrate properly if it was composed of antihydrogen. Hell, having antimatter shotgunned through the interior of a ship was probably more effective than a proper coherent integration, she supposed.

The problem with that tactic was, as always, the difficulty in making and storing antimatter.

They'd only get a few shots per cruiser, and that just wouldn't do.

Miram frowned, staring at the same numbers the commodore was looking at, and tried to work out the plan.

Weston was such an infuriating man.

———

The entity known as Odysseus felt a certain thrill of fear as he observed the entire situation playing out.

Unlike the others of his nature, those he'd met at least, Odysseus knew that he could *die*. His ship, his body, was vulnerable to things that even Gaia could, and would, laugh off. Certainly, there were planet killers as well . . . The Drasin were a well-known example in recent times, after all, but the ship he was contained within was so very much more vulnerable than even the Earth was, to say nothing of Saul's situation.

The commodore had committed the squadron and Odysseus to a battle they might not all survive. Likely wouldn't all survive.

It was something to be marveled at that so few of the crew, the crews even, found that objectionable.

Odysseus *was* the crew.

Their memories, experience, everything they were while they served aboard the *Odysseus*, was part of Odysseus.

Yet, he couldn't really explain that loyalty.

He knew it existed but couldn't *understand* it entirely.

The entity gave the mental equivalent of a resigned sigh and pushed those thoughts aside. There was work to be done now, if the crew . . . crews . . . were to have the best chance of survival.

He would attempt to decipher loyalty another time.

———

Eric found the situation a little amusing, really.

Oh, he was as concerned as the commander was, at least. Possibly more so. He knew the firepower arrayed against them, of course. He'd gone out of his way to put them in this position, so he'd better damn well know it.

That didn't keep him from recognizing the humor in the scenario.

His plan for dealing with the enemy was to burn them badly enough that they thought twice about coming back. He didn't know if the ploy would work, rather doubted it would to be honest, but an attempt had to be made before they could go looking at other options.

The Empire wasn't a normal nation-state. They had a social handicap, some sort of psychological impairment, that was making them irrational.

Rational polities didn't play around willy-nilly with the likes of the Drasin.

Oh, they might develop such weapons, sure. They might *test* such weapons . . . but they didn't *deploy* them so haphazardly. Not for moral reasons, of course. Few nations, or any organizations for that matter, were truly capable of being moral. Groups tended to average out things like morality, and then excuse that phenomenon with the idea that the ends justified the means.

However, certain things weren't an issue of morality. Rather, when dealing with decisions like deploying strategic weapons, it was an issue of economy.

Strategic weapons were a valuable commodity, but part of their value lay in their scarcity.

You had to be known to *have* them, and known to be willing to *use* them . . . but also be well-known *not* to deploy them without great need.

Everyone respected the power of a strong, confident man with a gun, and few would be quick to challenge him, but if that same man was prone to randomly shooting people for the slightest infraction against his person? Well, then *everyone* would group together and put him down.

That was what the Empire was risking with their actions, but somehow Eric didn't think they saw this.

That bothered him more than anything else. Imperial actions spoke to a lack of intelligence, a lack of understanding of consequence, that was damned dangerous to see in a person let alone an interstellar polity.

So far, he supposed some of it was explained by the fact that they'd been top of the hill for so long that no one else was even close to toppling them. It seemed that they'd all but eliminated all possible contenders, and maybe that was what gave them the arrogance to act as they had.

He didn't know.

One thing he did know, without question, however, was that nothing lasted forever . . .

And it's time for Rome to fall.

———

Bellerophon

Jason Roberts sat in the command station of the big cruiser, eyes stoically on the screens as he watched the numbers drop.

The enemy fleet was converging on their position with obvious intent, and he had to both admire and wonder at the sanity involved in the commodore's choice of tactics.

Eric Weston was one of the finest tactical strategists he'd ever served with, but more importantly, he was a man able to turn defeat into victory with often nothing more than a few well-chosen words. He had personally seen Eric talk a superior enemy into fleeing, and a weaker one into attacking, but this time Jason couldn't help but wonder if that trait had finally backfired.

The comm challenge he'd made had been classic Weston, taking a position of superiority that would make the enemy question reality, make them wonder what the captain was hiding. It should have made the enemy question their position of superiority, but this time it seemed to have done the opposite.

He always supposed it would happen, sooner or later. If not now, then eventually. When you bluffed . . . sooner or later you would be called on it. Still, while he was ready for that eventuality, he would make certain that anyone choosing to challenge them paid into the pot in full. He was certain Eric would make doubly sure of the same.

"System check clears, Captain."

"Good," he said. If this was his last fight at Weston's side, he would ensure it was one that the enemy would remember . . . those few who lived to report it. "Begin manufacturing antimatter, divert available power to laser capacitors, and rig the ship for a fight."

"Aye Skipper."

"*Odysseus* on open comm, Skipper!"

"Put her on the ship-wide," Jason ordered.

"Aye, aye!"

Eric Weston's voice came through loud and clear a moment later.

"The enemy thinks they have us cornered, and they do. They, in fact, have us *exactly* where I want them. Beam stations, charge and fire on my mark."

That was a little simpler than Jason expected from the man, but he was fine with simple.

"You heard the commodore," he said. "Find our targets and light up the black!"

"Aye, aye, Skipper. Beam out!"

———

Odysseus

Eric watched the augmented display light up with beams being plotted by the computer, showing him their passage as they burned through the vacuum toward their target. They had a good distance to travel at the moment, the two closing fleets still being several light-minutes apart.

The slow progress of the bars that represented the beams made him smile slightly as he noted the ludicrousness of watching *light* move so slowly.

Despite being within the technical range of the weapons, they were still at extreme distances, and even slight movements by the enemy before the beams crossed those distances would likely result in missing by thousands, or hundreds of thousands, of kilometers.

That was fine, however, because this was just the opening move.

Normally, it would be the enemy's move next, but Eric didn't want to let him think that he was going to play by the rules.

"All ships," he said over the squadron network, "stand by to engage with transition cannons. Targets have been sent to your stations, plot for a time on target operation and fire."

He watched as their destroyer screen pivoted, widening formation slightly and turning side-on to the enemy forces in order to bring all their guns to bear at once. The six cruisers stayed steady, having enough guns covering the front arc that they'd not gain anything by maneuvering for a broadside engagement.

Transition cannons, being FTL in nature, would engage instantly across any range they could traverse, but the nuclear warheads they'd originally utilized wouldn't reintegrate properly if fired close enough to the core of a cruiser to be effective. Gravity was one of the few forces that truly seemed to interact with tachyons, which was rather inconvenient.

Eric had been thinking about how to make up for that weakness for some time, however.

The numbers dropped, and when they hit zero, he silently said one word that he knew he didn't need and his crews didn't need, but which felt right all the same.

Fire.

———

Puffs of tachyons were the only evidence of the cannons firing, particles that existed for so short a period that it would take supreme effort and technical expertise to note that they'd passed.

Each of those nigh undetectable puffs signified a moment of fury unleashed as the *Odysseus* Task Group set all hell loose upon their enemies.

Chapter 18

Imperial Eighth Fleet Command Vessel

Birch flinched back as though she'd been physically struck when the first cruiser in her deployment belched fire into the abyss and began to waver in its charge. She twisted around to check, and alarms were suddenly blaring all around her as ship after ship reported damage ranging from minor to catastrophic.

The enemy was within their range, she knew, but at this extreme distance she'd *never* have wasted fire upon a military target. It would have been an unthinkable thing. No laser would penetrate proper armor at this distance, if only because you could never follow up the strike and really make use of the opening you'd just carved.

The convoy with noncombatant ships, those she was more than willing to engage at range. A lucky strike would disable or perhaps even eliminate such a target, and the results would be incredibly demoralizing.

Something she was now realizing was doubly true of losing a *military* ship at such a range.

"Damage reports from seven . . . no, nine ships, Fleet Commander!"

"What did they hit us with?!" she demanded, unbelieving despite the evidence of her own eyes.

Lasers would not have done this, not at this range!

"Some beam strikes are confirmed, Commander, but energy release indicates that they deployed antimatter ahead of us somehow."

For the second time, Birch flinched back.

How?

This enemy was determined to defy all the common rules of warfare in the great abyss, which was both fascinating and frustrating by levels she'd never before encountered. There was no way that they'd mined the approach she'd used. That was simply *impossible*.

Birch frowned, trying to parse it all together. She felt so *close*, knew that there was a missing piece to the enemy, something she needed to know before she could understand their actions and what resulted from them.

"Press the attack," she ordered firmly. "All ships, open fire!"

One way or another, Birch was going to get the intelligence she required.

———

Odysseus

"Enemy targets hit, we're registering three ships falling out of formation, Commodore," Miram reported.

"Excellent. Prepare another round of antimatter," Eric ordered, knowing it would take precious time to manufacture the material. "In the meantime, switch cannons to kinetic warheads and go to rapid-fire on all bores."

"Aye sir!"

The transition cannons across the squadron began loading tungsten and depleted uranium shells, firing as fast as they could load, aiming just ahead of the enemy ships.

The range was closing fast, and Eric was expecting . . .

"Lasers detected!"

That.

The drone screen detected the beams as they got within one light-second of the squadron, however, and reported on frequencies along the short-range FTL comm. That gave their computers the chance to adapt armor in the very last instant before the beams struck home and glinted off, reflected and refracted away.

"Enemy accelerating, still on intercept course."

Unsurprising.

Eric took a break, opening the squadron network.

"Reverse warp, all ships. It's time to center this fight."

Imperial Eighth Fleet Command Vessel

Birch continued to flinch as her ships took hits, now seemingly running into some type of kinetic munition that must have been fired so long ago that there was no chance they could have scored a direct hit. And yet somehow they had. She steeled herself to ignore the reports for the moment, eyes focused on the enemy.

"Enemy acceleration has changed, Commander!"

"Are they increasing relative velocity?" she asked, having expected that. Charging into her formation now would limit the engagement time, leaving them less exposed to her weapons at close range.

"No Commander, they've reversed acceleration. They're aiming for a zero-speed relative engagement!"

Birch almost *choked.*

This was *not* how this enemy had engaged the Third Fleet! Not at all.

They'd gone for hit-and-fade maneuvers against that fleet, refusing to give Commander Mich the opportunity for a definitive engagement. They'd focused then on bleeding his ships from him in a war of attrition, counting on their admittedly superior ranged weapons and tactics to give them the edge.

"Confirm!"

"Confirmed, Commander. They have made for a zero relative velocity engagement."

Mich was right. These people . . . No, she thought grimly as she recalled her conversation with the empress, *no people are so mad. These are Xeno in the truest sense.*

Her analytical mind wouldn't stop nagging at her, though.

What if they weren't?

Mad, that is.

"Full active scans," she ordered. "If they're hiding anything out here, I want to know it!"

Hiding anything else, that is.

"Yes, Fleet Commander!"

———

Odysseus

"Heavy scanner pings, Commodore," Miram said, surprised. "I'd say you've spooked them."

Eric nodded, unsurprised.

The Imperial Fleet had been hit by too many new surprises over the last few minutes for them *not* to be spooked.

"Any change in disposition?" he asked, not looking up from his calculations.

"No sign of that yet, sir."

"Hmmm . . ."

The engagement was ongoing, lasers passed back and forth as the ships converged. By reversing warp, he'd opened up the time that the enemy would stay outside the one light-second radius provided by the drones, which kept his squadron intact in the face of the overwhelming power of the enemy beams.

Once they got inside that range, which *was* going to happen in short order, Eric knew the fighting would get bloody for his side.

He glanced at the countdown, running the numbers quickly in his head.

Less than a minute before they cross the drone wall.

Come on. Make your call, he urged the commander of the opposing fleet.

Eric couldn't make his next move until he knew the enemy had made and committed to their decision. He didn't really care what that decision was, but he needed to know it.

————

Imperial Eighth Fleet Command Vessel

Birch glared at the numbers, showing that the enemy was still unflinchingly aiming for a zero relative velocity showdown.

The intensive scanning of the region showed nothing beyond what she already knew, and that did not sit well with her at all. By everything she knew she had the upper hand, and while this might be a costly engagement, the outcome should *not* be in doubt.

So why are they clearly moving to prolong the engagement?

She looked around. "Tactical! Report on damage to the enemy forces."

There was a brief pause, enough that she twisted around to look right at the man at the tactical station and stared until he swallowed.

"No damage detected, Commander."

Birch blinked.

What.

"What," she said, her tone flat.

"We've achieved direct hits multiple times, but their armor . . . it is more effective than the Third Fleet reported."

More effective.

"No damage? That isn't more effective," she snarled. "That's impossible!"

She'd been fully briefed on the enemy's adaptive armor. The Empire had deployed derivative technology within the advance scouts of the Eighth already, so she was quite familiar with it.

Though putting that tech to use did those scouts no good at all, she noted with some trepidation.

Birch was firmly aware that she was deploying and testing technology that the enemy had already perfected, which had clearly put her operations at a larger disadvantage than she'd expected.

Even so, the briefing was clear about the deficiencies in the armor, and the enemy should not have been able to completely escape damage. Not against multiple ships firing simultaneously at least, and not instantly. It took time to adjust the qualities of the armor, time that the enemy should not have had.

They've deployed new technology, clearly, she realized. Were the new changes sufficient to carry the enemy to victory?

This was ridiculous.

The anomalous species were *clearly* not human. They couldn't be. No human group in her knowledge was so chaotically insane as to introduce as many new changes as quickly as this group did.

The empress' intense dislike of Xeno now appeared to be an understandable position to Birch.

None of that helped her work out what to do next. Her cautious instincts were telling her to back off, regroup, and acquire better data for a future conflict. Her Imperial officer's side, however, was demanding that she close the range and *end* this, one way or another.

I need more data, she raged internally, eyes on the telemetry being fed to her station from all the ships of her fleet. *This makes no sense, which means that I am missing a key piece of the puzzle.*

Birch tried to ignore the slight plaintive tone she could feel her thoughts taking on, hoping she was right but rather worried that perhaps rationality was too much to ask.

Baring her teeth, the Imperial officer took over and pushed the intelligence officer in her aside.

"Adjust warp," she ordered. "Give them what they want. Bring us to a stop relative to the enemy fleet. If they want to settle this as we hammer one another from point-blank range, then I'm willing to let them die the way they choose."

Odysseus

Eric spotted the change in velocity a fraction of a second before the tactical station announced it. He smiled thinly, satisfied.

"The Imperial commander has made his choice," he said. "Looks like they intend to indulge us with a good old-fashioned close-range slugfest."

"I fail to see how this is going to benefit us," Miram said softly, pitching her voice so that it wouldn't be overheard. "Projections show that they'll penetrate the drone shield before coming to a stop. Should we adjust our acceleration to keep them out?"

"No." Eric shook his head. "That will fail shortly anyway, once they decide to really start hammering our position, unless you think we can keep up with that many simultaneous strikes?"

Miram grimaced, shaking her head.

Once the Imperials got their legs under them again and really set to conducting the battle, not all the drones in the galaxy would be able to help them. The ship's armor would never be able to keep up with that many frequencies, even if the drones could.

"Commodore, now would be a good time to reveal your master plan."

"And ruin the surprise?"

Miram sighed audibly, more at hearing the weak chuckles from those who'd overheard them than Weston's actual statement. The crew was too used to Weston's odd style of command, in her opinion, but at least they had faith. Little more than that had carried them through in the past. She just hoped it would again.

"Tactical," Eric said, pitching his voice to carry.

"Sir!"

"Go active on all scanners," he ordered. "I want to know the enemy position every second, by the second."

"Aye, aye, sir!"

"All ships, this is Commodore Weston," he said, flipping on the squadron channel. "All weapons free, fire as you bear."

———

Imperial Eighth Fleet Command Vessel

"Enemy fire density has increased significantly, Commander."

"Indeed." Birch examined the numbers. "That's an impressive density of fire. Kinetic impactors, though?"

They were tracking the high-speed rounds, taking evasive action as possible. Kinetic warheads weren't used by the Empire or any species she knew, for good reason. Armor could largely reduce their effectiveness to the point where they weren't truly worth the limited magazine capacity compared to lasers.

She flinched as one of the kinetic warheads impacted, however, and then stared in shock at the numbers.

That is no normal kinetic impactor.

"Shift to defensive fire," she ordered. "Burn those down before they strike!"

"Yes Commander!"

Order given, Birch twisted, and strode over to the scanner station.

"What was *that*?!" she demanded. "That was no mere kinetic impactor."

"I don't know, Fleet Commander," the tech said helplessly. "It impacted with far more force than the size and mass analysis would indicate."

She pushed him out of the way, examining the data. The technician was right. The scans detailed the speed and mass of the kinetic weapon with no sign of a significant energy source that might have augmented the blast. They read as purely kinetic weapons, but they didn't *hit* like that was their payload.

There's no possible way that a chemical warhead could significantly change the payload, and we would detect anything like antimatter or atomic weapons. What are these people?!

More frustrating than that, however, was that she was learning more in these few instants of combat than the Fifth or any previous fleets had managed to report back.

"Log *everything*!" she snarled. "I do not care how small. Log it all and share across the fleet. If we go down, I do not want that intelligence lost!"

"Yes, Fleet Commander!"

Birch refocused herself. Realizing just how much they didn't know reminded her of her true mission. She wasn't here to eliminate the enemy; she was here to acquire intelligence on them, and *that* job her fleet was managing quite well, albeit in one of the most expensive ways possible.

These people, or Xeno, or whatever they are . . . are like nothing we've ever dealt with.

Chapter 19

Odysseus

"The *Bell* was just hit! Enemy ships have broached the drone screen. We're vulnerable, Commodore."

"I see it. Refocus our fire on the closest ships," Eric ordered. "Try and make them flinch back a little!"

The two groups were exchanging weapon blasts with furious fervor, throwing back and forth enough power to light up entire continents on Earth. Eric felt his hands twitch as he saw the enemy ships on his displays *without* magnification.

They were still a long damn way off and resembled nothing more than a few extra stars peppering the darkness, but they were moving. Every now and then a glint would mark them as having fired a laser off in the general direction of the *Odysseus*.

The task group was giving as good as it received; of course, he would even argue that they were giving far better than that. The kinetic penetrator magazines were nearing empty, but they were still firing rapid-fire bursts. As the range lowered, his ships were getting more hits with the counter-mass equipped weapons.

Gigaton level payload deliveries were tearing into the enemy fleet, and more than a few of their ships were now drifting dead or disabled.

They weren't able to keep fighting, which was all that Eric truly cared for in that regard, but now the sheer weight of the battle was beginning to turn the tide against his squadron.

Once they'd penetrated the drone screen, the laser-detection system lost its utility, and they had started taking real damage. They'd lost several destroyers. Eric hoped they were merely disabled but it was impossible to tell now and wouldn't be possible until after the fight, assuming he was alive to check.

The *Bellerophon* had just been struck seriously as well, and he knew that the *Odysseus* was bleeding air from multiple breaches. If any of them came through fully intact, Eric would be surprised.

I'm actually shocked. For a moment there I thought they would flinch, Eric thought grimly.

It had been a short moment, but he'd felt like the enemy commander had hesitated there at the last second. Something had changed, however, and suddenly the Imperial Fleet was throwing itself forward, fully committed to the fight once more.

He felt a certain level of disappointment. He would have preferred to escape this with as few losses as possible, but Eric knew that would only have prolonged things rather than ending them.

No, he thought grimly. *This is the only way.*

———

Imperial Eighth Fleet Command Vessel

Birch grimaced as one of her cruisers vanished in a hail of fire that was beyond anything that should have been possible. She hadn't figured out how their kinetic weapons could possibly have had the effect they'd managed, but she was certain they *had* to be running low on munitions.

And it's about time. Who loads that many heavy rocks when they have unlimited energy for lasers?

The enemy ships had to be crammed so full of munitions that there couldn't be room for much in the way of crew at all. Why was this not more emphasized in the reports?

There were times when Birch honestly hated her fellow Imperials.

Automation had to be a critical factor in the anomalous ships, which went a long way to explain some of their actions and capacities.

"Press them harder," she ordered. "All ships advance!"

"Yes Commander!"

Her forces were starting to gain real traction too. She could see the damage her lasers were beginning to inflict. Ships were belching flame and smoke into the void, bleeding atmosphere from the holes gouged out in their armor.

It would appear that we've oversaturated whatever trick they were pulling off with their armor. Their defenses held up longer than I expected possible, however. We will have to recover samples to see if they've changed the technology from earlier ships.

For the moment, though, she needed to push them hard enough that they stopped holding back.

Show me what you can do, Birch thought as she stared intently into the displays that surrounded her. *Show me your secrets.*

———

Odysseus

"Hold the line!" Eric ordered as the Imperial ships continued to press in, more of them crossing the drone screen.

"We're running low on munitions, Commodore. They just keep *coming!*"

Inwardly, Eric had to concede Miram's point there. The Imperials were willingly absorbing more damage than he'd ask of his people, short of a truly critical mission. In the last twenty minutes or so, they'd lost more than *twice* the tonnage of the entire *Odysseus* squadron, and it hadn't made them flinch in the slightest. If anything, the Imperial ships had redoubled their efforts in just the last few moments.

This can't be the same commander who willingly let us pass just because I slowed the task group's velocity, can it?

If it were, then he was entirely wrong about what was driving the man. This wasn't the act of a cautious commander. This was someone who was more than willing to wade through the fires of hell to accomplish their mission, caution be damned.

So what the hell is his mission?

He would work it out later, assuming he had a later. Eric glanced to one side, eyes alighting on a specific display.

Only one thing left to do then.

He rose to his feet, opening the squadron command channel.

"Close the range," Eric ordered. "Continue firing, all weapons! Empty the magazines, bleed the core dry if you have to!"

He was working furiously on his console as the battle raged, gathering data and logging everything across the squadron. The Imperials weren't showing much new in terms of technology, though they'd clearly cobbled together a variation of the cam-plates from ships they'd destroyed.

Unfortunately for them, those armor modifications were not particularly useful against kinetic penetrators. Of course, he was about to run out of those, so the fight would be a lot more difficult once that happened and he had no more high-velocity missiles to chuck at the enemy.

Eric sneaked another glance to the display at his right and smiled.

Right on time.

Priminae Cruiser Zeaus

"The fleet reports transition was successful, Admiral."

Rael Tanner held a closed fist up to his mouth, forcing his stomach to settle before he tried to respond.

"Thank you, Ithan," he said finally. "All ships report in and prepare for battle. System scans to my displays."

"Yes Admiral."

He heard someone retching around him but intentionally didn't look because he wasn't certain he could keep from following suit if he did.

The scanners were flooded with new data, filling out the area of space around them in a growing sphere that propagated at the speed of light. Mostly.

Rael instantly spotted an exception to that limitation and smiled thinly.

Bravo, Eric my friend. You came through as always.

The entire area was *saturated* in tachyon particles, the results of the entire *Odysseus* Task Group just hammering their targets with pulse scans at an incredible cost of energy, and that effort was giving his ships a very clear and very real time image of the situation ahead of them.

He paled as he recognized the sheer disparity in forces that existed between the Terrans and the Imperial ships. Outmassed by incredible odds, however, the Terrans were not only holding their ground but actually *closing* on the enemy fleet.

He knew it was part of the plan, but while Rael had understood it intellectually, he had not quite made the visceral connections in his mind that would have allowed him to get what he was seeing until just then.

Incredible.

"All ships report in, ready for battle, Admiral!"

"Excellent. All ships, prepare to warp space to the following coordinates," he said, tapping in commands to send the data out to the fleet.

He had to force himself to keep from rushing, knowing that moving too fast would result in mistakes, possibly causing more loss of life than if he were too slow. Rael took time to issue the orders, then finally made the last call.

"All ships, engage warp. Maximum velocity, all weapons armed and *free*," he stated. "Check your fire until I give the order. Targets are being assigned."

Space *twisted* as the fleet powered their warp drives, making the local space-time distort and alter to unrecognizability as the fleet began to fall through it along the curve they carved into the very fabric of the universe itself.

———

Imperial Eighth Fleet Command Vessel

Birch heard a vicious cheer rise among her people as one of the enemy cruisers' armor failed spectacularly, gouts of flame spewing out into the void as the ship pitched off course and forced its fellows to react by moving aside before they could once again press their attack.

The enemy ships were undaunted by the loss, still pushing hard and firing everything they had. She was impressed by the fighting prowess and spirit shown, but now it was clear that Imperial victory was a foregone conclusion.

As good as they were, and there was no question that it was going to cost her far more than she would extract in turn on a ton-for-ton basis, the Eighth simply was too large a force for this small squadron to hope to overcome.

Her first warning that not everything was as it seemed was when one of her ships vanished from her tactical display . . . one of the ships at the *rear* of her formation.

———

Zeaus

"Targets struck!"

"Excellent work," Rael said firmly. "Continue to do so."

"Yes Admiral."

The Imperial Fleet had been intently focused on the fighting and better than half-blinded by the massive levels of scanner energy being thrown about by the Terran ships. So much energy abounded, in fact, that his own fleet had been able to close and target the enemy without using a single active scanner for the entire trip.

Weston is a terrifying person, Rael thought, his feelings on the matter mixed between legitimate fear of the man's ideas and clear admiration for the effectiveness of his methodology.

Not the least of which was his willingness, and that of his people, to place themselves at the center of such a bloody conflict, mostly just to make a very serious point to the Empire. That sort of determination, and willingness to sacrifice, unnerved him in very real ways.

Sacrifice was no stranger to Rael and those from the Colonies, but he didn't believe that they would have been so quick to do something of this nature, even if the idea had occurred to them.

The battle they were watching was vicious, he could tell that at a glance, with neither side giving anything nor, apparently, asking for anything. He knew why the Terrans were fighting that furiously, of course—to keep the Imperials focused on them. But what was driving the Imperials? Why were *they* so intent?

Rael suspected he would not like the answer.

———

Imperial Eighth Fleet Command Vessel

"Where did that come from?" Birch demanded as she reached out with a flick to reorient her display.

"Enemy fleet detected!"

Fleet?!

Birch paled, understanding instantly what had happened.

"Location, vector, and arrival!" she ordered.

"Approaching from Vector Six Four Niner Brek, three lights out, arrival within optimum range in . . . three beats."

Birch swallowed. The fleet was right on *top* of them. She brought up the wider display, realizing that she had real time data on the enemy fleet and briefly not understanding how that was possible. Then it hit her.

They blinded us with active pulses. While we were focused on the squadron we couldn't see anything else. But the enemy fleet would have been able to use those same signals instead of revealing themselves with their own scanners. Damn them to the abyss, and damn me with them!

The mass of the enemy fleet was more than enough to tilt the odds, and she knew that this was the end of the Eighth. If she stood and fought, they would all die or be captured.

One last duty.

"All ships," she ordered. "Scatter and return to the Empire with the captured intelligence. These are my orders."

Everyone turned to look at her. She recognized conflicting emotions on those faces she saw looking back.

"Primary squadron will provide cover," she said. "Initiate my orders."

A brief pause, then everyone jumped into action.

"Yes, Fleet Commander!"

Odysseus

Eric winced as the enemy formation exploded, ships peeling off in every direction.

Retreating was the only move they could do, aside from surrendering, but it still hurt to see them run like that. There was no way he'd be able to hunt all of the fleeing ships down, which meant that some would report back to the Empire.

That was unfortunate, as he was sure that they'd learned more than he would prefer in this encounter, but it was also largely unavoidable. They couldn't have just allowed them to run around attacking new colonies at their leisure.

"Break Three!" he ordered, initiating one of his contingency plans. "All ships, engage plan Break Three!"

"Roger, Commodore. Break Three is in action."

With the enemy fleet on the run, his own ships prioritized targets differently now, aiming to take out their drives and move on rather than focusing on disabling them entirely. Wallowing in space, they would be dealt with later. For now, he wanted as *few* of the enemy to escape as possible.

It was no longer about winning.

Now it was about sending a message. They might not be able to get all of the retreating ships, but he would see that they hunted down every last one that they could.

"I told you," he whispered, knowing that he couldn't be heard. "You should have turned back."

Chapter 20

Imperial Fifth Fleet Command Vessel, Free Stars Space

"Fleet Commander, there's an unusual level of communication traffic being bounced around the Hele Protectorate."

Jesan Mich looked up, the name catching his attention.

The Protectorate was so named because they were, technically at least, an Imperial Protectorate. In exchange for certain war materials, tribute, he supposed, the Empire largely left them be and was even known to occasionally intervene on their behalf if one of the other local polities were becoming a threat to said war material production.

"Have we decrypted it?" he asked, mildly curious.

"Yes, My Lord, that is why I brought this to you."

"Do not call me that," Jesan growled. "Not any longer."

"I'm . . . sorry, Fleet Commander."

Jesan sighed deeply, but nodded and gestured with his left hand. "Pass me the comm traffic."

"Yes sir."

He accepted the data plaque, dismissed the young officer, and settled back in his position to read.

His reassignment to the Free Stars, a term he personally found almost as distasteful as the area and people themselves, had been going acceptably well. Generally reminding the locals of why the Empire was feared and respected was almost relaxing work, particularly after his last assignment.

The thought of that was enough to make Jesan flinch involuntarily, remembering the mess he'd inherited and how it had been spiraling out of control when he arrived and that *nothing* he did made it any better.

What is all this about? he wondered as he read through the intercepted traffic.

Something had the Protectorate up in arms, that was obvious. They were being rather cagey about the affair, however. Even while using encryption, they were clearly using coded phrasing to disguise whatever it was they were referring to.

Still, some items were clear from context if nothing else.

One of the other polities must have gotten a little more aggressive than normal, Jesan decided.

Someone had captured one of the Protectorate's star systems, and whichever system it was had the whole damn group in a near panic. Jesan read the reports with interest, amused by some of the exchange.

Near the end, however, he noticed something that made him sit up and take serious notice.

They're discussing asking the Empire to intervene?

That was . . .

Jesan didn't *know* what that was, actually.

The Protectorate didn't ask for anything from the Empire. The Protectorate status was a joke, a fiction that the locals had come up with and the Empire simply never truly contradicted. Whatever the Empire did for them was entirely due to it being less of a hassle to allow them to mine precious material rather than for the Empire to maintain their own facilities this far from Imperial control.

He couldn't imagine anything that would cause them to think the Empire would actually intercede on their behalf except for . . .

They could not have been that incompetent, Jesan thought darkly, a thought hitting him.

He scoffed lightly.

It's the Free Stars. Of course they could.

Jesan tossed aside the plaque and rose from his station, walking across to the helm and navigation consoles where he nodded to the officers manning those stations.

"Fleet Commander." The sub-commander returned the nod. "What are your orders?"

"Devise a course for the Hele Protectorate," he said. "I want the fleet moving as soon as possible. Once we have better intelligence we will adjust, but let us move in the right direction immediately."

"At your command." The man turned to work.

Jesan left them to it, heading for the long-range scanners.

The young woman there stiffened as he approached.

"Fleet Commander," she said as he stopped.

"Analyze ship movement in the Hele Protectorate, coordinate with communications intercepts," he said. "They will be moving a fleet into action shortly, if I am correct. I want to know as soon as that happens."

"Yes, Fleet Commander."

He gestured absently in acknowledgment, turning away and heading back to his station.

If he was right, the Protectorate had just lost the only thing that made them of any particular interest to the Empire. The deep matter available from their mines was not the only source for such material in the Empire, but it was an important one nonetheless.

He would be remiss, Jesan decided, if he did not determine exactly what had happened . . . and who, if anyone, was now in control of that system.

And who will be in control of it when I am finished with them.

Mirran's Bane, *Hele Protectorate*

Jorra swore as he oversaw the repairs. Entire sections of the *Bane* had been burned away by the enemy lasers. Just sealing up holes in the outer hull so they could repressurize the ship had taken the better part of the destroyer's return trip to the Protectorate's home system.

The High Command's reaction to his news had been predictable, if certainly not something he'd ever wanted to experience.

As the highest-ranking officer to so far have survived whatever happened in the neutron system, Jorra had caught the worst of the blame, but at least command had quickly become too busy preparing the reaction force to continue tearing into him.

That hadn't saved him from being assigned to return, however, despite the damage to his ship.

Which was why he was fighting to get the *Bane* in as close to fighting trim as possible, running repairs while under power, barely able to keep up with the fleet that had been dispatched to reclaim the neutron system.

He was surprised and, though he would *never* admit it, shocked that High Command had managed to get ships moving as quickly as they had. Unfortunately, the speed of dispatch meant that they were hardly what he would consider a proper fleet.

More of an oversized squadron, Jorra supposed, but at least it was entirely a fighting force this time.

High Command couldn't risk not moving quickly; that was clear. If any of the Free Star polities got wind of the action and losses they'd sustained, not merely in terms of shipping power but more in terms of the system itself, then they would be scenting the blood of a wounded prey. Old enemies would act on their grudges.

Only the control of the deep matter and the threat of being able to lean on the Empire lest supplies of that material be interrupted had kept some of them from waging their little petty wars against the Protectorate already.

It was vital that the system be reclaimed immediately.

Former Protectorate Mining Facility

Steph looked over the assembled people, most of them new faces and none Terran human. He couldn't spare any of *his* crews for tasks like this, not with a likely attack looming.

After they'd taken the freighters and secured at least some of the area, he'd done the best he could to get things in order. That meant, first, completing the mercenary mission he'd accepted originally.

Thankfully, that was simple.

The Kingdom wanted a supply of strange matter.

No problem. They'd loaded up enough to more than meet the Kingdom's highest expectations, plus ten percent, and sent it off with one of the more damaged ships. That really just required a small prize crew, along with a few of his own people to keep everyone honest. Freighters didn't have much of a crew, and most of them were apparently fine with working for him as for anyone else, especially when he offered them standard wages for his little band of pirates, plus bonuses.

He couldn't trust them, of course, but it wouldn't take many of his own to keep them in line. They were as beaten down as anyone Steph had ever met, and he'd helped free some nasty POW camps in his day.

He was half sure that the freighter crew would have thrown in with him just for proper *food*.

That was only his assigned mission, however, and if that was all he cared about he could have been back within the Kingdom's space by this point with his mission complete and enough strange matter to ensure his legend for some time.

No, he had a bigger goal now.

His reputation as a man who completed the missions assigned him was, like that of his crew, secure. Now he wanted a legend of a different sort.

"You're all here because I've read your files," he said to the gathered people.

That was a lie. He'd actually had Milla filter the stolen files for key attributes he needed.

"The Protectorate took you from your worlds," he said, eyes sweeping the field of faces. "They took your *families*. You've been working for them ever since. Some of you have lost friends, but none of you lost family."

Steph lowered his head, shaking it silently for a moment. No one spoke, because they all knew why their families had survived.

The Protectorate couldn't trust workers without leverage over them. A worker only lived so long as his family did, and from what he could tell the reverse was just as true.

"Every man here has a reason to want to see the Protectorate bleed," he said, eyes blazing as he looked back up at them. "Work with me, and I promise you that is a future you can look forward to."

Steph could see some people shift, and eyes of the group seemed to gravitate to a small handful. He noted each of those and turned his focus to them.

"You have something to say," he said, picking the one that most eyes looked to. "Please, say it. No harm is going to come to you from myself or my men here."

The man hesitated, but Steph waited patiently. He could see the haunted look in the stranger, eyes that had seen too much. It wasn't quite the thousand-yard stare, but only because the man was strong enough to be here, in the present, despite his memories clearly walking alongside him.

While he was waiting, Steph examined the stranger closer. It was clear why he was considered one of the leaders. He wasn't in much better shape than the others, probably worse than many, but something made him stand out. He was a wiry little man still standing straight with a light of intelligence in his brown eyes. Steph could see defiance there too.

Perfect.

"Making the bastards bleed is worth looking forward to," the man admitted. "But we have family here. What do you have to protect them?"

Steph nodded. That was what he wanted to hear. People who were concerned more with others than their own welfare were people he could work with, whom he could make into something more. A mercenary was useful, but a patriot and a man with friends and family, that was someone who could be built into far more than just a man with a gun.

"Right now, we have my ships and whatever we can scrounge," Steph said honestly. "That's it."

The men murmured, real concern filtering back and forth through them. Steph let them murmur; he wasn't going to get what he wanted by forcing the issue, despite the time constraints.

"The Protectorate will be back, and in force," the speaker warned. "Our families can't be protected here."

"They have to be," Steph said. "I don't have the lift to evacuate them. The freighters are too small, in terms of living space. My ships as well. Only the *Dutchman* and the captured destroyer could carry any significant number of people, and of the two, only the *Dutchman* is fit for a long-range transit. If we abandon the system now, we'll have to leave nine in ten behind, at least."

"That's not enough!"

Steph didn't bother looking to see who the speaker was. It was someone in the back who'd yelled out in reaction. Nothing more mattered for the moment.

"That is the reality," he countered. "I have three choices before me. I can leave here, with my captured spoils. I can do that and take perhaps ten percent of you with me . . . or we can fight."

He paused, letting himself frown as he turned to look them all over.

"I cannot force this decision on you, and I cannot fight without your help," he informed them. "So I leave it to you. If you wish to take your chances with the Protectorate, then I'll leave. I'll even offer to take as many of your families with me as I can . . . But you know what will happen to those we have to leave behind."

They bowed their heads, aware of what he was referring to.

If he took their families out of the Protectorate's reach, then there would be no more leverage over them and thus their value to the Protectorate would be at an end . . . as would their lives.

"Or," Steph said, speaking up, "you can choose to fight."

All eyes were on him then, all murmurs stopped.

"Draw a line, here, now," he said firmly. "Teach the Protectorate that they should *never* have crossed you. I cannot promise you safety, of course. You all know I would be lying if I did. What I can promise you is that you can make the Protectorate *pay* for what they did to you. You can stand up and either walk out of their control as free men or die fighting as free men. Either way, you'll not be slaves to anyone if you choose to fight."

"What about you? You have the guns, you're telling us to fight. When this is over, if you win, you'll need people here just as the Protectorate did."

Steph again ignored the hothead, eyes on the man they'd unconsciously elected as their representative.

"Any promise I make would ring hollow," he admitted as he looked the man in the eyes. "I think you've probably been lied to too often for words to mean much."

The man nodded, almost imperceptibly, but Steph caught the micro-expression.

213

"So I'll just say this," he went on. "Fight with me, and you'll fight as free men. Be one of *my* men, and you'll never be slaves again. I don't care what happens, where you may wind up, but if you need me, I promise I'll come for you. I may come *late*, I may fail to save you, but I will *never* leave you to your fate without trying."

He fell silent.

"You have a short time to decide," he said finally. "When you do, pick your representative and send him to me. I will abide your decision."

Steph pivoted on his heel and marched out, all eyes following him as he did.

Only when he was out of sight did he stop and lean against the wall, wiping his face with his hand.

Jeez, Eric, how the hell do you do the whole inspirational speech thing? That was horrible.

He didn't have time to wallow, however. Whatever they decided, he would have to move fast to make things work beyond that. He knew what he hoped they would choose to do, if only because it was the best outcome for himself, his mission, and *them* . . . But ultimately, it had to be their choice.

Freedom wasn't handed off to people.

You had to stand up and *take* it.

———

Imperial Fifth Fleet Command Vessel

Jesan swore softly as he read the newly intercepted message traffic.

Those fools actually lost their most important strategic asset. Imbeciles.

He wished he could communicate with the Empire, but the Fifth was well outside the range of the communication relays that would allow something resembling a reasonable discourse with the distant capital.

He would have to make decisions that might determine Imperial policy, which was not something to be taken lightly even when he had the empress' favor.

At the moment, considering how much on the outs he was with the Imperial Court, even if he made the right call, Jesan was under no illusion that a positive outcome was guaranteed.

He had plenty of enemies in the politics of the court who'd use anything they could to see him thrown down from what was left of his career. He would have to be careful.

"Locate the main body of the Protectorate forces," he ordered. "Do not communicate with the Protectorate, do not be seen by their vessels."

"Yes Commander," his second confirmed. "It will be done."

"See that it is," he said coldly. "I have a message to dispatch to the Empire. They will not be able to provide advice or support within reasonable time, but they will need to know of this all the same."

Chapter 21

Imperial Capital, World Garisk

"Your Majesty, a report from the Fifth has drawn some attention to the Fleet over-commanders."

The empress looked up, eyes barely interested. "Oh?"

"It seems that the . . . Hele Protectorate?"

"Yes, I am aware of them."

"Well, it appears that they might have . . . lost their mining system."

The empress scoffed loudly, covering her face with her hand a moment later, before looking angrily at the messenger, daring him to comment.

He declined, wisely so.

"How does one *lose* a star system?" she asked, slightly amused, despite knowing the value of that particular system.

"It seems . . ." The messenger sighed. "An unknown force, presumably one of the other polities, managed to usurp control of it. The exact details are unknown, but it was enough to draw Fleet Commander Mich's attention."

"As well it should," she said sourly, despite her previous amusement. "That was one of the very few sources the Empire has for deep matter. If the system weren't so far outside our controlled space, we would never have allowed it to remain under the control of anyone else. Allowing the Protectorate to mine it and accepting their *tribute* was the best of several rather bad options."

She rose from her throne and walked to the projection of stars that floated in the center of the room.

A gesture brought the scene in close on the system in question.

"Jesan is moving on the system, I presume," she said, more a statement than a question.

"Yes, Your Majesty."

She smiled slightly. There were reasons why she had not had the man executed after all. "Good. For the moment, I believe we will leave this in his hands. I am interested in seeing what he can do with this test."

"Your Majesty?"

She glanced sharply at the messenger. "I have spoken. Give my word to the over-commanders."

"It will be done, Your Majesty."

She ignored the man as he practically fled the room, instead refocusing on the system floating in the air before her.

Let us see how you handle this . . . Lord Jesan.

———

Imperial Fifth Fleet Command Vessel

"More reports on the Protectorate . . . fleet, Commander."

Jesan heard the slight hesitation in the other man's voice but didn't comment, mostly because he would probably be a lot more blunt in his description of the gathering of forces than merely exhibiting a minor hesitation.

It was *not* a fleet.

He grudgingly admitted that it was a reasonably powerful assembly of ships, with more than sufficient capability to handle most anything the local region could muster. But calling such a gathering a fleet was an insult to every Imperial force so named.

He forced down his distaste, however, and continued to oversee the new data incoming from their shadowing of the Protectorate . . . battle group.

They were moving finally, after long *days* of idiotic wrangling, heading for the neutron system as he'd expected them to do quite some time earlier. That didn't speak well for his opinion of the Protectorate, which surprised Jesan, honestly. He hadn't realized that his opinion of them could fall any more.

No matter the depths these barbarians plumb, they always seem to find further reaches to explore in their idiocy.

Losing a neutron system to any force was a humiliation compounding the more tangible losses. A system of that nature should be the crown of any Empire's jewels, and to leave it so undefended as to allow this . . . He supposed there was only so much one could expect from barbarians.

It may be time for the Empire to move into the region more . . . permanently.

Mirran's Bane, *Hele Protectorate*

Jorra looked over the fleet arrayed around his ship, a swell of pride filling him. It was the most powerful force he'd ever seen assembled by the Protectorate, and he was fully confident that they would soon retake the neutron system through its power.

The fallout of having fled the system had certainly done his position within the Protectorate Guard Force no good, and so he had whipped his crew into the best shape he could manage to ensure that the *Bane* would distinguish itself in the next action. His career had been saved only because the system had already been lost by the time he arrived, and those in command of the station had already had their commissions stricken from the rolls.

That was *not* something that would happen to him. He would make certain of that, no matter what else occurred.

"The fleet is fully in motion, Commander."

"Thank you," Jorra said to the tech manning the scanner station before turning to the navigation controls. "Keep in formation with the lead elements. Pay attention to the over-commander's ship, take your lead from him."

"Yes Commander!"

If the lead ship, under the over-commander's control, were to falter, then it would be better for his career to ensure that his people kept formation with that ship and make anyone else who got out of position look as though they were at fault.

"Not a single step out of line," he ordered firmly, glaring around the command deck. "Mark me well, not one single step!"

"Yes Commander."

———

Cruiser **Mylen's Victory**, *Hele Protectorate*

Over-Commander Broche glared around the deck, making sure everyone felt his ire evenly, as he was rather pissed off with the universe at the moment. Those nearest to him were the only parts of said universe he could make feel his annoyance.

Of all the wastes of his precious time that might be demanded of him, this had to be one of the single *stupidest*, and thus most rage inducing.

He was an over-commander of the Protectorate *fleet*. His job was to take systems from the enemy, *not* to retake systems that should never have fallen in the first place.

At least it shouldn't be too difficult, he supposed.

They'd scanned the records of the "battle" as documented by the destroyers that escaped the system. While it had been difficult to locate the enemy ships, his forces had eventually been able to find evidence of no more than six ships in addition to the single destroyer that had led the fight against the convoy.

That was a pitiful weight of steel to take a star system, a point that Broche had made quite strenuously to the Council of the Protectorate. The defeat made it clear that they had relied far too strongly on the threat of the Empire to secure their holdings, and that was simply an unacceptable state of affairs.

Still, reality was reality, and he would have to deal with it.

"Time to arrival at the mining system," he asked softly, his voice still carrying.

"At current velocity, we are several days out yet, Over-Commander."

Broche grimaced but nodded.

He had expected such news but didn't like hearing it even so. Their supposed fleet was a mishmash ensemble of everything the Council of the Protectorate had been able to summon at the spur of the moment. That meant they had been saddled with a lot of older ships that really shouldn't be in space but had not been broken down for various budgetary reasons that he was certain made sense to *someone*.

The effect was that, while his ship could arrive at the system in a few hours, his fleet was going to be dragging itself across space for the next . . .

He checked the exact time and closed his eyes.

Four days.

Unbearable.

Imperial Fifth Fleet Command Vessel

"Please, by the empress, tell me that this is not their maximum velocity."

No one jumped to answer him, which told Jesan all he needed to know.

Free Stars.

He spat on the deck, furious at the time he was wasting.

I should go ahead and secure the damn system myself.

Unfortunately, if he did that he would be committing the Empire to a position he wasn't certain it would be willing to maintain, and that would require him to hand the system back over to the Protectorate when he was through. That would be the equivalent of surrendering Imperial territory to a minor polity.

Unthinkable.

Treason, even.

So instead of doing things the easy way, Jesan had to settle himself in as he trailed the Protectorate fleet at a snail's pace through the stars.

He grumbled, shaking his head.

"Very well. We know where they're going," he said as he walked to the navigation console. "Fall away from pursuit of the Protectorate forces, then enter a course to bring us to the neutron system. We'll evaluate the situation there, make decisions with better intelligence."

"Yes Commander. Course being prepared."

Jesan found himself rather irritated that current Imperial policy precluded him from culling a few of the Protectorate ships as part of his mission. It would certainly alleviate his frustration.

Perhaps we'll get to see whomever took over their system tear a few ships down before they retake it?

Doubtful. No one in the Free Stars had a fleet capable of holding the system, not even against the paltry force the Protectorate had scrounged up. Most likely, they'd arrive to find the system empty of invaders, the conquerors having looted the facility of everything they could and fled.

I will at least enjoy having . . . words . . . with the Protectorate council members over their losing the empress' tribute.

Something to look forward to.

"Course prepared, Fleet Commander."

"Proceed."

Chapter 22

"They'll be coming soon."

Steph didn't look up from his work. "I know."

He and his crews had been running preparations nearly nonstop. Days had gone by since the ships fled their defense of the recently captured system. Days of work, hundreds of thousands of man-hours, a veritable *fortune* in materials that the Admiralty would give their first-borns for . . . and Steph still wasn't sure if it would be enough.

They'd loaded another of the freighters, sending it off with a small prize crew that was mostly pulled from his Archangels. They were ulti-mately going to a somewhat different destination than the first, though the initial leg of their mission would be nearly identical.

Before arriving in the Star Kingdom, they would alter course and set up station at the rogue world the Archangels used as a staging area within the Free Stars. They'd wait there for the heat to die down a little, then move on to Priminae space and, from there, home to Earth.

He was acting as a privateer and a pirate, and enjoying every bit of it, but Steph's first loyalty hadn't changed.

He knew that they'd be able to do a *lot* with a few tera-tons of strange matter.

Steph just wished he had dared send it all off.

That was not something he dared to do, however.

No, he needed some in reserve. A lot in reserve, unfortunately.

"What are you working on, Stephan?" Milla asked, looking over from where she had set her own work aside for the moment.

"Calculations," he answered. "We don't have time to establish a Kardashev Network in this system, so we have to be strategic in the deployment of the replicators."

"We know the safe corridors, do we not?" Milla asked, frowning.

"They won't use those," Steph said confidently. "Though I'll mine them just in case the enemy is either more clever or stupid than I believe them to be."

Milla raised an eyebrow. "I've heard you complain about how stupid everyone from these Free Stars are, Stephan."

"Sure, but there's stupid and then there's *stupid*," Steph said. "And you don't actually fight battles without learning the basics, no matter how badly you flub the advanced course. No, they'll have some idea of basic strategy and tactics, so they won't use the cleared approaches. They'll expect them to be mined."

"Which they will be," Milla said slowly.

"Well, I can't let them down, now, can I?" Steph asked, grinning.

"You are a very strange man, Stephan."

"Why thank you."

Milla rubbed her face, leaving Steph amused as she finally gave it up and just sighed.

"Do you believe we can do this?" she asked instead, her voice quiet.

Steph looked around, mostly just flicking his eyes, ensuring that no one was in earshot.

"I don't know," he admitted. "That's why you'll be on the *Revenge*, and all of my people will be in positions to retreat in case anything goes wrong."

There were a lot of ways for things to go wrong; he was not in any way blind to that. More ways it could go wrong, in fact, than ways it could go right. He was gambling, for truly high stakes, but it had only taken a couple glances at the system here to tell him that the gamble was worth it.

He doubted he could actually *hold* the system, though anything was possible. That would depend far more on the strength of the slaves and other locals, and he would do his best to lift them up to make them capable.

The Free Stars had been in a state of war for so long that Steph doubted if they truly had any idea how to handle peace anymore.

Many people thought that conflict brought innovation, and they weren't completely wrong . . . just mostly. The right sort of conflict had a way of truly compressing technological development, bringing about miracles in almost no time at all.

The kind of war that had crushed the Free Stars, though, wasn't the sort of conflict that drove innovation. If conflict were all it took to breed technical superiority, Africa and the Middle East would be the most technically developed areas on Earth.

To really drive innovation, you needed a period of conflict that was intense enough to push people to surpass their limits, but short enough that you didn't burn through the resources that development truly needed. Then you needed time for people to begin leveraging how to use those developments.

Peace was at least as important to the development of society and technology as conflict was.

When he looked around the Free Stars, he saw a people who had been burned to the ground so many times that they didn't know how to grow anymore.

The inventors had been killed, enslaved. Their children driven into poverty, the brightest minds of *many* generations snuffed out before they could bloom. What was left were the warlords, the monsters who saw nothing of the world but advantages they could press to gain themselves a little more power.

That didn't make them any less of a people, though.

Steph was certain of that. The spark was still there, waiting for the right mix of fuel and air.

Embers can be buried in the dirt for a long time, waiting for the right puff of wind to breathe life back into the blaze.

Steph looked out of the command deck at the mining ships moving things back and forth around the captured station.

He'd found his embers.

Now he just needed to provide the breath that brought the blaze back.

———

Archangel Two

Alexandra Black wiped her eyes, blinking away the itch. She needed some sleep but figured she'd get caught up on missing naps when she was dead.

In the meantime, the mission was just starting to get interesting.

Of all the assignments she'd ever expected, this wasn't exactly on the list. She'd hoped, eventually, to be assigned a NICS-enabled fighter and be given a berth on a carrier. That had been her goal almost her entire life, ever since she'd seen the Archangels turn the tide of the war.

She'd been a teen, too young to sign up during the war, but had wanted to fight all the same. Everyone she knew did, after Okinawa at least.

Her career hadn't exactly turned out as she'd planned. It had its ups and downs; sometimes she felt more of the latter than the former, but it had led her here.

She couldn't figure out exactly what her current assignment really was. It wasn't a pilot's gig but more like something she'd only heard about from before the war. A long time before.

Alex was reminded of the histories of the Cold War during the twentieth century, when the big boys didn't dare mess with each other directly for fear of nuking the whole planet. Instead they fought proxy wars, slipping forces into different parts of the world that were important to their opponents and forcing them to dedicate more and more resources to a fight they didn't want and sure didn't need.

Stephanos was *really* getting into it too, and that worried her at times.

Hell, it worried her *all* the damn time.

His enthusiasm for the pirate captain role was becoming squadron legend, something that the Marines found endlessly hilarious once they'd gotten over their knee-jerk reaction to being called pirates.

Now what was she doing?

Laying the foundations for system defense of a system that she couldn't *imagine* how they could actually hope to hold, in order to do . . . what?

That was the crux.

Alex wasn't much of a fan of slavery, of course, and she wanted to help these people as much as anyone else, but it wasn't their mission. More than that, it wasn't something they were equipped to be able to accomplish.

Orders were orders, however, and she wasn't going to bitch about eliminating a few slavers when she had a chance at them.

She just hoped that the effort didn't come back to bite them all.

"Commander, next replicator is ready to deploy."

She swallowed the last gulp of her coffee and hit the button on the intercom. "I'm on my way up."

Philosophizing could wait. There was work to do.

Archangel One, Gaia's Revenge

Tyke put the last of his replicators into position, ensuring that the system was active before he left it on a collision course with an appropriate asteroid.

He didn't know much about the tech, but the brief had been interesting in a vaguely horrific sort of way, to his mind. The tech was based on the alien invaders that had damn near taken out the whole freaking *planet* Earth not that long ago.

It was an example of how scientists didn't always stop to ask themselves whether they *should* do something as far as he was concerned. He'd been especially creeped out when he found out that they'd deployed the damn things in Earth's solar system.

Sure they needed defense, and sure the things had *worked*, but how long before something went wrong?

Hopefully he wouldn't be around to see it.

In the meantime, he did his best to treat the tech like it was just another tool in the arsenal. Like it wasn't self-replicating, alive for all intents and purposes, if not sentient.

Need to stop thinking along those lines. He shuddered. *Already sleeping badly enough.*

Compared to the hardware he was deploying, Tyke was in love with the mission.

Playing pirate, only the idealized version that rarely, if ever, truly happened in history, except in extremely narrow and contained instances. Freeing slaves, leading a genuine revolt against an oppressive government, and getting to fly a damn *spaceship* the whole time?

Childhood fantasy stuff right there.

Tyke noted that the replicator had landed on the asteroid and deployed correctly, so he shook off his musings and hit the radio.

"*Revenge* here," he said. "Last device is deployed. Am RTB."

"Roger, *Revenge*. Good work."
Yeah. It is good work.
He was happy to be doing it.

———

Command Station

A soft buzzing caused both Milla and Steph to look up, then over to the computer.

"What is that?" Milla asked as she rose to her feet.

"Gravity anomaly," Steph said. "I tied in the scanners here with our destroyers and the Archangels, so we have a decent array out there."

Milla nodded, unsurprised. They hadn't been able to repair the latest "prize" ship they had captured, this time from the Protectorate, to say nothing of either finding a crew for it or converting the current one, but they had been able to take control of the computers and get a skeleton crew on board to manage her weapons and the limited functions still intact.

With all those ships linked together and spread out decently, they would have a fairly effective gravity array for detecting inbound vessels. Still, destroyers wouldn't be so easily spotted.

"Cruisers?" she asked with trepidation.

Steph grunted.

"Yeah," he said finally. "Look at this."

She leaned over his shoulder, reading the numbers off.

"That's a large fleet," she said softly, swallowing. "We cannot win against that."

"No, we definitely cannot," Steph confirmed.

Milla frowned. "Why are they just sitting there?"

They were, in fact, sitting quietly out in the comet shield, such as it was. Unlike Earth or any inhabitable system, as a rule, the comet shield of this system had been all but blown away by the explosion of the neutron star a very long time ago.

Only small chunks had survived or, more likely, reverted and coalesced after the explosion, eventually being drawn back in by the high gravity of the collapsed star. There wasn't much out there anymore, and even less of it was anything remotely like water, but some material still existed.

"I think," Steph said after a moment, "that the Empire has come calling."

Milla paled. "We must escape."

"No."

"Stephan! We cannot defeat the Empire, we do not have the strength here . . ."

"I know, Milla, relax. I know." He frowned. "I don't think they're here to fight. Not yet, anyway."

"They are the Empire, Stephan."

"Yeah, but we know they left this system in the Protectorate's control for a long time. I don't think they're in any hurry to get directly involved," he said.

Milla stared at him, unbelieving. "Stephan, whether they fight us themselves or help the Protectorate fight us, it ends the same."

"True."

Steph took a deep breath, wondering if he shouldn't just *leave*.

Grab everyone they could and evacuate.

They couldn't save everyone, but they wouldn't be able to save everyone anyway.

No.

He wanted to see this through.

"Not yet," he said. "We're going to let this play out a little more, Milla."

"This is reckless, Stephan."

"I know," he confirmed. "It's high stakes. Let's hedge our bets, though . . ."

"Hedge our . . . What are you talking about?" Milla didn't seem to understand the phrasing at all.

Steph just smiled, used to Milla still occasionally missing some of his idioms. "Come on, we have some orders to issue and things to prepare."

Milla growled softly, but gave up.

"You Terrans are so frustrating."

"Yeah, I know."

———

Imperial Fifth Fleet Command Vessel

"They're still here."

Jesan was surprised.

He had honestly expected the raiders to be long gone by the time they arrived.

Of course, it seemed that they weren't raiders after all.

"Are they attempting to secure the system?" he asked, leaning over the tactical map of the neutron system. "That seems . . . foolhardy with so few ships."

His intelligence commander, Kandrus Low, laughed softly and derisively beside him. "I was thinking of slightly less flattering terms, Fleet Commander."

Jesan could see why. The system might not have as many weak points as a generally inhabited one might have, but it was still a rather difficult proposition to hold off a superior enemy under the limited defensive conditions the area offered.

"The Protectorate likely won't want to damage infrastructure if they can avoid it, but if given the choice between retaking the system and saving the facilities, I have no doubt what they'll choose."

Kandrus nodded. "Agreed. Cheaper to rebuild than to lose the status of such a high-value resource. The raiders are fools."

"Perhaps. Do those ships look familiar to you?"

Jesan glanced up as Kandrus looked closer, frowning.

"Are those the same ships that escaped us . . . ?"

"Precisely." Jesan filled in the quiet as the man trailed off. "They did not strike me as fools then."

"No, but reckless, that they were."

There was truth there.

"Agreed," Jesan said.

"What are our plans, then?"

Jesan wondered if he should go in and eliminate the ships that had given him the slip before, but discounted the idea quickly.

"We wait, we watch," he said finally. "If we were to charge in, they would escape again. They are fast, as I recall."

Kandrus nodded, expression sour. "That they are."

"For now, let us see what they have in store for the Protectorate," Jesan decided. "I see no reason to spoil their fun just yet. It would be more amusing for me to do so later, if the opportunity presents. For now, I believe we will have some entertainment in the coming days."

Kandrus chuckled softly. "On that I do not disagree, Fleet Commander. These raiders against the Hele forces? Do we care who wins?"

Jesan shrugged. "Not particularly, though I suppose that ultimately it is in the Empire's interest that the Protectorate regains control here."

"I suppose."

"In the meantime, adjust our formation for optimal scanning," Jesan ordered. "And inform the crew that we will make the coming battle available for their viewing . . . pleasure."

"As you command," Kandrus responded, grinning.

Morale required occasional gifts of magnanimous intent, after all. And, as they'd said earlier, who truly cared which side won here?

Chapter 23

Mylen's Victory, *Hele Protectorate*

The target system was laid out before him as Broche stood at the front of the planning room, examining the projection with a stern glare. Around him, his closest advisers stood while the commanders of each of the ships in his fleet observed from their own vessels.

"The system appears to be unchanged," a young sub-commander offered, looking between the projection and his notes.

The assembled group murmured mostly in agreement.

In fact, they couldn't even find the smaller ships that had made such a hash of the convoy.

"Is it possible they left?" the same man asked after a moment.

Broche grunted unhappily. "It is more than possible, it is likely, I suppose. I hope they have not, however."

"Why is that, Over-Commander?"

"Because if they have, it likely means that they completely cleaned out the available stores of deep matter, and since it was due for a convoy pickup, that means we've lost *uncountable* tons of material." He glowered at the projection. "I would far prefer having to fight to retake the system over having lost that much material."

The gathered shifted uncomfortably, both at realizing the likely loss and at the idea that the material was worth that much more than their lives being put out quite so openly. Most of them had been aware of that, of course, but it was still unpleasant to hear.

"We proceed as planned," Broche ordered sternly. "Assume nothing. The enemy is awaiting us, and we *will* clear them from our system. Is that entirely clear?"

"Yes, Over-Commander!"

"Good. Proceed."

———

The Protectorate fleet broke their extrastellar orbit and began the descent into the system, various squadrons of ships associated mostly by type as they pierced past the gravity limit of the neutron star and set their sights cleanly on the command station that had supervised their mining operations.

On the over-commander's orders, the fleet spread their formation over a large area without getting so far that overly long communications delays would disrupt coordination.

This decision was noticed almost immediately.

———

Imperial Fifth Fleet Command Vessel

"The Protectorate is maintaining close communications across the entire fleet," Kandrus noted, his voice bland.

"Their over-commander has no confidence in the capabilities of his underlings," Jesan grunted, unimpressed but not particularly surprised. He'd often done the same, particularly given some of the people assigned to him. "He is attempting to keep any of them from doing anything spectacularly stupid."

"Will that work?" Kandrus asked. "It is my experience that stupidity is exempt from such restrictions."

Jesan scoffed with amusement. "No, it won't work, but it will allow him to mitigate the effects of any such stupidity, assuming that the over-commander himself isn't the source. The latter case will propagate his stupidity at the speed of light to the rest of the fleet."

"A common problem, I have no doubt."

Jesan shot his intelligence officer a sharp look but said nothing.

Kandrus quickly corrected himself. "Among the Free Stars, I mean."

"Of course." He sighed. "Apologies, old friend. I am growing too sensitive."

"You have had a bad turn of events, Fleet Commander," Kandrus said. "The events in the Priminae space, and especially within the anomalous system, they were unprecedented."

Jesan nodded, his dark eyes shifting back to the display.

There was work to be done. He would deal with those issues in good time.

Archangel One, Gaia's Revenge

"Here they come," Tyke said softly, speaking mostly to himself though he was sending his comments over the ship's comm to Milla and a few others.

The *Revenge* was running a skeleton crew at this point, like almost all of the Archangels. They had their Marines back, but most of the shift crews had been seconded to other duties. Some manning the prize ships, some on the station. The setup was going to make things a mess if it all went to hell, he supposed, but for the moment that wasn't his problem to deal with.

"Enemy ships are keeping a close formation, less than two light-seconds' separation at the widest point," Milla commented.

"I see it. The commander is a micromanager," Tyke said. "Or they're worried that we have enough forces to take out their fleet piecemeal if they break it up too much."

More likely the first than the second, he assumed.

"Either way, that fits the primary approach plan Stephan devised," Milla reminded him.

"Agreed," Tyke said. "So far we're on course for plan Alpha, no derivatives. Predictable, but that's all for the best, I suppose."

Tyke examined the time, then idly tapped at the hard-light holograph in front of him, feeling the tingle of the quantum locked photons as they impacted on his finger.

Anytime now, Crown . . .

He didn't have long to wait, as a focused pulse of tachyons painted the inbound fleet, marking them all in real time for anyone in the system to see.

"Set combat clock to synchronize with mark at . . ." Tyke checked the clock. "Fourteen forty-three and twenty-nine seconds."

"Combat clock has been synchronized," Milla said. "We are officially cleared to engage operations."

"About damn time."

Dutchman

Steph set the clock and let out a slow breath.

No turning back now.

Well, that wasn't technically true. He had one way to pull the plug on the operation, but if he used that, it meant everything had gone to hell and would be a hit to the professional reputation he'd been cultivating in the region.

Not with his client state, of course; that had already been locked in by delivering the materials he'd promised them, and then some. However, with his local crews, using the GOTH plan would be a bad thing. They'd have to leave too many people to the nonexistent mercies of the Protectorate.

They were still a long way from that being a factor, he reminded himself.

The Imperial ships were still sitting out there. He didn't know if they thought they were being stealthy. Maybe by the local standards they were, but they'd made no move to join the Protectorate forces when they arrived, and that was good enough for Steph to decide to move forward with the plan they'd concocted. The Empire opting to sit out was the first hurdle they'd cleared, and now it was time to deal with the next.

"Enemy fleet has redirected their course, Captain Teach."

"Understood, crewman," he said softly, keeping the urge to cackle under control as he heard his chosen moniker. "As predicted?"

The man nodded nervously.

"Yes sir."

Steph didn't blame him for being anxious.

The predictions were that the fleet would vector directly onto one specific target once they'd painted the enemy ships with their active scanners.

The *Flying Dutchman* herself.

———

Mylen's Victory, *Hele Protectorate*

"Source of targeting located."

"Redirect all ships to that vector," Broche ordered. "Show me the enemy."

On the screen a single destroyer was visible, resting in space some distance from the command station of the system.

"One destroyer? Is that all?"

"All we can detect, Over-Commander."

Broche didn't like it, not one bit, but for the moment they didn't have anything better to track. He settled back, orders already given. There was nothing more for him to do.

The Protectorate fleet was descending into the system, looking to meet the enemy, and it seemed that at least one of the enemy was willing to give them what they wanted.

"Look for the other ships," he ordered, however. "They're here somewhere. If they'd left, the destroyer would be gone as well."

"Yes, Over-Commander."

It was to be an ambush, of course. He knew that, but he'd been aware of that from the start. Assaulting a star system was always an ambush of one sort or another. In space combat, however, there was only so much that clever tactics could accomplish.

Ultimately, *power* would rule the day.

———

Imperial Fifth Fleet Command Vessel

Jesan snorted softly as he watched the Protectorate ships alter their approach.

His team had been observing the defensive preparations within the system for some time and knew that the Protectorate were sailing right into the teeth of their enemy's defenses. He could warn them off, he supposed, but honestly didn't care to bother at the moment. His forces were the supreme power in this system, and thus he was confident that the battle would end only one way.

His way.

Until that point, he was curious to see how things ran through.

Besides which, it is clear that the Protectorate needs something of a spanking. They've clearly become too confident due to their connection to the Empire.

He observed the smaller ships where they were lying in wait, their signature quite difficult to spot. But as they'd been observed in motion, it was simplicity to maintain clear observation. They were small but impressive for their size, and not for the first time Jesan wondered what polity in the Free Stars had created them.

They were not what he'd expected from the locals, who had largely shifted to fleets composed primarily of destroyers with a smattering of cruisers, largely following the Empire's example in as much as they could afford.

These ships were *not* of Imperial example, however. In fact, they resembled nothing he'd ever encountered, and that fascinated Jesan deeply.

He had spent most of his career learning the rote examples of the modern military, and until very recently had never encountered anything truly *new*.

Now he'd encountered new things twice in two far-flung places, at what was effectively very nearly the same time.

The anomalous species was bad enough, but for a new thing to appear here as well? The new ships were impressive, but their weapons seemed to be exactly what he would expect in the region. Lasers, powerful certainly, but just the same sort of lasers that the Empire and the Free Stars used. The ship class was fast, but nothing really unusual.

"Protectorate forces are entering the outer perimeter, Fleet Commander."

"Put it up across the fleet," Jesan ordered. "No reason not to let everyone watch the entertainment."

"As you command."

Mylen's Victory, *Hele Protectorate*

The fleet had crossed a third of the distance from the outer system to their target, and tensions were slowly ratcheting higher. Broche had taken to pacing as he waited for *something* to happen. Almost anything would do.

Across the command deck, he could tell that he wasn't the only one on edge, and that only made him more irritated and set him pacing faster.

"Is it still just *sitting* there?" he demanded for the third time.

"Yes, Over-Commander," his scanner officer said firmly. "No change in the target."

"Fine," Broche snapped out. "Inform me when we're within range to engage."

"Yes, Over-Commander."

He scowled, stomping back to his station and dropping heavily into the seat as he continued to do the only thing he could.

Wait.

Broche was about to ask for another update when an alarm caused him to twist just as the cruiser was suddenly pitched hard to one side and his entire world exploded in alarms from every direction.

Imperial Fifth Fleet Command Vessel

Jesan snorted, shaking his head, the sound of laughter among the other officers filtering to him.

He was unsurprised. He was tempted to laugh as well and certainly would later when he was recounting this among equals.

What fool just follows the path the enemy sets for them?

The Protectorate commander *had* to have known that it was a trap, that was spectacularly clear from the start, yet he just calmly flew a *direct course* at the only ship he could see?

Absurd.

"I think they lost a couple smaller ships there, Fleet Commander," Kandrus said casually.

Jesan nodded. "If that's all they lose in this operation, they're luckier than any have the right to be in this universe. Fools."

Kandrus nodded silently in agreement.

There were reasons why the military officers of the Empire considered the Free Stars to be largely a joke, and this was a direct example.

———

Archangel Two

Alexandra shook her head.

She could hardly believe that the enemy had just walked right into a minefield. It boggled her mind, even after hearing Steph explain why he thought the strategy would likely work.

She was too young to have fought in the wars that he was referencing, but then again so was Steph.

"All hands," she said. "*Two* Actual speaking. Stand by, we're about to go active."

Time to see if he was right about other things as well. She closed her eyes, taking a deep breath.

After a moment, her deep blue eyes snapped open and Alex leaned forward in the projected harness, feeling the ship come to life under and around her.

"*Archangel Two*, initiating operation."

Chapter 24

Dutchman

Steph let the crew whoop it up as they watched the Protectorate fleet stumble right into the mines they'd laid out along the approach. Working out how to place those effectively had been far easier than it should have been, but the one thing Steph had realized about the Free Stars was that they had long been crippled by the Empire.

The locals didn't realize it, and he even wondered if the Empire itself knew what they were doing.

In the end it probably didn't matter, but he suspected that most of the Imperial officers probably had no idea why the Free Stars were so damn incompetent. They likely just thought it was an example of Imperial superiority, and he supposed from a certain point of view they weren't exactly wrong.

After speaking with his recruited crews, as well as the officers and officials of the Kingdom, Steph had come to realize that the Empire treated the Free Stars like their own private sandbox, likely using this area of space to train their own officers' cadre, and crews, with something resembling "real combat."

What they didn't seem to realize was that calling what they got here "real combat" was like calling scrapping with a child a fistfight.

It's no wonder Eric had them dancing to our tune the whole while, Steph thought darkly. *Though it does make their relative strength all the scarier. Giants with clubs.*

He remembered Eric referring to the Priminae and the Drasin that way. Big dumb giants, wielding BIG damn clubs.

Easy enough to fight if you could avoid getting clobbered, but one hit from the club was enough to end things.

The Empire was like that again, only more so.

They *thought* they were military strategists, as best he could tell, but they had no real experience to show them the truth. They'd ground the Free Stars down so much that development in this cluster of stars had actually been dragged back to near feudal levels.

That type of devolution of society brought with it a lot of issues, especially if the stressors were maintained.

The people here just don't stand a chance, Steph thought darkly.

He hated the culture of the Free Stars deeply, in ways that he knew the locals would never be able to understand. Even if he were to bring them out of it, show them what things *could* be, they wouldn't get it. It was something they were born into, raised in, and considered *normal.*

Worse, he understood *why* they were that way, even if they didn't . . . and couldn't.

And he was going to make things worse for them, in his own small way.

"Unit Two has commenced operations, Captain Teach."

"Very good, thank you."

That was the hell of it, Steph supposed. He wished that he could blindly believe he was here to bring freedom to the Free Stars, but he was better educated than that.

All he could do was bring more death, and the only hope he really had was that he might be able to tip the scale of death and destruction more to those who truly had it coming than the innocent who had no choice in things.

A forlorn hope, but he would do what he could to see it achieved. "Power to the drives," he ordered. "Warp space, full military power." "Yes Captain, as you command!"

———

Archangel Two

Archangels Two and *Four* moved in unison, accelerating at their highest level as they warped space toward the enemy formation.

Coming in from the flank, they were in among the fleet while the Protectorate crews still dealt with the nuclear mines they'd tripped, taking the crews entirely by surprise.

"*Archangel Two* . . ." Alex announced, thinking to herself that she needed a nice nickname for her ship. There was no reason that the *Revenge* should get all the fun, after all. "Beams beams beams!"

Lasers cut out from the ship's emitters, more powerful than any of the enemy's destroyers could manage by half again, at least, vaporizing armor as they targeted key points. She distantly heard *Archangel Four* announce their own attack, and peripherally saw more targets blink red as they had their thruster vents destroyed and beam emitters slagged by the two fighter-gunboats that slashed through the formation.

They were two-thirds through the fleet before the Protectorate forces managed to mount a counterattack.

Beams slashed around them, but they were moving fast and erratically and at such a range that they were able to outpace the enemy system's ability to track their motions.

Alex briefly wished that they could trick the enemy into shooting each other, but despite the Protectorate ships being in "tight formation," that still meant the enemy ships were spread as much as a couple full light-seconds apart, farther than the distance from the Earth to the moon by a good fifty percent.

In that volume, you could stack a *lot* of ships and still have essentially empty space.

So she wouldn't be tricking the enemy into potting their own ship, sadly enough.

Alex twisted as she floated in the control space, her fighter-gunboat carving a hard-g turn upwell, climbing away from the star and crossing out of the forward beam arcs of the enemy ships. Imperial designs didn't have much in the way of chase armaments mounted to the rear arc, which had filtered down to the Free Stars' choice in design.

Which was fair enough. The *Odysseus* and other Terran ships didn't have near as much rear firepower either. In space it wasn't usually a problem, since accelerating backward was as easy as to the front.

Now, however, it did give her and hers a place to run that was relatively safe unless the enemy ordered their ships around, which she doubted they were going to do, since she'd just spotted the *Dutchman* light off her drives.

"*Archangel Two*, attack pass complete."

"Roger, *Two. Archangel One*, engaging the enemy."

———

Mylen's Victory, *Hele Protectorate*

"Shoot them!" Broche ordered, eyes wild as he watched the pair of fast-moving ships dart right through the center of his formation, tearing apart three destroyers and heavily damaging a cruiser in the process.

"Fleet is responding. However, the enemy is very fast and *very* close, Over-Commander," one of his men said.

"They're not faster than *light*, shoot them!"

There was a pause, no one wanting to explain to the commander that while the enemy couldn't outrun light, they apparently *could* outrun the targeting capacity of the laser emitters at this range, which Broche intuitively knew.

"Yes Commander."

Broche grunted, turning to glare at the profile imagery they'd managed to get of the new ships. They were highly unusual, that much was certain, but he vaguely recalled reading some report about them.

"Where have I seen this design before?" he demanded of his aide.

"The design matches descriptions of a group of pirates that recently caused some problems in, or near, the Star Kingdom, Over-Commander."

"Right, I remember that report now," Broche said. "No one knows where they came from, but they mixed it up with an Imperial Fleet, didn't they?"

"Ran from one, but yes, Over-Commander."

Broche grunted.

Of *course* they ran from the Imperials. He'd run from an Imperial Fleet too. The fact that they'd been in the same system as one and were still around was proof that the commander giving them orders wasn't a complete idiot.

"Were there any other reports about them?" he demanded.

"Nothing of significance, Over-Commander," his aide admitted. "Some speculation that the Kingdom had employed them in their little conflict with the Belj, but reports seem clear that they're independent."

"So either they came after us on their own, or someone hired them to." Broche shook his head. "Unlikely they did this on their own, but . . ."

He was interrupted by another alarm and more ships suddenly going red just before the *Victory* herself bucked violently.

Archangel One, Gaia's Revenge

"*Archangel One*, beams beams beams," Tyke said calmly as he opened fire, picking his targets on the fly as they went through the enemy formation, warping space with full military power.

The Protectorate fleet was a mess. He'd seen better organization in the Middle East, and that was saying something.

It was harder to read, mostly due to the sheer volume of space the fleet occupied, but Tyke was pretty certain that he could see their discipline starting to crack.

With *Archangel Five* covering his six, Tyke wound through the enemy ships, leading the way as both burned out one ship after another.

The Protectorate thought they could just wade in with numbers and win the battle with nothing more than a weight of metal.

They might even be right, if it were a simulation.

Sims don't bleed, though . . . and they don't panic.

"*Archangel One*, attack pass complete."

"*Archangel Three*, beginning our attack run."

———

Imperial Fifth Fleet Command Vessel

"It seems rather one-sided, does it not?" Kandrus asked, sounding slightly surprised.

"They're picking the Protectorate apart like they're the amateurs they are," Jesan replied. "The test will be what happens once the fight shifts, and it will."

Kandrus nodded.

As effective as the opening salvos had been, the weight of metal was too strong for the Protectorate to lose. All they had to do was wade in and make the enemy come to them, which was exactly what they were doing.

No matter how fast and nimble the enemy was, they couldn't keep ahead of a beam forever.

"Of course," Kandrus said. "The outcome is certain, but the opening is still impressive."

Jesan leaned in, bringing his tented hands up in front of his face. He looked over his fingers at the Protectorate formation.

"Is it?" he wondered. "It should be . . . however . . ."

He trailed off, thoughtful.

"You believe they have a chance against the Protectorate?" Kandrus asked. "The pirates have nowhere near the weight of metal to take the Protectorate fleet, as pitiful a formation as it actually is, Fleet Commander."

Jesan nodded. He truly agreed, but something was wrong. Something he couldn't quite place.

Finally he sat back. "We'll see. Be sure to record everything, I want to review this later."

"Of course, Fleet Commander."

———

Mylen's Victory, *Hele Protectorate*

"Bring in that wing formation," Broche snarled. "If they don't get back into position, I'll burn them down myself. They won't have to worry about the enemy!"

"Yes, Over-Commander!"

His fleet formation was turning into a mess as the ships lost their nerve and tried to get away from the enemy attacks or got angry and tried to chase them. He'd be willing to tolerate the latter, except that they inevitably ran into the *next* strike as the enemy led the foolish commanders into traps.

Worse, *no one* had managed to score a strike on the enemy ships thus far, despite them scoring up ten disabled ships.

"Over-Commander, the destroyer is moving."

Broche twisted. "What course vector?"

"They're coming right at us, Over-Commander."

Impossible.

"Impossible!" he snapped. "They cannot be that suicidal. A destroyer cannot face off against a fleet our size!"

"Over-Commander . . ." The scanner officer was at a loss. "They're accelerating in our direction, full military power."

Broche fell silent, unable to quite believe what he was dealing with.

Ships that came from nowhere, moving so fast they couldn't be targeted, explosive mines in open space, and now a *single destroyer* charging his fleet?!

None of it made any sense.

"We're fighting crazy people."

The men around him exchanged nervous looks, but no one said anything.

———

Dutchman

Steph sat back in his station, leaning to one side to pull a telemetry display over to where he could better see it. The *Dutchman* was making a big show, charging an enemy fleet, and he had no doubt that they were all now wondering what the hell was going on.

"It's a trap, sir," Steph whispered. "There's *two* of them."

He noticed that the men around him had overheard, and were exchanging confused glances, but didn't worry about it. He'd tell them the joke that came with the punch line sometime, assuming this worked out, and they'd probably have a new favorite for themselves as well.

"Open broadcast," he ordered. "No encoding."

"Yes Com—Captain," the communications officer said. "Channel open to your control."

Steph leaned forward slightly with a smile on his face as he began to speak.

"This is the *Flying Dutchman*," he said softly, no heat or emotion in his voice. "If you were intelligent, you would *run* now. Thankfully for us, you're clearly not that intelligent. Just stay where you are, we're coming to you."

He closed the connection, smiling as everyone turned to stare at him, unbelieving.

"Stand by for targeting orders," he said, calmly shifting subjects.

When his crew didn't immediately return to their tasks, Steph's expression grew stern as he met their eyes one at a time until they each looked away.

Steph looked at the clock.

Too slow. We get to move again.

———

As the Protectorate fleet continued its downward plunge into the neutron star system, the ships slipped into the second layer of defenses that had been prepared for them.

Still trying to figure out exactly what was happening, the ship commanders of the Protectorate completely missed the surge in power around them until it was too late. They ended up caught in a net of beams from the remains of the former defense network that had once belonged to *them*.

Massive laser emplacements that were supposed to be *much* closer to the command station and slave pens suddenly burned hotter than the surface of a star, and the Protectorate had only a few seconds to respond before they were cut in two.

Chapter 25

Mylen's Victory, *Hele Protectorate*

Broche held on to his station with a white-knuckled grip as he watched ships burn around him.

"How did they place those?!" he demanded. "There's not enough of them in the entire system to protect the system from this far out!"

None of it made any sense to him.

The enemy had placed a minefield so *far out* from the star that it should have been *impossible* to achieve sufficient field density in any position that would be useful!

Now they did the same with what were intended to be orbital beam emplacements?

Insane!

Did they somehow mine the whole damn system? No one had that many resources, certainly not to complete such an operation in so little time with so few ships.

He paled.

They had to have more ships.

It was the only thing that made any sense.

Broche looked around, examining the telemetry displays, trying to find what he was sure *had* to be out there.

"Where are they?" he mumbled.

People around him looked at one another, nerves growing as the commander started talking to himself.

"Where are who, Over-Commander?"

"Focus on your task!" Broche snapped, driving his people back to their stations before he looked back to what he was searching for.

They have to be there somewhere.

———

Imperial Fifth Fleet Command Vessel

"This is pitiful." Jesan sighed, resting his head on his hand as he watched the Empire's supposed allies being marched around the battlefield by the nose. "They haven't yet worked out that the enemy is leading them around like children."

"The Protectorate *is* an Imperial asset, of sorts at least, Fleet Commander," Kandrus offered reluctantly. "Perhaps we should involve ourselves?"

"Eventually. I see no particular reason to save any of these fools, however, unless you have a reason I should?"

Kandrus grimaced. "I cannot really say that I do, Fleet Commander."

"Well, at least you're confirming that I'm not seeing things," Jesan muttered. "I was hoping for a good battle, see the Protectorate lose a few ships, but this is going to be a *rout* if it continues. Worse, it's not even because the Protectorate's enemy was that much more powerful. The Protectorate commander is simply an imbecile."

Jesan was a man who respected power; it was in the nature of being a hand of the empress, to his mind, so this situation was doubly irritating to him. Yes, he could find some respect in the cunning of the invaders, and certainly in their ambition, but they were a weak force and that should dictate the place in the hierarchy. The fact that the Protectorate were allowing these *pirates* to play above their station was unforgivable.

"The crews find it all rather amusing, if nothing else," Kandrus offered up.

"Not the intended entertainment, I admit," Jesan said. "However, it will do I suppose. The least we can do is let it play out to the end before we intervene."

"The men will be grateful to you, Fleet Commander."

"Let something of value come from this idiocy."

———

Mylen's Victory, *Hele Protectorate*

"Over-Commander! Two of our ships have broken ranks!"

Broche twisted, stomping across the deck. "Where are they?"

"Far on our flank. They're angling for an escape vector."

Broche felt himself shaking, unable to believe what he was being told.

"Cowards," he hissed. "Have the closest ships burn them down."

"Over-Commander?"

He ignored the shocked question, face set white with rage.

"You heard me! Execute the cowards."

———

Dutchman

Steph felt his jaw go slack.

Are they actually . . . ?

Alright, so he knew he had little to no respect for the Free Stars. That was something he'd been dealing with ever since the squadron had arrived and discovered just how screwed up this particular section of space was. Pocket empires, slavery writ large, with no real sense of what he'd come to accept as military decorum . . . all part of a formula for the worst sort of situations you could get, to his mind.

He hadn't thought they'd be stupid enough to engage their own ships in the middle of a fight, however. Hunt them down after? Sure. Probably do really nasty things to them at that point too, but actually taking more of their ships out of the fight in order to kill them now?

"This is insane."

The whole damn place was just sick.

Which wasn't to say that he was unwilling to make use of opportunities when they presented themselves.

He quickly brought up the encrypted squadron channel.

"Archangels, engage any ships that are firing on fleeing vessels," he ordered.

He wasn't above sowing a little discord in the ranks, after all.

Archangel One, Gaia's Revenge

"Are they . . . firing on their own people?"

Milla's voice was disbelieving, and Tyke wasn't sure he could blame her. He'd seen a lot of crazy stuff in his time, during the war as well as before and after, but this was something he'd only *heard* of in stories that always seemed to be a couple people removed.

He knew of incidents where deserters had been *shot*, of course, but he'd never witnessed an enemy force actually sacrificing the effectiveness of their own line of battle to do it on the spot.

Despite his disbelief, however, Tyke smelled an opportunity.

"*Four, One*," he said calmly. "Follow my lead, I'm shifting our strategy."

"*One, Four,*" *Archangel Four* replied instantly. "Roger. Have your six."

The Archangel platform had always been the most freeing experience of his existence, from the first time he'd strapped one on back in a ratty old hangar in North Dakota. The NICS interface let machine respond to man in ways that had been imagined but never remotely possible in any previous control system.

The new platform, however? It wasn't merely freeing. He *was* the Archangel.

Tyke leaned into the controls, suspended in the air, and the scene around him changed in response as the fighter's drives flared brightly and they dived forward in a tight arc that brought them to bear on the closest of the ships firing on those fleeing.

He mentally haloed the ships, causing the system to open an enhanced view of the targets as though looking through a wormhole as he rushed through space.

"Lock targets," he ordered. "Maximum impact."

"Roger," Milla responded. "Should I disable or eliminate the target?"

"Eliminate."

In for a penny, in for a pound, Tyke decided. He reached up to the hard-light display that stayed still relative to him and flipped the security switches that secured his weapons from misfire, making everything live for the duration of the attack run.

"Roger," Milla said again. "Key points targeted. You are clear to engage."

"Thank you. *Archangel One*, beginning my attack run."

"Roger, *One*. The fourth is with you."

Tyke winced.

"Bad joke, *Four*. Bad joke."

"Says you." Burner laughed at him.

He sighed. "We will be having words later, trust me."

257

Burner just laughed again, leaving Tyke to focus on the target as it actually began to show up without enhancement. A dot at first, barely visible by reflected light, the ship abruptly began to grow *fast* as he approached at high speed, still accelerating.

"*Archangel One*," Tyke intoned. "Beams beams beams."

Lasers slashed out from the fighter-gunboat, striking the enemy ship, a destroyer, amidships as Tyke cut in across the aft quadrant and charged forward before arcing away. He looked over his shoulder at the burning ship just as he heard Burner follow his lead.

"*Archangel Four*, beams beams beams."

Invisible focused energy from *Four* finished what Tyke had started, effectively slicing the destroyer in half as they completed their pass, collapsing its core in turn. The explosion lit the black like a nova for a few seconds, then vanished, leaving nothing where the destroyer had been.

Upwell of them, the fleeing ship continued to run, no longer under fire.

Tyke let him go.

Cowards were of no value to him, but they would *hurt* the Protectorate's forces in multiple ways.

"Message from *Dutchman*," Milla said. "Steph orders that we intercept any ships firing on fleeing vessels."

Tyke laughed sharply.

"Great minds, Ms. Chans. Great minds."

"Should I inform Steph that you consider him to be a great mind?"

"No!" he objected sharply. *Seriously, what is it with the bad jokes?*

"Roger that, sir," Milla said.

I miss the days when a fighter had a one-man crew.

———

Mylen's Victory, *Hele Protectorate*

Broche stared in blank-faced, open-jawed shock as he watched the running ships escape from his fleet's range, running for freedom at perpendicular course to his current velocity. He knew he couldn't catch the vessels, and knew that they would keep on running. The Protectorate had likely seen the last of those ships. Odds were they'd wind up pirates themselves unless they had someone willing to take them in.

Worse, though, was that he was now certain several more ships were likely considering desertion as well. He could see, in how they were edging away from his formation without actually running for it, that they were laying the foundation. More obviously, several of his vessels had now actively opted to *not* fire at the pirate ships that had eliminated the vessels he'd tasked with punishing the cowards.

It was all going wrong, and he still didn't know how.

———

Dutchman

Good man, Tyke.

Steph had smiled the moment he saw Tyke moving, knowing that the orders he'd dispatched wouldn't have gotten there remotely that quickly. He liked working with professionals in a deep and abiding way.

That thought forced him to mask a sigh as he glanced around at the men he was currently commanding.

"Com—Captain?"

"What is it, Lieutenant?" he asked, using a mangled version of "sub-commander" in Imperial to represent the rank that they didn't really have. He would be damned if he were to start calling everyone "commander" in some way or another.

"We are about to come into range of the enemy fleet."

Steph raised an eye, giving the man . . . and all the others watching . . . a crooked grin.

"I believe you phrased that wrong, Lieutenant."

"I . . . pardon, Captain?"

"You said that we are coming into range of the fleet, correct?" Steph asked.

The young officer, who looked vaguely ill at the attention he was getting from the ship's commanding officer, nodded. "Y-yes Captain."

"What you *should* have said, young man," Steph said as he climbed to his feet, "was that the enemy fleet was entering *our* range. Prepare for beam engagement!"

That startled the crew back into action.

"As you command!"

At least they take orders reasonably well.

It was a start.

Imperial Fifth Fleet Command Vessel

"Well."

Jesan didn't know what more there was to say, frankly.

The Protectorate had lived down to every bias he had against the Free Stars, and then managed to dig out a hole to find more. The pirates were opportunists, as all pirates were, though more clever than most if he were to offer an opinion in that direction.

The Protectorate fleet, as he expected, did not deserve the term even slightly. They were a straggling band of loosely affiliated ships that barely had any cohesion while things were going in their favor, and none at all when events moved against them.

"Should we get involved, Commander?"

Jesan sighed. "I believe at this point we have no choice. Issue the orders to the fleet, prepare to move out."

"Yes Commander. I will see to it."

It chafed at him, saving such incompetence, but what was he to do? The Empire wanted and needed those materials.

One day the Empire will stop playing with these damn fool Free Stars. Perhaps I may even live to see it.

That would be a good day, he was now quite convinced.

Chapter 26

Mylen's Victory, *Hele Protectorate*

"Over-Commander! The enemy has altered their pattern. They're coming at us together now!"

Broche was startled.

So far the enemy had taken care to maintain only hit-and-run tactics, moving fast enough that his ships couldn't properly engage them in turn, and they had been moderately successful using such methods. He didn't understand why they would choose to make such a large change in their strategy.

Perhaps they realized that cutting away at my fleet would only slow the inevitable?

That made some sense, he supposed. Broche didn't think the enemy had enough force to properly win this battle no matter what they did, but perhaps they expected that changing methods would throw his people off enough to give them a chance?

Or, a darker side of him wondered if they weren't counting on more cowards fleeing from a massed attack.

Something he was rather afraid might be true.

I will hunt those cowards down to the last, he swore angrily.

First, though, he had a battle to win.

"Target the destroyer ahead," he ordered. "Tighten the formation. I want *all* ships back in close. Now."

"Yes Commander."

That would not be a popular order, he knew, but he saw little choice. If he left the ships out on the flanks where they'd "drifted," he was certain to lose at least some of them if anything untoward happened at all. As it was, he expected some to bolt just at the order itself.

They would be dealt with, when the time came, that he would ensure. For now, though, he could waste no more time on cowards.

"Fire full barrage."

"Firing, Commander!"

Dutchman

Timing. Space combat was all about timing.

Steph eyed the clock, wondering if the enemy commander was punctual or not. He thought not, actually, but he couldn't really count on that with the stakes being what they were.

"Target acquired, Captain."

"Fire."

"Beam out, Captain."

Steph nodded, eyes still on the clock. The moment he'd entered the enemy range, the clock had started. Now it was just a matter of making the seconds count.

"New course," he ordered. "Slide five zero zero kilometers, port side! Engage now."

"At your command!"

Steph grabbed the edge of his station, as the ship felt like it was tilting dangerously to one side, the warping of space slightly out of sync with the ship. Partly, he knew, that was due to the smaller size of the destroyer over a cruiser, which was the preferred ship scale based

---

on warping technology. Partly, though, Steph was fairly certain that the drives were slightly out of alignment.

Need to get the Dutchman *into some kind of dry dock eventually and have that checked. It'll be straining the hull if I'm right.*

He kept counting down the seconds as they moved, one eye on the clock as the other watched the telemetry of the battle that was still raging in the odd slow and methodical way of space combat.

"Laser detected!"

He's a little late, but not bad, Steph noted idly as he picked a point at random before issuing new orders.

"Fire again."

"Beam out!"

"New course, slide three zero zero kilometers, down relative to the system plane!"

"At your command!"

Huh. I think I'm getting used to their odd mishmash of human and Imperial terminology. It might even be growing on me.

Mylen's Victory, *Hele Protectorate*

"Laser strike!"

The *Victory* shuddered as the beams broached the space-warp at the front of the vessel, burning into the armor and bleeding atmosphere out into the void. Broche snarled as he gripped his console. "Continue firing!"

"Enemy shifted course. We missed, Over-Commander."

Broche swore. "Retarget and fire!"

That will only buy you time, and little enough of that, you irritating insignificant pest, he thought savagely.

The beams from the destroyer were powerful, but they were striking right into the heaviest armor of his ship, attenuated a great deal by the most potent point of the warping of space. He could take the damage, and would, rather than risk allowing the enemy a shot at the more vulnerable flanks of the cruiser.

All he needed was one good hit, Broche knew, and the destroyer would be done.

Then he would turn his focus to the little pests buzzing around.

Swatting them would be a pleasure.

"Increase warp, close the range," he ordered.

"Yes Commander!"

———

The smaller pirate squadron was outmassed thousands to one, easily, by the larger and more numerous ships of the Protectorate, yet they continued moving quickly in through the spread formation of the larger fleet while inflicting damage in small degrees before flashing out of range again with incredibly quick converging velocities.

The Protectorate ships became more demoralized with every passing engagement, more choosing to run rather than face the ghostlike attacks of the smaller foe.

That still left an overwhelming weight of metal facing the force that was led by the destroyer, enough of a force that only a fool would think they could win such a fight.

A fool, or a man with yet another ace up his sleeve.

———

Dutchman

Steph kept up the pattern of stick and move, keeping his ship mobile as the range closed, but he knew that was a losing game in the long-term. The enemy had already scored some glancing strikes, mostly turned aside by the gravity warp, he would guess. As they got closer, it would get worse, Steph knew that for certain.

If he could mask, the way the *Odyssey* had back in the day, and keep his range, then he could likely keep this fight up almost indefinitely. Bleed the enemy ships until they were forced to withdraw, or do something stupid.

Instead, he would be forced to close the range eventually or flee the system himself.

However, he'd known that was the outcome he was playing to from the start, and he'd had a few days to prepare his battlefield.

The weapons the Protectorate had left in the system were a godsend, not so much because he wanted to use them as that they provided him with a cover to deploy technology that he otherwise could *never* have risked under the eyes of an Imperial Fleet.

His Kardashev Network was nothing like the one that protected Earth. He'd only had a few days to get the system building, and that was barely enough for a half dozen generations to pass. On the other hand, the neutron star had left a far richer system than what they had to work with in Sol, at least in terms of ease of access.

The lesser elements had been burned off, blown to atoms, or in various other ways ejected from the system. What was left were the heavier elements. Metals in particular, giving his Kardashev drones a leg up that had been unaccountably valuable.

Even so, all he had in the end was barely enough to mount a single effective trap.

A trap that the time had come to spring.

Steph didn't voice the order. None of his crew had any idea what the weapon system was. They would assume it was just repaired scrap from the Protectorate's own defenses. He issued the order over a secure comm, encrypted and pulsed in a fraction of a millisecond.

Just one word.

Initiate.

Practically the moment he sent the signal, his ship bucked like a wounded beast, and Steph could hear the screaming of people and alarms as doors slid shut automatically.

"Report!"

Mylen's Victory, *Hele Protectorate*

Broche glowered, hating the little destroyer with everything he had in him.

They had bracketed it with everything they could muster, and yet the damn little beast kept managing to maneuver *just* clear, it seemed. He was almost certain, judging from scanner returns, that they'd inflicted some minor damage, but it seemed like nothing that would actually have any significant impact.

His rage was threatening to grow beyond his ability to control it just as they received a clear and obvious scanner return.

"Direct hit!"

The destroyer was spewing atmosphere and flame into the void, pitching hard to one side as its drives were thrown out of balance.

Finally!

"Good." Broche rose to his feet. "Now finish this! End them where they drift!"

"As you ord—"

The response was cut off as his own ship suddenly was torn out from under him. A force unlike anything he could recall threw Broche out of his station and sent him tumbling along the deck. Alarms screamed in the distance, but he was too busy trying to fight off an encroaching darkness that he could feel closing in on him.

He struggled to his feet, ears ringing and head dizzy, barely able to keep his feet under him as he staggered over to the scanner station.

"What . . . happened?"

The scanner tech was bleeding from his forehead, eyes dazed as he tried to focus on the system in front of him.

"We . . . I-I'm not sure," the tech admitted. "We were hit by a laser. Powerful, it burned through our hull . . . Sir, reports coming from across the fleet. We're not the only ones struck!"

"How many?" Broche croaked out.

"Still counting, some are not responding, but . . . a lot."

He forced himself across the command deck, reaching the weapons station. "Do we have a targeting lock on the destroyer?"

"Yes sir, but . . ."

"No buts. Fire."

"Over-Commander, we can't."

Broche snarled. "Why not?"

"Power is down. We're running emergency systems."

He slumped. "Fine. Issue the order to the fleet. Anyone who can fire, destroy that damned ship."

"As you comm—"

"Over-Commander!"

Broche twisted and immediately regretted it as his head screamed in protest. "What is it?"

"Sir, we're scanning a large fleet approaching from out system."

He paled, even more than he likely already was.

That was not something he wanted to hear.

"Scan and put visuals to my station," he mumbled as he stumbled back.

"As you command."

The telemetry was waiting for him when he got there, and it took only a few moments for him to work out who and what it was. He slumped, mostly relieved, though it likely wasn't a great situation all the same.

The Empire. Of course they're taking an interest, he realized. Broche also knew that he could make that work in his favor.

"Give me a wide comm," he ordered. "No encryption."

"As you command!"

With the comm open, Broche forced himself to stand upright.

"This is Over-Commander Broche of the Protectorate fleet," he said firmly, keeping any hint of a slur out of his voice. "I would like to thank the Imperial Fleet for their intervention in this illegal operation, and pledge the Protectorate's gratitude and continued cooperation concerning our agreement in this system. To the *pirates* afflicting Protectorate space, if you surrender now, you may hope to serve out your lives mining our system here rather than facing an execution squad. Over-Commander Broche out."

He killed the audio, leaving the comm open for any responses.

"Video response, Over-Commander. From the pirate's destroyer."

"On the main display," Broche ordered.

They watched as a sandy-haired man in black armor sat silently in the destroyer's command station, eyes not wavering from the screen as he calmly and deliberately punched in a series of commands at his station without saying a word.

"Signal pulse, Over-Commander. It's encrypted."

"Break it," Broche ordered as he watched the man on the screen lean forward and rise up to his feet.

The pirate captain stepped forward, taking several deliberate steps, then fell into a wide stance that left him facing the screen as he clasped his hands behind his back. He said nothing, just looked at the screen and seemed to be waiting.

"What is he doing?" Broche asked, eyes darting around as he tried to figure out what the other man had done. "Are we being fired upon still?"

"Negative, Over-Commander. All combat has ceased."

The Imperial Fleet was almost upon them, and Broche knew it didn't matter anymore anyway. With the Imperials there, they'd won. The Empire wouldn't give up access to the deep matter, and they didn't want to have to take the system for themselves or they would have done it already.

In a moment the Empire would fire, and the enemy would die.

Broche grinned a death's-head smile as he waited for that to happen.

The Empire loomed in the scanners, then the fleet was upon them. It didn't pause, it didn't fire. The fleet just continued on past without even transmitting a single word. Broche felt his jaw drop as he watched the fleet fly past the pirate's destroyer, angling slightly to make for a docking approach with the system's command station.

Sound came through the pirate's channel then.

The sandy-haired man leaned forward slightly, and spoke in accented Imperial, almost whispering.

"The *Dutchman*, she *owns* this star now. I would run if I were you."

The signal died, screen going black, and every alarm they had left seemed to scream to life.

"Over-Commander! We're being targeted! All vectors!"

Broche swallowed, unbelieving.

"Over-Commander!"

"Withdraw," he ordered, his voice croaking. "Withdraw."

Epilogue

Imperial Fifth Fleet Command Vessel

This is one of the strangest things I've ever done, Stephanos had to admit to himself as he walked the corridors of the Imperial flagship.

They'd let him keep his armor—no weapons, of course. He'd been marginally impressed with how efficiently they'd searched him and his one "guest."

Seamus Gordon had insisted on joining him, something Steph couldn't really gainsay him given the nature of the meeting. It was his business in both his official pirate role as squadron purser, and the far more important role as chief intelligence analyst on the mission.

Steph still rather wished that he'd had a better working relationship with the enigmatic man before having to work with him in such conditions, but that was the way things went sometimes.

The pair walked in silence, escorted by three guards each, all brandishing arms, of course.

It was a pretty decent intimidation play, if Steph were being honest. He couldn't even pretend it wasn't working on him. They were laying *everything* on the line, and there was no out here. If the Empire decided to end them and the squadron, there wasn't much he could do. Maybe one or two of the Archangels might escape, flee back to Earth with the intel they'd gathered so far, but that was the best-case scenario if it all went bad.

Best make sure it doesn't go bad, then.

The escort came to a stop in front of a set of larger doors, not speaking as they took up positions on either side. Steph exchanged glances with Gordon, who just shrugged. He took a nervous breath, noting the smirk on the faces of the guards with some annoyance that he pushed aside as he stepped closer and pressed his hand on the door caller.

Silence reigned for a long moment, and Steph knew he was being made to wait. A power play, obviously, but effective.

Finally the doors slid open, and a voice from inside spoke up.

"You may enter."

He stepped forward, feeling Gordon do the same at his side. They walked into a rather palatial office by starship standards at least. He'd seen larger on Earth, and certainly on Ranquil, but it would be impressive even planet-side just the same.

"So," the man behind the desk said without looking up. "You're *pirates*, or so I'm told. The Empire takes a dim view of pirates."

"I would say that we are . . ." Steph chose his words carefully. "Independent warriors in the employ of carefully chosen clients."

The man behind the desk looked up at him, and Steph saw his face for the first time and paled.

Oh shit.

It was the man who'd *led* the assault on Earth.

What the hell is he doing out here?

Steph forced himself to calm. The man he was facing had been the focus of every officer in the fleet, which was how he knew that face. He'd been a nearly anonymous pilot sunk into the *Odysseus'* helm pit, barely visible when Eric had exchanged words with the enemy commander.

"The Empire takes a dim view of *mercenaries* as well," the commander said.

"I'm certain we can come to an arrangement," Steph forced himself to say.

"Indeed," the commander said lightly. "Your proposal was . . . fascinating. You can hold up the initial offer?"

"Two bulk freighters are awaiting the Empire's prize crews," Steph said. "We secured them against any possibility of combat by hiding them in the mining fields on the other side of the neutron star. They each have been filled to capacity and represent, I believe, one and a half times what the Protectorate normally delivered. A bonus for . . . your trouble, Fleet Commander, is it?"

The commander rose to his feet, nodding. "Mich. Fleet Commander Jesan Mich. Very well, you've bought yourself a chance. Now, why should I leave *you* in charge of this system?"

Steph raised his eyebrows. "You shouldn't. I'm a military man. What I know of running a mining facility wouldn't impress a child of any man in this system."

"Interesting, I admit, you fascinate me . . . Commander, is it?"

"That works." Steph shrugged. "Teach is my chosen name. Commander Teach, or Captain, as you like."

"Captain," Mich said slowly. "That is an old word."

"I know," Steph said. He'd had to dig *deep* into the archives to find a word that matched up with the role of a captain in Imperial speech that wasn't some variation of commander. "It's an affectation. I like to present a different sort of image to my crews."

"Ah." Mich nodded. "So what do you suggest, then?"

"Mr. Gordon?" Steph gestured.

Seamus Gordon smiled. "We suggest that the former slaves of the system run the mines on the Empire's behalf, of course."

Mich's eyes widened.

"More and more interesting," he said. "I admit, I did not see that coming. You must know that the Empire has no interest in securing this star at this time."

"No reason you would need to," Gordon offered. "Station a single squadron, potentially a single ship, merely to show the flag. The rest could easily be handled by the locals and our own forces on your behalf. The Empire would, of course, claim the bulk share of the material. We would take a small share to cover our expenses, and the rest would see to the needs of the miners as they continue to keep the system running appropriately."

Mich laughed softly.

"You are going to be a true pain for me, I can see it now," he said. "However, I have little left to lose and the only alternative is to turn the system back over to the Protectorate . . . Something I am loath to do after that shameful showing."

He looked at them evenly. "You have until the empress requires my report. Prove you can deliver, and I will speak on your behalf. Be warned, she may not listen. If I am so ordered, I will wipe out every man, woman, and child in this system and rebuild."

Gordon tilted his head.

"Of course, Fleet Commander. We expect nothing less."

Odysseus

Fleet Commander Birch slowly opened her eyes, climbing out of the darkness that had encompassed her gradually and as if with great effort.

She didn't remember much.

Her fleet had been pinned down, and she ordered an escape, then . . .

Battle, darkness . . . nothing.

She looked around the room she was in, clearly a detention facility of some sort. She could feel the hum of a ship's core under her, so she was still in space.

They must be hoping for intelligence on the Empire.

It was the only reason to take her alive, in her opinion. Not that it would benefit them. She had enough experience that she wouldn't give them anything they could use.

She wondered what had happened to her crew. To the rest of the Eighth?

So much of my life, all blown away . . . because I could not contain my temper. Blast it, I'm no better than the rest of those damn fools. Worse even, because I thought I was better and took pride in it.

———

"She believes she can keep information from us indefinitely, Commodore," Odysseus said curiously.

"If you weren't here, she probably could," Eric admitted as he watched the woman sit up and examine her surroundings. "We don't know enough about the Empire yet to judge lies from truth."

"She's worried about her people," Odysseus offered, sounding sad.

"That's not unexpected, but it is encouraging," Eric said. "I was worried, from our previous prisoners. I'd begun to wonder if some form of sociopathy was the norm in the Empire."

"As I understand such things, she is not a sociopath," Odysseus said. "She is blaming herself for what happened."

"She was their commander. Their safety was her responsibility. Just as the lives lost on our side were mine."

Odysseus nodded.

The entity was wearing his more formal uniform, one that consisted of modern armor with no helmet to block his features. His face was done with tasteful makeup, but noticeable, all within the letter of regulations.

Eric approved, and saw it as proof that the entity was growing up . . . or at least faking it nicely.

"What will we do with her?" Odysseus asked. "She is expecting . . . not nice things."

"Nothing like that," Eric said. "Especially with you here. Even if you weren't, though, there's little point to enhanced interrogation in this case. We'll interrogate her, hard at first, but nothing like she's probably expecting. Eventually we'll lighten up, offer luxuries . . ."

"If she talks? That will not work."

"No, just to be nice. We'll play the long game," Eric said. "No one can be on guard forever, Odysseus, and everyone slips up from time to time. It's the slips we want."

Odysseus nodded, eyes falling back to the woman in the cell.

"I . . . understand."

ABOUT THE AUTHOR

Bestselling Canadian author Evan Currie has an imagination that knows no limits, and he uses his talent and passion for storytelling to take readers everywhere from ancient Rome to the dark expanses of space. Although he started out dabbling in careers such as computer science and the local lobster industry, Currie quickly determined that writing the kinds of stories he grew up loving was his true life's calling. Beginning with the techno-thriller *Thermals*, Evan has expanded the universe within his mind with acclaimed series including Archangel One, Warrior's Wings, the Scourwind Legacy, the Hayden War Cycle, and Odyssey One. He delights in pushing the boundaries of technology and culture, and exploring the ways in which these forces intertwine and could shape the future of humanity—both on Earth and among the stars. For more information, visit www.evancurrie.ca.